Wonderful reviews for award-winning author Helen Brenna

"Brenna combines nonstop action and great sexual tension for a story readers won't want to put down."
—*RT Book Reviews* on *The Moon That Night*, nominated for a Reviewer's Choice award for Best Harlequin Superomance of 2010

"I've found a new series romance writer to put on the auto-buy list."
—*All About Romance* on *Along Came a Husband*

"One book you must have on your list...don't miss it!"
—*Romance Reviews Today* on *Along Came a Husband*

"In this touching story about the power love has to heal all wounds, Brenna's characters have terrifically real depth and emotional appeal."
—*RT Book Reviews* on *Then Comes Baby*

"A talented storyteller, Brenna has a gift for writing category romance. She understands how to create intimate, heart-touching stories with the kind of vigorous writing that makes a series romance a satisfying little peek into the lives and loves of unique people and families. If you don't know her work, *Next Comes Love* is a nice place to start."
—Michelle Buonfiglio, BN.com

"Highlighting the eternal tension between safety and risk and the familiar and the unknown, this poignant, sweet, gently humorous story focuses on a pair of deeply conflicted protagonists and nicely sets the stage for the Mirabelle Island books to come."
—*Library Journal* on *First Come Twins*

Dear Reader,

Wow. Number five in the An Island to Remember series. It's finally Sarah's turn!

The first time Garrett Taylor popped into my mind for book two, *Next Comes Love,* I had this feeling he had brothers, and by book three I knew at least one of them was going to make his way to Mirabelle. Jesse, though, was a truly larger-than-life surprise.

Sarah and Jesse. Jesse and Sarah. No matter how I look at it, these two simply belong together. I hope you enjoy the journey of them discovering what was so clear to me from page one.

Two more An Island to Remember stories are coming in August and September 2011. I promise *Her Sure Thing* will shake up the life of entirely-too-content Dr. Sean Griffin. And *Redemption at Mirabelle* has Missy Charms's sister, Marin Camden, getting a little more than she bargained for when she comes to the island for some R & R.

Without giving too much away, Mirabelle Island itself is going to face its toughest challenge yet in the midst of these three stories, so keep reading! And check out my website at www.helenbrenna.com. I'll be adding pages of Mirabelle Island detail, pictures, maps and a character chart.

I love hearing from readers. You can contact me at helenbrenna@comcast.net, or P.O. Box 24107, Minneapolis, MN 55424.

My best,

Helen Brenna

The Pursuit of Jesse
Helen Brenna

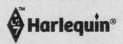

TORONTO NEW YORK LONDON
AMSTERDAM PARIS SYDNEY HAMBURG
STOCKHOLM ATHENS TOKYO MILAN MADRID
PRAGUE WARSAW BUDAPEST AUCKLAND

Recycling programs
for this product may
not exist in your area.

ISBN-13: 978-0-373-71719-4

THE PURSUIT OF JESSE

This edition published by arrangement with Harlequin Books S.A.

For questions and comments about the quality of this book please contact us at Customer_eCare@Harlequin.ca.

www.Harlequin.com

Printed in U.S.A.

ABOUT THE AUTHOR

Helen Brenna grew up in central Minnesota, the seventh of eight children. Although she never dreamed of writing books, she's always been a voracious reader. So after taking a break from her accounting career to be an at-home mom, she tried her hand at writing the romances she loves to read. Since she was first published in 2007, her books have won many awards, including the Romance Writers of America's prestigious RITA® Award, *RT Book Reviews* Reviewer's Choice Award, the HOLT Medallion, the Book Buyers' Best Award and the National Readers' Choice Award.

Helen lives happily ever after with her family in Minnesota. She'd love hearing from you. Email her at helenbrenna@comcast.net or send mail to P.O. Box 24107, Minneapolis, MN 55424. Visit her website at www.helenbrenna.com or chat with Helen and other authors at *Riding With The Top Down.*

Books by Helen Brenna

HARLEQUIN SUPERROMANCE	HARLEQUIN NASCAR
1403—TREASURE	PEAK PERFORMANCE
1425—DAD FOR LIFE	FROM THE OUTSIDE
1519—FINDING MR. RIGHT	
1582—FIRST COME TWINS*	
1594—NEXT COMES LOVE*	
1606—THEN COMES BABY*	
1640—ALONG CAME A HUSBAND*	
1672—THE MOON THAT NIGHT	

*An Island to Remember

For Johanna Raisanen
Thanks for making that first big leap of faith!

Acknowledgments:

He doesn't yet know this, but I have to thank
Adam Gadach, once again, for inspiring me to
write this story. He's a real live hero who truly
knows how to forgive.

Adam was hit by a drunk driver one night and, as
a result, lost his leg.

The man who hit him was Adam Lunn,
and I do need to thank him, too, for showing me
how a man starts to find the courage
to face his mistakes.

Believe it or not, these two men stand side by side
and talk to DWI offenders about their experience,
hoping to make a difference, hoping to save lives.
I have to believe they've saved more than one.

My best to you both,
Helen

"To err is human, to forgive divine."
—Alexander Pope

CHAPTER ONE

"THIS WISCONSIN OR the tundra?" Jesse Taylor chuckled as he glanced through the windshield of the four-wheel-drive SUV and into a blinding swirl of white. The bus had only taken him as far as Bayfield. From there, he'd hired a taxi.

"Oh, heck, this ain't nothing," the driver said, his voice cutting through the twang of an old country-and-western song playing on the radio. "We're only gettin' six inches of snow today. I remember once we got eighteen in a coupla hours."

Six inches or eighteen didn't make a bit of difference to Jesse. It'd been a long time since he'd experienced a Midwestern blizzard. Frost built in the corners of the windows and wind twirled the snow, obscuring visibility and causing dangerous drifts. Black ice formed on the frozen road.

"Dang, it's cold out." Even for January. He flipped up the collar of what was proving to be a woefully inadequate jean jacket and hunkered down for the ride.

His skin prickled with more than goose bumps as a sense of uneasiness spread through him. Instinct screamed at him to head south and get as far away from the state of Wisconsin as his thumb would carry him. Nothing here for him except snow and cold. And the past. Reality was, though, he needed some traveling cash, and a job, he hoped, was waiting for him at the end of the line.

"Here." The driver grabbed a knit cap from his center console and tossed it toward Jesse. "Keep your head warm, anyway."

Jesse glanced at the hat and stiffened. In his world, at least the world he'd been living in for the past three years, ten months and sixteen days, there was no such thing as something for nothing.

Relax, man. He doesn't want anything from you.

Carefully taking the hat, Jesse pulled it down over his frozen ears. "Thanks."

"Thought you said you was from Chicago. Heck, you should be used to this kind of weather."

"I've been...away for a few years."

Simple. Evasive. Good job, Jess.

Suddenly, it looked to Jesse as if the road was ending at the shoreline, but the driver wasn't slowing down. "You planning on going right across the lake? I didn't think Lake Superior froze over completely."

"It don't. Chequamegon Bay does most winters, though."

"*Most* winters?" The old truck bounced over an icy ridge and headed out onto the snow-covered ice. "Let's hope this is one of them."

"Don't worry." The man smiled. "I'll get you to Mirabelle Island in one piece."

It wasn't long before the SUV approached a dark blur getting larger by the minute. "That the island?"

"Yessiree."

It was bigger than Jesse had expected and more iso-lated. A cluster of homes and businesses occupied only one corner of the island. The rest of the land appeared undeveloped and thickly wooded with hardwoods and tall, stately pines heavily laded with snow. A winter wonderland kind of place.

"You got someone meeting you at the pier?"

"Yeah." Jesse sighed. "My brother."

"That's good."

Not necessarily. When their father died a long while back, Jesse's oldest brother had snubbed the family patriarch role, but now that he'd gotten married and settled down, he'd become damned near insufferable.

The driver reached Mirabelle's shore. He slowed, put the vehicle in low gear and then drove right up an embankment and into a parking lot. "There you be."

"Thanks." Jesse hesitated. The weather he'd find a way to tolerate, but his brother's cold disapproval would be another thing entirely. Not to mention that this town looked about as welcoming as the frigid temperature. Despite the fact that it wasn't even dinnertime yet, there was absolutely no sign of activity. Only the dim interior lights of a nearby restaurant, the Bayside Café, were any indication there was life on this island.

"You want to wait in my truck for a few minutes? At least until your brother shows up?"

"A little snow never hurt anyone." He'd arrived a bit earlier than he'd expected, but he had an address. He could hike up the hill, if necessary. Even so, he couldn't seem to make himself move.

"Well? You getting out or what?"

Jesse glanced through the falling snow. Quaint little town. Most likely nice people. A community, where everyone knew everyone else. He might've been better off in a city where he could be anonymous.

"Mister? You okay?"

The bottom line was he had no place else to go. "Yeah. Sorry. Thanks for the ride." He handed the guy a twenty, one of only two in his wallet. "Keep the change." Then he took a deep breath and opened the door.

As he stepped into several inches of light snow, wind whipped up the legs of his jeans and up the back of his jacket. He grabbed his bag and slammed the door. The truck pulled away and headed to the mainland, leaving him alone on this apparently deserted chunk of snow and ice. How his brother had ended up here in the north country was anyone's guess, but he sure sounded as if he was here to stay.

"Well, hell," Jesse muttered to himself. "Time to face the music."

He'd taken no more than a few steps when the drone of a small, noisy engine sounded from a short distance away. Seconds later, a snowmobile zipped around the corner and came straight for him. The driver, dressed in an insulated one-piece suit and stocking cap, wasn't wearing a helmet. Jesse took one look at the man and stopped in his tracks.

The machine pulled up next to him and the driver hopped off. "Hello, Jesse." There wasn't even a glimmer of a smile in the man's tough eyes or in the severe set to his lips, but then he was the chief of police. Having a guy like Jesse for a brother sure as hell wasn't a feather in his cap.

"Garrett," Jesse said, reaching out his hand. He realized belatedly that he would've liked a hug, some kind of more meaningful human contact after all these years, but it didn't look as if that was about to happen. "Good to see you."

Garrett stood there for a moment and then he reached out and shook Jesse's hand. "Good to see you, too, Jesse."

A knot formed in Jesse's throat, but he sucked the emotion back into his chest and grinned. "I hope you got a coat I can borrow, 'cause I'm freezing my ass off here."

"Come on." Garrett gave him a half smile. "We'll stop at the station and find you something."

Garrett hopped onto his snowmobile, and Jesse climbed on behind him and held on as they drove a couple blocks into town. Crossing what looked like the main avenue, given the shop fronts and ornate black lampposts. The first thing Jesse noticed were the three bars located within a two-block stretch.

Immediately, the skin on the back of his neck broke out into a cold sweat. *Oh, for crying out loud. Lighten up, Jess. Just because you don't drink anymore doesn't mean you can't have a little fun while you're here.*

Garrett turned down a side street and stopped in front of an historic-looking white clapboard building. The police station. This place was a laugh a minute.

He followed his brother through the front doors and suffered through introductions to Renee, the receptionist, a well-preserved middle-aged woman, and Herman, a lanky old deputy, all the while swallowing the knot of apprehension growing tighter in his chest. He couldn't believe his own brother had become a cop.

They went to the corner office, and Garrett opened up a closet. "Here." He tossed Jesse a winter coat. "Keep it. I got a couple others."

Jesse held out the heavy parka. There was no doubt he was going to need something warm and serviceable, but handouts didn't sit well. "You got anything in red? Or black?" he joked. "Military green has never been my color."

Garrett ignored Jesse's meager attempt at humor and

glanced at his watch. "Before we head up to the house to get you settled, I need to make a stop at that job I told you about."

"Right now?"

"Yep. Sarah will be waiting for us."

"Sarah, huh?" Jesse grinned. "Pretty? Single? Available?"

"All of the above." Garrett frowned. "And a good friend of mine. That's exactly why you'll be steering clear of her and all the rest of the single women on this island. And with the influx of new residents we've had over the last couple of years, there are quite a few."

"Thanks for the vote of confidence."

"Look," Garrett said. "I don't want any trouble."

"Trouble's my middle name, big bro. You know that," Jesse said, trying to make light. From the time he'd been a little boy, he'd been the comic relief. You could always count on Jesse to lighten any tense situation. Bad habit, he knew, but a tough one to break.

"I mean it, Jesse."

"Don't worry." Jesse spun around, wanting out of here as quickly as possible. "Your precious island's safe from me."

"Jesse?"

There is no wave without wind. Jesse repeated his mantra. *Don't cause a wind, you won't have the waves.* He turned and forced out a grin despite the fact his skin felt as if it might crack.

"Don't pull any stunts here on Mirabelle," Garrett whispered, his tone deathly serious. "Brother or not, you screw up and I *will* put you back in jail."

Jesse refused to let his smile dim. "Wouldn't expect anything less from you, Garrett."

CHAPTER TWO

"THIS IS IT, BRIAN." Sarah Marshik, her cheeks sore from smiling nonstop since she'd woken up that morning, glanced through the falling snow at the old Victorian cottage nestled at the edge of Mirabelle Island's forest.

"It's kinda small," Brian said, grimacing. "And old."

"I know, honey. But it's ours. All ours." She looked past the peeling paint and the porch's broken gingerbread trim and imagined the possibilities. "No more apartments. No more rent. You'll have your own yard. A bigger bedroom. And Garrett promised it'll be as good as new by the time he gets done with it. We'll be able to move in before school lets out."

And, she hoped, before this year's wedding season kicked into high gear the first weekend in June. She climbed the snow-covered steps, and pride at her accomplishment swelled in her heart, even as tears blurred her vision. It'd taken her years of scrimping to save for a down payment on a house and even more years of working her butt off building her wedding-planning and flower-shop businesses so that her income would be steady enough to qualify for a loan, but she'd finally managed to pull together all the parts of the equation that made for a good life.

A safe community. Check. A job that paid the bills.

Check. A house. Check. Finally. A little more than ten minutes ago, she'd signed the mortgage papers at Mirabelle's tiny bank. Now this was *her* house.

She put the key in the lock, tapped the snow off her boots and opened the weathered oak door. Then she stepped inside and glanced around. Make that her *dilapidated* and *vermin-infested* house.

The place looked even worse than when it had first come on the market two years ago. There were water stains on the ceiling from a leaky roof. The kitchen countertop and sink were discolored. The walls were pitted with nail holes and large dents as if they'd seen one too many parties, and it looked as if some kind of wild animal had set up camp in the fireplace. She didn't even want to look at the bathrooms or the carpets. On top of the grunge, everything appeared dated, including the countertops, the light fixtures and all the appliances.

The old couple who had owned the cottage had long since stopped spending summers on the island, and had, instead, been leasing the place. As the cottage had fallen into disrepair, the renters had stopped coming and the house had sat dormant for the past several years. No one had wanted to buy it. No one had been able to see what she could see.

Silently, she prayed that Garrett was right and the basic structure was solid and therefore worth remodeling. If he was wrong, she'd just signed her life away for nothing.

Brian followed her inside and took a step toward the kitchen.

"Ah, ah, ah," she said, closing the door. "Stomp that snow off your boots before you start traipsing around."

"Seriously? What difference does it make? This place is a dump."

"Dump or not, it's our dump." Gingerly, she picked up an old wadded-up towel from the corner and laid it in front of the door. "Step on that." The towel was dirty and smelled musty, but it would have to do for now.

"This place is disgusting, Mom. And it smells. You sure you want to live here?"

It was going to take some time, most of her savings and a lot of elbow grease, but this house was eventually going to look perfect, like the home of her dreams.

"Yes, I'm sure." She reached out and ruffled his hair.

"Moooom!" He ducked away. "I'm not a baby."

No, he was nine now. Almost a man, he'd been insisting lately. Well, he could insist all he wanted. Nothing could change the fact that he'd always be her little boy.

"I know the place needs a lot of work before we can move in," she said. "But Garrett's sure he can get everything done before the wedding season kicks into high gear. He'll put in new kitchen cabinets and countertops. New bathrooms. New carpet. You can help me paint. By the time we're finished, it'll be beautiful."

"If you say so."

The sound of a snowmobile coming up the hill filled the quiet outside and Sarah pushed aside the moth-eaten curtain to see Garrett pulling into the yard. Excited to hear when he could start, she didn't give the fact that he had a stranger with him much of a thought. She opened the front door as Garrett came up the steps. "Right on time."

"I knew you'd be excited." Although there was a slight smile on Garrett's face, he looked preoccupied.

He stomped the snow off his boots and stepped inside. The other man followed suit and closed the door behind him. "Sarah, this is my youngest brother, Jesse."

As in the rolling-stone, smart-aleck, ladies' man youngest brother? "No kidding?" she said, warily eyeing the man.

Everyone knew Garrett had three brothers, but she'd never expected any of them to come to Mirabelle, at least not during the winter months. She'd gathered from the past comments Garrett had made that his siblings weren't much for islands, at least not the non-Caribbean variety. While many of the single women on Mirabelle had been after Garrett to talk his brothers into coming north, Sarah had never been one of them. At least not seriously.

"You didn't say anything about him coming. Or did I miss that?" she asked.

"Kind of spur-of-the-moment," Jesse said, holding her gaze.

Then he smiled at her, and her stomach pitched. The way his lips curved in a lopsided grin, the way his eyes twinkled, this man reminded her so much of…Bobby, it was frightening. She hadn't thought of him in years, and she sure as hell didn't want to think about him now. The man—that time—had been the worst mistake of her life.

"Nice to meet you, Sarah." All at once, Jesse took off his hat, ruffled his short dark hair and reached for her hand.

Uh-oh. "Nice meeting you, too," she somehow managed to murmur.

Garrett was the more traditionally handsome of the two brothers, but Jesse, with his rugged features, including a nose that looked to have been broken more than once, dark, scruffy stubble and a tiny silver hoop in his left earlobe, was far more fascinating. At least in Sarah's book. If the way he'd held her hand—a little longer than technically necessary—was any indication, Garrett was right. This brother was the flirt in the family, a fact that likely made up for in spades what he might be lacking in the looks department.

Once upon a time, she would've been tripping all over herself to get to this man, but times had changed. She'd changed. Fun-loving rolling stones didn't make good husband or father material. And if Sarah was attracted to him? Therein lie the first sign Jesse was no good. No woman on earth could pick a good-timing loser faster than Sarah.

She forced her gaze away from Jesse's face and glanced toward Brian, reminding herself of her priorities. *You had your fun with bad boys, and remember how that turned out? Mother first, woman second.* Or *woman never* as had been the case living on an island the size of Mirabelle all these years, but then that had been why she'd moved here in the first place. Very little to no temptation on Mirabelle, the tiny destination wedding spot of the Upper Midwest, and that was fine by her.

"This is Brian," she said, smiling. "My son."

"Hey, there, Brian." Jesse feigned a serious look. "Aren't you supposed to be in school?"

"School's over for the day," Brian said with a scowl on his face. "But I think I'd rather be there than here, anyway."

"It might not look like much right now," Jesse said, glancing around. "Wait a few weeks. You won't even recognize the place."

"I told you, honey, Garrett's going to take care of

everything." She glanced up at Garrett and noticed his frown had deepened. "What's the matter?"

"I don't know how to tell you this."

"Straight-out is usually best."

"There was a young couple here on Mirabelle this past summer. They stayed in one of the honeymoon suites at the Mirabelle Island Inn and expressed a lot of interest in the furniture I'd made for Marty Rousseau. I wasn't going to hold my breath for an order, but…" He ran his hands over his face as he paced. "They called me yesterday, Sarah. Out of the blue. They're buying a new house and want me to make their master bedroom furniture, a dining room set and some other pieces."

"That's great, Garrett! Good for you."

"They want everything ASAP."

"So what does that mean?" As she held her breath, she had the feeling she knew exactly what he was trying to say.

"It means I have to get at the order right away, and it's going to take several months."

Her excitement fizzled like a candle flame doused in a bucket of water. "So you can't help me with my house."

"Sarah, I'm sorry, but this is the biggest order I've gotten since I moved up here. There's potential for a lot more orders. It's just what my furniture business needs to get off and running."

"So now what?" she asked.

"I can do it," Jesse said.

She was supposed to put her house in the hands of Garrett's baby brother? What were the chances he'd actually follow through and get her house done on time? On top of that, she'd expected to spend a lot of time for the next several months at this house helping Garrett.

Day in and day out, side by side with a confirmed ladies' man would be Sarah's nightmare come true.

"Anything Garrett can do, I can do better." Jesse chuckled. "And I won't charge you as much."

Sarah frowned.

"You know what?" One look in her eyes and Jesse turned around. "I think I'll just go outside and let you two talk this over." He crammed his hat back on his head and slipped through the front door.

"Can I go with Jesse, Mom?" Brian asked.

"Sure," she said before thinking about it, but the last thing she needed was for Brian to get friendly with this guy. Who knew what kind of influence he'd be? Unfortunately, her son was already racing outside.

The front door closed and Sarah turned to Garrett.

"I know, I know," he said, holding up his hands. "You probably feel as though I'm backing you into a corner, but the honest-to-God truth is that this is for the best. Jesse's a better all-around carpenter than me."

It wasn't his carpentry skills she was worried about. "If he's so good, why can't he build the furniture and you do my house?"

"Because he's never made so much as a bookshelf. He can do everything from plumbing to finishing work. Lay carpet, install windows, fix that leaky roof." Garrett pointed to the ceiling. "But there's a difference between all that and the detail involved in designing and building one-of-a-kind furniture. This order's too important to leave in the hands of a novice."

Sarah glanced out the window to find Brian throwing snowballs at the side of the storage shed and Garrett's brother watching him, looking as if he didn't have a care in the world. Her apprehension built. Through the years she'd been careful to ensure the male influences in Brian's life had been good men, solid and dependable. She'd bet her bottom dollar Jesse was neither.

"If I remember right," she said, turning back to Garrett, "this is the brother you said went through women like other men went through socks. He moved around so much you were never sure where he was from one day to the next. 'Everybody loves Jesse, but the guy can't hold down a job to save his soul.' Ring a bell?"

"Yeah, I probably did say all those things." Garrett sighed heavily. "But that was then. This is now. Sarah, give him a chance. Please. You and I have laid out every detail of this remodeling project. We've ordered all the supplies. All Jesse has to do is follow through."

"That's the problem. *Will* he follow through?"

"Yeah." Garrett held her gaze. "This time I think he will."

"You *think?*" She had at least one wedding scheduled for every weekend throughout the summer. Come June first, she'd be so busy, she wouldn't have time to take a breath, let alone move into this house. "This is too important to me for you to guess, Garrett. I need you to know."

"What I *know* is that if he doesn't come through, I will. One way or another. I promise."

If there was a man whose promise meant the world and then some, it was Garrett's. He and his wife, Erica, were two of her best friends, and his troubled gaze spoke volumes. Sarah had the distinct feeling she was going to regret this, but if the positions were reversed, Garrett would do this for her in a heartbeat. "Take the furniture order. I'll deal."

He looked only slightly relieved.

That, more than anything, set her on edge. "There's more, though, isn't there?"

"Yeah," he said. "Before you make up your mind, you should know…Jesse…well, he's had some tough luck." Then Garrett shook his head. "No, that's not true. He brought it on himself."

"Brought what on?"

"There's no easy way to say this." He held her gaze. "Jesse just got out of prison. Today."

The words had a hard time registering. "What? Did you say prison? As in guards, bars, cells? Criminals?"

Garrett nodded. "He served an almost four-year term. Was released this morning."

She sucked in a breath, absorbing what he'd said. "What did he do to deserve going to prison?"

Garrett took a couple steps away from her and then looked back. "I promised Jesse I'd let him decide when and how much to tell the islanders. But, Sarah, he's not dangerous to you or Brian. I swear. On my life. On the lives of my family. I care too much for both you and Brian to put either one of you in harm's way."

"So you want me to welcome an ex-con into my home, into my life. Into my son's life." She pointed out the window. "Without the slightest indication—"

"Jesse's done his time. He deserves a chance to get back on his feet, and I know the most important part of the process for my brother is going to be keeping him busy."

Outside, Brian was laughing and talking with Garrett's brother as he threw snowballs at a tree in the woods. Jesse stood there for a moment, watching Brian before picking up a handful of snow and tossing it, then he glanced up and caught her looking at him through the window. His grin brightened for an instant, and an answering wave of attraction pummeled her. As he held her gaze, he clearly sensed her apprehension and his smile slowly disappeared.

Mentally, she kicked herself. *Snap out of it!*

The irony of the fact that she'd even dated a couple of felons a long time ago wasn't lost on her, but no one here on Mirabelle knew about her wild days. She'd moved to Mirabelle to get away from all that, to put the past behind her and start over, start fresh.

She turned back toward Garrett. "I don't think—"

"You know I wouldn't ask if it wasn't important. Please, Sarah. This is the best opportunity I've had yet to get my furniture business going. Give Jesse a chance. For me and Erica."

Garrett had never asked her for anything, and he'd given so much back to this small community, to her. Could she really turn her back on him simply because she was worried that one man was all it would take to ruin the good life she'd built here on Mirabelle? "The Setterbergs need me out of my apartment by the end of May," she said. "If this house isn't ready, I'll have no place else to go."

"It'll be ready. Even if I have to drop my furniture order and do it myself."

Suddenly, she was sick of looking into the faces of men like Jesse and having to fight the urge to run like hell in the opposite direction. She had a good life here on Mirabelle. It was time to prove to herself once and for all that she wasn't going to risk it all over a man, any man. "All right, Garrett. For you. I'll give Jesse a chance."

CHAPTER THREE

JESSE CLIMBED OFF the snowmobile and stared at the log home sitting in the middle of at least an acre-size lot bordered by massive evergreens and bare-branched hardwoods. The structure was old, but clearly solid as a rock. Whoever had taken the time to restore it had done a good job. "Did you do the work on this place yourself?" he asked Garrett.

"Naw, it was mostly finished when I bought it. Did some of the interior work, though."

This setting was a far cry from the inner streets of Chicago where they'd grown up, but somehow this rustic lifestyle seemed to fit the new, settled Garrett.

"My woodworking shop." He pointed to a stand-alone building. "I have duplicates of all my tools, so take whatever you need to work on Sarah's house. With one condition. I want everything back when you're finished. Okay?"

That stung. "What? You think I'm going to skip the island with your tools?" Jesse may have pulled a lot of stunts through the years, but he'd never stolen a damned thing in his life. Well, except for those couple packs of bubble gum he'd snitched from Wolter's candy shop when he was ten.

"Come on," Garrett said, letting the issue hang between them. "It's freezing out here. Let's go inside."

Feeling more than a little out of sorts, Jesse followed

his brother up the steps and onto the wide porch. Though the wind had let up a bit, the snow was still falling steadily and the sun had all but set, leaving behind frigid temperatures. The moment the front door opened, a blast of warm, garlic-and-meat-scented air hit Jesse square in the face.

Quickly, he glanced around. A mudroom combination laundry room was positioned to their left, and a large kitchen opened in front of them with a family room off to the right. Pots and pans bubbled on the stove, a fire sizzled in a stone hearth and a kid's video game quietly played out on a wide-screen TV.

An attractive dark-haired woman came toward them from the kitchen and Garrett grinned as he shrugged out of his coat and hung it on a nearby hook. "Hey, you." Garrett planted a kiss on his wife's lips.

Jesse would've expected a quick peck on a closed mouth given the couple had been married for a while, but, no. This contact was instantly intimate. The petite woman nearly disappeared when Garrett wrapped his big arms firmly around her.

Caught off guard, Jesse found himself staring. What would it feel like to be welcomed home that sweetly? Hell, it'd been so long since he'd been kissed, he'd surely forgotten what a woman's lips felt like. Although the exchange lasted only a second or two, it was long enough for Jesse to feel as if he were intruding.

Garrett stepped back, his arm still draped over his wife's shoulder. "Jesse, this is Erica."

Jesse nodded and reached out to shake her hand. "Nice to finally meet you." Per Jesse's orders his family and friends had not been allowed to visit him while he'd been behind bars, and suddenly, he felt awkward and shy, meeting for the first time this woman who'd become so important to his brother in such a short amount of time.

Chuckling, she glanced at his hand. "That's a joke, right? We're family." Then she threw her arms around him and hugged him. "I'm glad you're finally...here."

Jesse made an attempt at hugging her back, but it didn't feel right. After so many years of holding the world at arm's length, he wasn't sure he remembered everyday niceties.

"Daddy, Daddy!" A toddler sat in a high chair near the kitchen's center island, his arms impatiently outstretched toward Garrett.

"And this is David." Garrett kissed the cheesy-sauced cheek of his young son and scooped him out of the high chair. *Cute kid.* Reminded Jesse of baby pictures of Garrett. His brother sure did seem comfortable around all this domesticity.

"Zach?" Erica called. "Come and meet your uncle, kiddo."

A young boy popped up from the family-room floor and came toward them, his hands hanging awkwardly at his sides. "Hey."

"Hey, Zach." Jesse reached out and shook the boy's hand.

From what Garrett had written in his infrequent emails to Jesse, Garrett and Erica had adopted her nephew after Erica's sister had been murdered by her husband, Zach's dad. Damn. And Jesse thought he'd had a tough childhood. The kid's real name was Jason, but he went by Zach or Zachary, the name he'd chosen when he and Erica had first come to Mirabelle to hide from her abusive brother-in-law. Sounded to Jesse like a way to evade the past and all its pain, but who was Jesse to judge? The kid looked as if he was doing okay.

"You look like you're about Brian's age, huh?" Jesse said. "Sarah's son. You two friends?"

"Yeah." Zach's eyes lit up. "Best friends."

"That's cool. He seems like a nice kid." For a moment, Jesse stood there, unsure of what to do next.

"Well, settle in quick," Erica said, heading back to the stove. "Dinner's ready in a few minutes. Hope you like pork chops. Mashed potatoes and gravy."

Jesse's mouth watered at the thought of his first home-cooked meal in almost four years.

"Come on, Jess." Garrett started toward the back of the house. "I'll show you to your room before we eat."

Jesse picked up his bag and followed Garrett down a hallway off the kitchen. "Erica and I are upstairs with the kids," he said. "You're in the spare room down here. We'd been using it for storage, so it's nothing special."

Jesse walked through the doorway and flicked on the light. Unlike the rest of the house, this room was sparse and plain. There was a bed, dresser and bedside table. The closet was still full of boxes, camping gear and luggage.

"I know it's basic, but—"

"It's clean," Jesse said. "It has a bed." He threw his bag onto the mattress. For years, he'd dreamed of this moment, he'd dreamed of being free, but now that he was out it all seemed terribly wrong. He didn't belong here. This was all too perfect. Too nice. Too good for the likes of him.

"And there aren't any prison bars," Garrett said softly.

"Nope." Jesse glanced out the window into the dusky early evening, saw the snow falling more gently now and felt sweat break out on his brow. Most of the men he'd gotten to know in prison would've been leaping for joy right about now. An open window. Open door. A couple of open bars down on Main Street. And from what Garrett had said a few ready-and-willing single women.

Women like Sarah with her long, straight black hair, piercing blue eyes, made almost fierce with those thick arching eyebrows and dark lashes. And those lips with their dramatic fullness. It'd been almost four years since he'd touched a woman, four long years since he'd been touched with anything even remotely resembling tenderness.

Abruptly, the look on Sarah's face as she stared at him through her window just a short while ago flashed through his memory. He glanced back at his brother. "You told her about me, didn't you?"

Garrett held his gaze. "You mean Sarah?"

Jesse nodded.

"If you're going to be working in her home, she deserved to know."

"Forewarned is forearmed. That's fair." Jesse was going to have to live with being a felon from here on out, so he might as well get used to it. "What exactly did you tell her?"

"What we agreed on. Only that you'd gotten out of prison."

"She was okay with that?"

"Not entirely, but Sarah's one of our best friends. She trusts me." He sighed. "Erica's the only one who knows the whole truth. I haven't told anyone else on this island anything about you. Now that Sarah knows you came straight from prison, that's bound to get out.

It's up to you how much more you want to tell anyone else."

Jesse looked away for a moment. "What about Zach?"

"He doesn't even know the prison part. Kids ask a lot of questions, Jess. I thought it best you told him when you were ready, but I wouldn't wait too long. He's bound to hear rumors, and it's probably better if he hears the truth from you."

"Look, if me being here is going to cause you too much trouble, I'll go someplace else." Already his feet were itching to hit the road. All he needed was an excuse. On second thought, maybe what he *wanted* was an excuse.

"You don't have any place else to go and you know it."

"I can find a job someplace else." Someplace where no one knew him. Where no one knew what he'd done.

"Don't you dare start thinking about cutting and running," Garrett said. "I stuck my neck out for you. Promised Sarah you'd finish her house."

Jesse hadn't made any promises, so he sure as hell couldn't break any. All he wanted—all he needed—was some traveling cash. Just enough to get him a long, long way from Wisconsin. Hell, before he'd gone to prison the longest he'd ever stayed in the same town had been three months. He gave Mirabelle two months, tops. As soon as spring hit he was history.

"Jesse, I mean it. She needs that house finished before the end of May."

"Don't worry about it, bro."

Garrett studied him for a moment. "I'm not going to lie to you. Mirabelle's a small island. This whole place is going to be buzzing with the news about you coming. Why you're here. Where you came from. This place is just like any other. Some will cut you some slack. Some will hate you on sight. But if there's ever a place that'll give you a chance to start over, start fresh, Mirabelle is it."

"Dinner's ready," Erica called from the kitchen.

His chest tightened. The last thing in the world Jesse could stand in that moment was sitting around a cozy table with Garrett in his perfect house with his perfect family. Maybe starting over, starting fresh wasn't at all what Jesse deserved. Besides, four years of sucking it up while guards told him what to do and when was enough.

"You know what?" Jesse said, smiling. "I think I might head downtown." Just because he could. "I'm feeling a little antsy. Figure I'll get the lay of the land. Check out Main Street."

Refusing to look at Garrett's face, knowing all he'd find in the depths of his brother's eyes was disappointment, Jesse put his head down and walked toward the front door. "I won't be too late. Don't bother waiting up for me."

He tugged on the coat Garrett had lent him, walked through the kitchen, keeping his gaze averted from Erica and the kids, and slipped out the front door. He was halfway down the hill before he felt as if his chest wasn't going to cave in on him. *Breathe, Jesse. Breathe.*

The rush of cold air recharged his senses and he went on his way. Having absolutely no idea where he was going, Jesse let his feet take him wherever they wanted to go. Before he knew it, he'd passed the pier, hit Main and headed down the middle of the deserted, snow-smattered cobblestone street.

He walked a few blocks, passing stately black lamp-posts and the picturesque storefronts of Main Street Mirabelle businesses, a few even trimmed with under-stated but colorful winter lights. Everything was neat and tidy.

Hell, even the snow seemed to understand it had better behave on Mirabelle. Every sidewalk had been shoveled clean, and just enough of the picturesque white stuff had accumulated on windowsills, signs and bare tree branches to give all of Main Street the appearance of a holiday greeting card. This place really had to be something in the summer. Too bad he wouldn't be around to see it.

He glanced up and saw Duffy's Pub scrolled in large brass letters across the front of a brick building. That was Erica and Garrett's place now that they'd bought it from the previous owners. Not what Jesse wanted tonight. What he needed was the peace of at least one night of anonymity.

Pushing himself onward, he passed a bright red candy store, a gift shop that looked as fanciful as its name Whimsy implied and a flower shop. *Weddings and Flowers by Sarah.* Garrett had explained that Sarah needed to get into her house before her wedding season started. This had to be her store.

With a display of the trappings of a wedding—photo albums, a towering cake, sample invitations, floral bou-quets, even a pair of lacy bridal gloves and glittering sandals—it was clear Sarah had an eye for pretty in-nocent things. She'd taken one look at him and had known he didn't fit in her world. She'd been right.

He was about to call it a night and head back to

Garrett's when he glanced down a side street and noticed light emanating through frost-covered windows a couple blocks down. There just might be a bar or restaurant off the beaten path that better suited him and his mood.

Making his way down the sidewalk, he read the sign out front swinging in the bitter wind. The Rusty Nail Tavern. Either the place had fallen on hard times, or the owner preferred a low-key, somewhat tacky appearance. In any case, Jesse had something in common after all with at least one establishment on this island fantasyland.

He opened the door and hesitated. Immediately, his senses were assaulted by the sounds of rock music, laughter and conversation, the slight scent of stale beer and even more stale cigarette smoke. He hadn't been in a bar, let alone around people drinking, since…

Go back to Garrett's, idiot. You don't need to do this. Things can be different. Better.

Yeah? How? This is what you do. This is what you always do. I'm not going to drink, anyway. Even if I did there are no cars on this island, so what could possibly be the harm?

He plastered a smile on his face, stepped inside and headed right for the bar. The first thing he noticed was a cute blonde sitting a few stools away and nursing a tall pink concoction. She honed in on him like a hunter with a twelve-point buck in his sights.

"What can I get for you?" the bartender asked.

Even on a cold evening like this a beer sounded damned good. Then again, screwing things up the first night in Dodge probably wasn't a good idea. There'd be plenty of time for that later. "Cola, please."

"You visiting Mirabelle?" he asked, filling a glass with ice.

"Here for a couple months. Some construction work."

"Tom Bent," he said, setting the soda in front of Jesse.

"Pleased to meet you. Jesse." Just Jesse tonight. Even whispering the name of Taylor was bound to put a damper on the evening.

"Well, don't be a stranger." The owner wandered off.

Predictably, the blonde slid off her bar stool and walked toward him. Garrett be damned, right along with his order for Jesse to steer clear of the single women on this island. As long as Jesse was stuck here on Mirabelle, he might as well have some fun. She wasn't really his type, but there was no wedding ring in sight and she'd certainly help in passing the time.

"Well, hello, stranger," she said. "I may have just moved to Mirabelle last spring, but I'm sure I've never seen hide nor hair of you on this island before."

"Hello, yourself. I'm Jesse."

"Sherri Phillips."

"Did you say Sugar? Sugar Phillips? 'Cause you sure look sweet."

"Sherri, silly." She laughed and moved a little closer. "I own a hair salon a couple doors down, and I can't wait to get my hands on your…head."

"You can get your hands on any part of me anytime you want," he said softly.

"That's what I like to hear." She slid her hands along his arms. "Just so you know, though, strings don't stay on this little package. Understand?"

"Perfectly."

This was more like it. Finally, after four long years, Jesse was back in his comfort zone.

HER ELBOWS RESTING on the counter and her head in her hands, Sarah sat in her tiny apartment kitchen late that night with her laptop in front of her. She'd waited until Brian was sound asleep before logging on to the internet, and although she'd been at it for almost an hour searching for information, she'd had absolutely no luck.

Naturally, she'd located several people with the name Jesse Taylor, including a teacher at a martial-arts studio, a couple of teenagers with social-networking pages, a doctor at a medical clinic in Cincinnati and the president of a seafood company in Alabama. None of the individuals listed were of the same approximate age as Garrett's brother, and she could find no record of a Jesse Taylor ever having lived in the Chicago area. It was as if Garrett's brother didn't exist.

On top of that, she couldn't find a single mention of a legal issue or newspaper report involving a Jesse Taylor. Four years, though, was a fairly long prison term. Whatever he'd done, it'd been serious.

She searched for the types of crimes leading to four-year terms and discovered any number of infractions he could've committed. He could've been convicted of a robbery or rape. Maybe he'd been dealing cocaine, or gotten busted for operating a meth lab. It was possible he'd embezzled tens of thousands of dollars from little old ladies. Some of the crimes were violent, others were not.

She conjured the image of Jesse's face in her mind. That smile. Those eyes. His hand had felt so warm, his touch so engaging. It was difficult to imagine that someone as fun-loving as he appeared could've done anything to deserve prison time, let alone something violent. Not knowing what crime Jesse Taylor had committed worried her. Finding herself even remotely attracted to him in spite of it worried her much, much more.

CHAPTER FOUR

THE SOUND of heavy rock music blaring from a radio in the kitchen, Jesse ignored the two boys standing in the corner of one of the bedrooms in Sarah's house watching him work. Every day since he'd arrived on Mirabelle more than a week ago, they'd come here wanting to help and every day Jesse had done his best to ignore them. Today, although Zach was clearly interested in the ins and outs of ripping out old carpet, he rifled through the tools in the toolbox lying on the floor. Brian, on the other hand, watched Jesse's every move.

"Don't you boys have anything better to do than stand there staring at me day in and day out?" The presence of an audience was a bit disconcerting as far as Jesse was concerned, but at least they were kids. He didn't feel the need to make nice with a couple of nine-year-olds.

Zach glanced hopefully at Brian. "We could go up to the community center and shoot some hoops."

This small island had a community center? Jesse might have to check that out.

"I'm sick of basketball," Brian muttered.

"Yeah, I guess you're right."

"I'm so ready for baseball to start I can taste the hot dogs," Brian said. "You ever play any ball, Jesse?"

Hell, yes. There was a time the Taylor boys had dominated the game of baseball in their Chicago neighborhood. With Garrett pitching, Chris on first, Drew catching and Jesse at shortstop, it got to be no one within a couple-mile radius would play ball with the Taylors unless they split two and two between teams.

He almost smiled as the memories flooded his senses. The hot sun on the back of his neck. The dusty, dirt fields. The smell and feel of an oiled leather glove. Back then the worst things he'd had to worry about were skinned knees and how bad of a mood their dad would be in when he got home from work.

"Yeah, I played baseball when I was a kid," Jesse blurted out before remembering he shouldn't be engaging these boys. The last thing he needed was for the two of them to think he *wanted* them hanging around here.

"Zach pitches and I play shortstop," Brian said. "What position did you play?"

"You boys need to move." Jesse yanked up the last corner of the carpet and started rolling it. "You're in the way. You don't want to play b-ball, fine. Figure something else out. Anything not here is better than nothing."

"We wouldn't be doing nothing if you let us help," Brian said, raising his eyebrows.

"And what if you get hurt? Or screw something up?"

Zach's shoulders slumped as if Jesse had hit a nerve, and a pang of guilt niggled at his conscience. That kid had had a tough enough start to life. Jesse sure didn't need to make things worse.

"We're not stupid," Brian said, undaunted. "We know how to do things."

"Yeah," Zach added. "Even Garrett lets us help with stuff sometimes."

"Yeah, well, I'm not Garrett." Jesse crossed his arms. "So hit the roa—"

"You lift weights, don't you?" Brian asked, his attention instantly redirected to the bulk of Jesse's chest.

Jesse kept his mouth shut. The answer to that question would go over like a lead balloon. Other than work out what the hell else was there to do in prison? Except for read. In fact, he'd read so much he'd managed to get a two-year community-college degree through online courses. At least one good thing had come from his incarceration.

He considered telling the boys about his stint in prison. Better they get the truth from him rather than rumors and lies from someone else, as Garrett had said. What explanation could he give that wouldn't make the boys think less of him? The fact that he cared the slightest bit about what they thought of him was an entirely different matter.

"We have free weights at our house," Zach added. "But Garrett won't let me lift the heavy stuff yet. Says my bones aren't ready."

As far as Jesse was concerned, weight rooms were things from his past. He'd quite happily get his workouts through physical labor from here on out. Wiping the sweat from his brow with the back of a gloved hand, he rolled up the rest of the dirty green shag and hoisted it up and over his left shoulder. His biceps screamed, his quads burned, he was dirty as a bum and he'd never felt better. He was a free man with a job and a place to stay. Life was about as good as it was going to get. At least until he got off this frozen rock of an island and moved as far south as he could.

Moving south. That thought more than anything suddenly improved his mood. A nice balmy breeze, sand between his toes. Girls in bikinis, golden skin slathered in oil. *Mmm, mmm, mmm.* How long had it been since he'd kissed a woman? Smelled a woman's hair? Felt soft, warm feminine skin under his fingertips? And he wasn't talking about anything like what had happened last week in the bathroom of the Rusty Nail between him and Sherri. That had amounted to nothing more than soothing a physical need. No, what he had in mind was something softer, more tender. He flashed on the way Sarah's hand had felt in his, and the heavy carpet wobbled, nearly toppling him over.

Steady, man. Rebalancing the roll over his left shoulder, he slowly made his way out of the bedroom and down the hall.

"I'll get the front door!" Brian said, running down the hall.

The kid seemed so hungry for male attention, but for the first time since they'd shown up almost an hour ago, Jesse was glad they were around. Still, he couldn't help but wonder about the kid's father. Garrett had said Sarah was single, but did her ex live on the island? If not, where was he?

Jesse carefully angled the length of carpet through the front door and across the porch before flipping the roll into the Dumpster Garrett had delivered Jesse's first morning on the island. When he turned, he noticed Brian's mom, her shoulders squared and her head held high, walking across the snow-covered yard.

Poised. That was the first word that came into his mind the moment he saw Sarah. Hot on its tail were three more. *Curvy, confident* and *sexy in a very serious way. Okay, a few more than three.* A blast of cold winter air hit him in the face, cooling his skin, but it wasn't enough to cool the thoughts running through his head.

No woman should look that good in a turtleneck, serviceable down jacket and, of all things, mukluks. With her long black hair falling in loose curls past her shoulders, her lips painted a dusky red and her dark eyebrows arched inquisitively, she was the best thing he'd seen in a damned long time. Except that she wasn't his type. Not by a long shot.

From the classy dress pants to the perfect makeup, Sarah had *good girl* written all over her. Sherri Phillips, on the other hand, while not perfect, was more his style. Hearty, gutsy laugh. Easy way. Sweet. Fun. Uncomplicated. What more could a man want?

He took a deep breath and put on his game face. That's when he noticed Sarah was carrying something bulky in her arms. "Afternoon, Sarah. Need some help with whatever you got there?"

"Hello, and no, thank you." Despite her half smile, she didn't look very pleased.

Most people probably figured her for the calm, serene sort, but the intensity of her pale blue eyes blew that image to hell and back as far as Jesse was concerned.

She came up the porch steps and, virtually ignoring Jesse, zeroed in on her son. "Brian, have you been coming here every day after school?"

The kid looked at Jesse, quickly calculated whether or not Jesse would back up a lie and just as quickly came to the conclusion he was on his own. Stubbornly, he straightened his shoulders. "Yeah. So?"

"We talked about this." She stomped her boots, dislodging the snow, and then stepped inside the house, carefully unrolling an indoor-outdoor-type carpet runner in the foyer area as she went. "You're supposed to come home after school and get your homework done."

"I can do it after supper."

"You're supposed to come home to check in with me, then do homework and then play, right?"

Brian crossed his arms over his chest. "I'm not a baby, Mom. I should be able to decide when I want to do my homework."

"That's not our deal," she said. "Go on home now."

"But—"

"No buts. It's almost time for dinner. We'll talk about this later."

As Sarah talked with her son it was impossible to not study her. Manicured hands with deep red nail polish. Makeup so perfect he wondered if she used a magnifying glass in the application process. Not a hair out of place in those relaxed curls hanging past her shoulders. What struck him the most was the fact that she was doing her damnedest to send Jesse the message that she wasn't interested in him as a man.

"Can Zach eat over?" Brian asked.

"Sure, but he needs to call home and make sure it's all right with either Garrett or Erica." She put her hands on Brian's shoulders and pointed him toward the door. "Now go."

Poised *and* classy. She probably couldn't pound in a nail to save her soul. *Not your type.* Those hands had probably never seen the likes of dirt let alone a dish, so why was it he wouldn't have minded seeing her with a hammer in her hand? A tool belt hanging around that slim waist. And nothing else. Naked as the day she was born.

Mmm, mmm, mmm. Wouldn't that be a sight for sore eyes?

"Bye, Jesse!"

The sound of his name snapped his thoughts back to the present. "Huh? Oh. Bye, boys."

Zach and Brian both shrugged on their coats and ran out the door, calling in unison over their shoulders, "See you tomorrow."

"No, you won't. Homework, remember?" She turned toward him. "I hope they haven't been getting in your way."

"Naw." He shook his head. "They're nice kids."

"Yes, they are. Mirabelle's a nice quiet island. A lot of good people here."

He didn't miss the edge in her voice, but if there was one thing he'd learned in the past four years it was to not go looking for a fight. If he could avoid it, anyway.

"I'll make sure they don't come up here anymore," she said. "So they won't get in your way."

Fine by him.

She glanced from his shirt to his hair. "Looks like you've been busy today."

He brushed self-consciously at the layer of dirt and dust covering his long-sleeved black T-shirt. "Yeah, well, best to have everything out of here before all the supplies you and Garrett ordered are delivered. So I've basically been gutting the place."

"Good idea." She slipped off her boots, walked into the kitchen and turned off the radio.

"Sorry," he said. "It's been pretty quiet around here. I found that in the basement. Hope you don't mind."

"Not a problem." Slowly, she walked through the

house, glancing around, seeming to take note of his progress.

He struggled for something to say. Put him in a bar with someone like Sherri and he could talk up a blue streak, but this woman made him uneasy. He might be drawn to her, but he was uneasy all the same.

"So...Garrett said you needed to be all moved in here by the end of May. Before your busy season starts," he said, hoping to start the ball rolling. "Wedding planner, huh?"

She nodded. "I do a fair amount of business through my flower shop, as well."

While it was crystal-clear she wasn't interested in casual conversation, she wasn't as immune to him as a man as she wanted him to think. Her gaze would drop to his lips or linger on his arms and chest. He ran his hand along the back of his neck, feeling more edgy with every passing moment. Best to follow her lead and stick to business.

"Things don't seem to be moving very quickly," she said. "I was hoping the carpet would be in by now."

If he'd had feathers, they'd have been ruffled, especially after the week he'd had. Starting work on Sarah's house well before sunrise and working until past dinnertime, he'd put in close to sixty hours. But then that had been entirely his choice.

After the first morning of waking up in Garrett's house to the sounds of everyone else up and about, he'd sworn he'd never do that again. Just listening to the warm coziness of the Taylor family routine through his closed bedroom door—the smell of fresh coffee, the sounds of happy, rested kids, cereal bowls clinking and cartoons on TV—had been enough to make his skin crawl.

From then on he'd gotten up and headed off to work before anyone else had even stirred. To make sure he'd avoid Garrett's family as much as possible, he'd been bringing a bag lunch and eating by himself at Sarah's house. Then it was off to one of the bars downtown for a bite to eat for supper. By the time he'd been getting home, the Taylor house had settled in for the night and he'd been able to sneak back to the guest bedroom without disturbing Garrett, Erica or their kids.

Even with all those hours, Sarah's house was a big job for one man. "Well, for one thing," he said, trying not to sound defensive, "new carpet will likely be the last thing you'll want to do in the house. Wouldn't want it getting dirty, would you?"

"Good point."

"The first thing that had to be done was to fix your leaky roof, remember?"

"Oh, right."

"It was quite a job." Icy wind whipping up his back, hands freezing even in the thick leather gloves Garrett had lent him, Jesse had been on a ladder shoveling snow off a large chunk of the roof that'd apparently been damaged by high winds last fall. The entire roof would need to be replaced come spring, but for the time being he'd had to patch things up to protect the interior.

There was no point in elaborating with the fact that he'd twice nearly slipped off the icy rungs of the ladder, not to mention the roof itself. Or that he'd capped her chimney and patched up a hole in one of her basement windows, ensuring there'd be no more critters nesting in her house. She would've had to be here to appreciate the fact that the time he'd spent outside had been miserable. "That alone took me an entire day."

"I suppose."

After that, he'd cleaned out all the junk the previous owner had left in the basement, taking advantage of the Dumpster while it was available. Then he'd taken out the old toilet, sink and countertop in the main bathroom. Today, he'd pulled up all the ratty carpet.

"So what's next on your agenda?"

"Strip all the linoleum from the floors in the bathrooms and kitchen. By tomorrow the house should be ready for new subflooring."

"New sub—" She stopped. "Can't you save time and money by putting new flooring over the old?"

"Sure. I could do that." He bit back the smart-ass comment on the tip of his tongue. Was this the way it was going to be for the duration of this job? Him having to justify his every move? "But then you'll be stuck with every single creak and groan the old place has developed through the years." To prove his point, he crossed the master bedroom floor, setting off a round of squeaks that would've made anyone cringe.

"And this new…subfloor will get rid of all that?"

"Yes, ma'am."

"But I don't remember that being on Garrett's plan."

Could he really blame her for trusting Garrett more than him? "Well, it should've been. I'm guessing Garrett would've realized you needed new subfloors as soon as he got going on things in here."

"That may very well be." She turned away, put her head down and crossed her arms. When she spun back around her blue eyes had turned stormy. "But from now on I'd appreciate it if you'd stick to the way Garrett had things laid out, okay? If you think you need to deviate from his plan, please run it by me first."

"Yes, ma'am." Uneasiness turned to outright wariness. Apparently, this fight was coming whether he wanted it or not. Might as well get it over with sooner rather than later, so they could move on to more important things, like this attraction he could feel burning up the air between them. "But then this doesn't have anything to do with my construction abilities, does it, Sarah? You got something to say to me, why don't you get it off your chest?"

"Another good idea." She held his gaze. "Garrett said you just got out of prison."

"That's right." Straightening his shoulders, he prepared himself for the question he knew would follow.

"I want to know why you were there," she said. "I want to know what you did to deserve prison time."

He turned away and ran a hand over his face. He'd hoped he'd have more time to settle in here on Mirabelle before being confronted. Suddenly, his palms turned sweaty. His heart raced. He opened his mouth to explain and the words simply were not there. How could he explain that he'd made the worst decision of his life? One minute life was dandy. Then in the blink of an eye he'd almost killed another human being.

It wasn't happening. Not today. Not with Miss High and Mighty. "Sorry, boss." Grinning, he turned toward her. "I'm not in the sharing mood today."

"That's not good enough."

"Well, that's all I got. For the moment. See, I'm not feeling a connection yet between you and me. You know? As a matter of fact, I'm feeling kind of vulnerable." He took a step toward her. "You want me to bare my soul, maybe you should go first. Like…I don't know…you want to tell me about Brian's dad?"

"Brian's dad is none of your business."

"See? There you go. Looks like neither one of us is in a sharing mood."

"So that's the way it's going to be." She frowned. "Then let's get something straight between us right off the bat."

Jesse's spine stiffened, but he managed to plaster a grin on his face. *Here it comes.*

"I don't have the slightest interest in getting to know you." She cocked her head at him. "I've hired you as a favor to Garrett. That's all there is to it. Get my house done and move on."

"Whatever you say, boss." He mock saluted her.

"For that matter. Don't move on. Move *off* the island. For good."

Now he was pissed. "Trust me. The minute your house is finished, I'll be gone. I have no intention of staying on this boring, frozen hunk of rock any longer than necessary."

"Good." She stalked outside, shutting the front door loudly behind her.

That's when the worst of it hit him. This was only the beginning. She was no doubt going to be on his case until this job was done. So why was it he still wanted Sarah, not Sherri or any other woman like her, in bed, under him, and calling out his name?

CHAPTER FIVE

"GOLD CALLA LILIES," Sarah said. Her flower-shop phone on speaker, she talked to Megan, one of the more psychotic bride-to-be clients with whom she'd ever had the pleasure of working. This wedding would be the first of the season, and Sarah couldn't wait until this one was over. "They'll look amazing."

"But I want white daisies," Megan said decisively.

Normally, what the bride wanted, the bride got. Unless what she wanted might end up reflecting badly on Sarah. In this business, reputation was key, and she did her best to make sure every wedding was perfect.

"I know you want daisies, Megan, but remember your dress is classic in design. You wanted a very formal wedding." As she talked, Sarah prepped a mixed vase of stargazer lilies, irises and Bells of Ireland—one of her favorites—for the Mirabelle Island Inn.

Although winter was the slow season on Mirabelle, the island enjoyed a steady stream of snowmobilers, cross-country skiers and snowshoers given the miles of scenic, groomed trails that crisscrossed the many acres of state park land covering more than half of the island. That meant Sarah's shop did a small floral business over the winter providing the hotels, bed-and-breakfasts and a few other businesses on the island with freshly cut arrangements. Most of her time over the winter, though, was spent planning weddings for the upcoming summer season.

Sarah adjusted an iris stem. "White daisies may detract from the dramatic, stylish impact you've said you wanted." Insisted was more like it. Over and over again. "Instead, I'd add a few sprigs of amaryllis," she went on. "A shock of green."

"That sounds terrible." Megan's voice was turning pitchy, a sure sign she was close to drawing a line in the sand.

"Remember the two-toned Leonidas roses? You fell in love with them at first sight. I'm not sure they'll go well with daisies."

"Then maybe the roses weren't the best choice."

Oh, no. If Sarah had anything to say about it, the woman was not changing her mind on the focal flower in her cluster bouquet for the *fifth* time.

"I still think the roses were the right decision," Sarah said, easily keeping her voice steady and calm. "They match your color scheme and the style of your wedding, but before you decide, let me email you some pictures. I think you'll absolutely love what you see." She removed the pollen stamens from the open lilies with a tissue, ensuring the pollen wouldn't drop and stain anything and everything in its path.

She'd been working on the flowers much longer than she should have, but that was par for the course. Weddings and Flowers by Sarah hadn't gotten one of the best reputations in the Upper Midwest for no good reason. Nothing—fresh or silk arrangements, potted plants or the like—left her hands until everything was just right.

The flower shop's front door opened, letting in a burst of cold air, and Sarah glanced up. Her best friend,

Missy Charms Abel, who owned the gift shop next door, had, thankfully, stopped by to break up the monotony of her day. Smiling, Sarah put her index finger to her lips and then pointed to the phone.

"Lunch?" Missy silently mouthed as she held out two takeout bags.

"Yes!" Sarah mouthed back, nodding vigorously, and then spoke into the speakerphone. "So I'll send you the photos of the design I have in mind?"

"I insist on something unique, Sarah." Megan's voice echoed over the speakerphone and through the small flower shop like nails down a chalkboard. "Absolutely unique."

Missy rolled her eyes as she slipped off her boots and walked sock-footed across the tiled floor.

"I promise I've never done this arrangement before," Sarah said to Megan as she smiled at Missy. "I'll email you those pictures as soon as we get off the phone. Let me know what you decide. No rush. Take your time." Sarah disconnected the call before Megan could find something else to obsess over and glanced up at Missy.

Her friend shook her head. "She sounds like a winner."

"Guess how old she is?"

"To be that particular? Forty."

"Eighteen."

"You're kidding. What's her story?"

"High-school sweethearts. He's in the military. She's just graduating from high school this spring. Around New Year's, they found out Brandon was scheduled to ship off to Afghanistan on July first. That's when they got engaged."

"So why wait? Why not just run out and get married?"

"She insisted on a Mirabelle wedding. In spring. Period. She wants the perfect wedding," Sarah added. "And Daddy's made it clear that the sky's the limit for his only child."

"I don't know how you deal with all those crazy brides."

"Very carefully." Sarah laughed, prepping an email to Megan. "Honestly, though, I don't mind." Her years of experience with stressed-out brides-to-be and their stressed-out mothers had taught her to take their wacked-out moods in stride.

"Better you than me." Missy set the bags on the counter.

Sarah attached a photo of the arrangement she had in mind for Megan and sent the email. "There you go, Megan," she said, breathing a sigh of relief.

Only a second later, her computer pinged with received mail.

"Is that her replying back that quickly?" Missy asked, looking surprised.

"Yep. She thinks she likes this one. But she wants to make sure the bridesmaids' bouquets are in sync with hers."

"I swear," Missy said, shaking her head. "Your brides get more obsessive every year."

"Don't tell anyone I said this, or I could be out of a job. But sometimes I think couples these days are entirely missing the point of the day."

"So what's your idea of the perfect wedding? What's your day going to be like?"

A woman didn't dream of her wedding day if she never expected to get married. Besides, Sarah had once upon a time planned the perfect wedding. Pulling out all the stops never ensured a blissful union. "Who says I'm ever getting married?"

"Oh, come on."

"Seriously. I've got Brian. Great friends. A successful business. I love Mirabelle Island. Soon, I'll have a house. What more could a woman want?"

"A man she loves to share it all with?"

"Not gonna happen, but I'm so glad you stopped by," she said, abruptly changing the subject. People who were happy in their marriages always wanted everyone else to get married. "I really needed this break. What wonderful thing did you bring me to eat?"

Missy looked reluctant to let the topic of a possible Sarah-wedding go, but she did. "I've been dying for Dee Dee's cranberry almond salad with tofu crumbles. So I brought you her Caribbean chicken."

Missy was the island's only resident vegetarian, and she'd started off a bit of a health kick for Sarah. "Yum," Sarah murmured. "Sandwich or salad?"

"Salad, of course."

"That's going to hit the spot." The mango, black beans and jicama mixture over a bed of mixed greens sounded wonderful. "I just need to finish this arrangement before I eat, but you go ahead."

Missy took off her coat, unwrapped the colorful scarf around her neck and hung them both over the back of her chair. "You coming to yoga tonight?"

Missy taught twice-a-week classes up at the community center. Sarah tried to make it as often as she could, but she never seemed to have enough time in the week for consistent workouts.

"I think I can come after I get Brian to basketball practice. You might have to start without me."

"We can wait. I don't think anyone will mind. Oh, that reminds me. Did you hear the latest?" Her voice took on a conspiratorial tone. "Sherri cut my hair this morning and she said Garrett Taylor's brother moved to the island. She was in the Rusty Nail a couple nights ago and out of the blue this guy she'd never seen came walking in from a virtual blizzard. She said they talked and danced…"

Just talked and danced? That'd be the day.

"…said something about a quick trip to the bathroom…"

There you have it.

"…and all she knew was his first name. She didn't find out he was Garrett's brother until the next day when Crystal Stotz came in for a color. His name's Jesse. The baby in the family, and Sherri says he's as different from Garrett as curly from straight."

She had that right.

"She said he's going to be here for a while."

"Yeah, I know."

Missy's eyes widened. "You knew about this and you didn't tell me?"

"There's nothing to tell. Garrett can't do the work on my house, so Jesse's taking care of it."

"You don't sound happy about the situation."

Sarah shrugged.

"Has he started working on your house yet?"

"Apparently."

"Is he not doing a good job?"

"I've gone up there a couple times." After their run-in the other day, she'd done her best to go to the house only when she knew he was gone. She wasn't sure she could handle again the way he looked at her, as if he knew his touch would very likely set her skin on fire. The way he called her boss, as if she was no such thing, as if with a flick of a wrist he could get her to do his bidding. "The job seems to be getting done in a...competent manner."

The fact was she'd been surprised by how good a job he was doing, and had been hard-pressed to come up with improvements. Still, she'd wanted him to know she was keeping a close eye on him, so she'd—basically—manufactured things for him to do in the notes she'd left for him.

"Buuuuut?" Missy said, pressing for more.

"I just...I don't like him," she said decisively.

Missy raised her eyebrows.

Sarah held stubbornly silent. Although they'd moved to Mirabelle within a few months of each other and had been best friends since, there were things about Sarah's past she hadn't shared with Missy. Sarah had wanted to start fresh here on Mirabelle. As time had gone on, it'd gotten easier to let the past lie.

"What's this all about?" Missy said softly.

"Let's just say that you're not the only one with a past you're not too proud of and leave it at that."

"Tough to argue with that."

Missy's skeletons had rattled their bones in an effort to come out of the closet late one evening last summer when her presumed-dead husband, Jonas Abel, had shown up on her doorstep. It wasn't long after that Missy had felt compelled to share everything with Sarah, even the fact that she'd come from an extremely wealthy family. Sarah had been angry at first, but their friendship had been too important to toss aside.

"Does this have anything to do with Brian's dad?" Missy asked.

It had everything to do with him. Everything. Avoiding Missy's gaze by fussing instead with the flower arrangement, she pulled out one stem after another only to replace each one in the same spot.

Jesse's smirk. His deep voice. His laugh. The look in his eyes that made her skin flare with heat. How could she explain that Jesse reminded her a little of every man she'd ever dated before coming to Mirabelle, of the recklessness with which she'd once lived?

"Sarah, you're my best friend." Missy touched her hand. "There can't possibly be anything in your past that will change our relationship today."

"I wouldn't be too sure about that." If Missy knew the whole truth then she would never look at Sarah the same way again. In the back of her mind, it would be there. Always.

"If it's something you did, didn't do, I don't care. You forgave me, didn't you?"

Not the same thing. All Missy had been hiding is that she'd once been listed as one of the richest kids in America.

"You're not giving me much credit," Missy said.

Maybe she could share part of the truth. Only part. "It's a long story, Missy." She stuck one last iris stalk into the vase and called it a day. She could mess with this arrangement forever and it would never be perfect. "You sure you want to hear?"

"Come on, Sarah." Missy smiled gently. "Tell me what's going on with you."

CHAPTER SIX

SARAH PUT THE ARRANGEMENT in the cooler and then turned. This was it. Time to get this off her chest—at least some of it—once and for all. "You knew I grew up in Indiana," she said, leaning back against the wall and letting her thoughts wander back in time, an indulgence she rarely allowed herself. "But I've never told you much about my childhood. My family."

"No," Missy murmured.

"Well, as wealthy as your family was? Is, I should say. Mine was on the other end of the spectrum."

"I've met your mom and dad," Missy said, confusion on her face. "They seemed…middle-class."

"You met my stepdad," Sarah said. A few years back, when Brian was too small to take care of himself, her mom and stepdad had driven to Mirabelle to help with Brian during a particularly busy wedding season. "My real dad died when I was ten."

"I'm sorry, Sarah. I didn't know."

"It's okay." It really wasn't, but maybe talking about him might help. Sarah's real father had been the only bright spot in an otherwise dreary childhood, and she still missed him with a vengeance. "Before my dad died, we were dirt-poor."

"That's nothing to be ashamed of."

"It's nothing I'm proud of, that's for sure. Maybe if my parents had only had a couple children things might've been different, but I'm smack-dab in the middle of seven kids. They could never afford a house, so all of us were crammed into a second-floor apartment, above a drugstore.

"My dad worked at an orchard. Long, back-breaking hours during certain times of the year. We hardly ever saw him at harvest time, but in the winter he made up for it with all of us. Work hard and play harder. That's what he'd say."

She smiled, remembering. She had only a few pictures of her dad, but in every one of them he was smiling or laughing. "He was always happy. I don't think I ever saw him angry. At us kids. Or my mom. God, he and Mom were so much in love. He could make her laugh like no one else.

"I remember them talking quietly about buying a house. My dad wanted to start his own apple orchard, and my mom used to say that a house was the key to happiness." Sarah looked away. "She also used to say, after he died, that he was all talk and no action."

"Oh, Sarah." Missy reached out and briefly squeezed her hand. "How did he die?"

"He got sick. Had a low fever. Didn't seem to be a big deal." She paused, not wanting to remember anything more than that. The rest was too painful. "A few days into it, he got really bad, but we couldn't afford a doctor. By the time my mom realized how sick he was, it was too late. He died of complications from pneumonia. How stupid is that? All because we didn't have enough money to pay for a doctor."

"I'm sorry."

"I was devastated. Heartbroken. We all were. My mom didn't come out of her bedroom for days. Not long after that, we moved back to my mom's hometown to be by my grandparents and she met my stepdad. He was an okay guy. Quiet and dependable. Nice enough—a banker—but boring, especially when compared to my dad. I understand now why she married him, but at the time I couldn't forgive her."

"For marrying again?"

"For betraying my father. More than that, for, I guess, settling. It wasn't long before I started to feel… almost…claustrophobic. I couldn't wait to get away from Indiana."

"So you left," Missy said.

Sarah nodded. "Right after high-school graduation, I went to Miami. When I got there, I felt shell-shocked. I'd been so sheltered."

"A good girl in a big, tough city," Missy murmured.

"I did okay at first. Picked up a lot. Fast. I got a job within the first week working for a well-known wedding planner. Her clients were only the richest and the most famous."

Having grown up as a Camden, one of the wealthiest families this country had ever known, Missy had probably run in the same crowd until she'd turned her back on her family and tried for her own fresh start.

"I wasn't as strong as you were, Missy. Before I knew it, I'd fallen in with a crowd that loved to party. Damn, I met some men who knew how to have a good time. But then, I guess, so did I." She glanced at her friend, hoping to gauge her reaction. Instead of judgment, there was only compassion and understanding. Still, she knew she couldn't share everything.

It'd been a long time since she'd let herself even think about the past, let alone talk about it, but as she relayed her story to Missy, it hit Sarah. She was lucky to be alive. "I did a lot of crazy things back then, you know?"

"Didn't we all?"

There was no way Missy had stepped out like Sarah, and Sarah's brief step out of line had been the biggest mistake of her life. "That's when I met Brian's dad." Along with a few other bad boys she hadn't been able to resist.

"You told me he died. I figured the rest would come when you were ready." Missy frowned. "He is dead, isn't he?"

"Yes." Sarah chuckled. "This is one man who won't be coming back from the grave. Good riddance to him, too."

"That bad?"

"Robert Coleman, Jr. Name ring a bell?"

"Coleman and Coleman Enterprises?" Missy asked.

Sarah nodded.

"That company's the largest health and beauty manufacturer in the world," Missy went on. "That's a lot of money. And power. How did you meet him?"

"At a nightclub. I was out partying with girlfriends when he and a couple other guys asked us to dance. Before you know it, we were all heading to Bobby's yacht. Turned out I was a real sucker for a man's smile. His was something. The kind that could charm a rosebud into blooming. Or a woman into bed. It wasn't long before Bobby singled me out. One thing was for sure, that man knew how to have a good time."

"When you have that kind of money, it's one temptation after another."

"For him or me?" Sarah shook her head and decided it was best to leave out a piece of the next part of her story. Just one small detail. "Then I got pregnant." She held Missy's gaze. "Overnight everything changed. Bobby mostly cleaned up his act and asked me to marry him. I agreed."

Missy's eyes misted with tears. "You loved him."

"I suppose, in a way. There must've been a part of me that knew it wasn't going to work because I set the wedding date for after the baby's due date."

More likely a part of her had known what she was doing had been wrong. She'd justified it by saying Bobby was cleaning up his act, but that had been no excuse.

"The wedding plans zipped along. Bobby and his mom pulled out all the stops and I fell deep into the quicksand, getting caught up in all the excitement. Saffron flowers and orchid bouquets. A handmade wedding gown. Over seven hundred guests at his mother's estate in Miami Beach for a sit-down dinner."

"Then Bobby screwed up."

"Yeah. He completely disappeared for a few days. When he came back, he was like a little boy he was so sorry. Went straight again. Promised me the world. I believed him. That happened at least three times before Brian was born.

"He was out partying when I went into labor. Bobby showed up at the hospital the next day, all smiles and apologies, but looking like death warmed over. Still, I didn't call off the wedding. I kept thinking that being a father would change things. It didn't. I couldn't even trust him to babysit."

"So what happened?"

"A month before the wedding, he went off the deep end. Got busted with so much cocaine and heroin he could've supplied a small army for a few months. That's when his mom entered the picture in a big way."

"Trish Coleman?" Missy asked. "One of Fortune 500's most powerful women?"

"That's her." Sarah nodded. "Since I'd signed a prenup, she'd been cordial throughout the engagement and Brian's birth. But when they charged Bobby, she went on the warpath. When she couldn't get the police to drop the charges, she turned on me. Blamed me for what happened. Said that if I hadn't gotten pregnant, Bobby would've been fine. That the pressure of being a father was too much for him."

"So it was all your fault."

"Basically. She said I'd been a bad influence and hired a private investigator to dig up anything he could on me. And, trust me." Shame swept through Sarah as she glanced at Missy. "He found plenty."

"Did she threaten to take Brian away from you?"

"Not right away," Sarah whispered.

"Was Bobby in jail yet?"

"No. He was out on bail."

"He did nothing to stop his mom?"

"Worse than nothing. He told me she didn't matter. He told me that the possibility of going to jail had scared the hell out of him. He promised he'd straighten out. He promised he'd be there for me and Brian. He promised everything I needed to hear. And I believed him."

It was his damned smile.

"I always knew you were a softy at heart," Missy said.

Sarah sighed. "He went to jail, but Trish got him out on probation. He spent one night with me and then took off with friends. They found him dead a day later in the back room of some club. Heroin overdose."

"I'm sorry, Sarah."

"Probably the best thing for everyone."

"Did Bobby's mom sue for custody of Brian?"

Sarah looked away. "Yeah. She did."

"But you won."

She nodded. "That's when I moved back to Indiana." In truth, she'd gone back to her mom and stepdad's house defeated, her tail between her legs, and stayed there for years. Until she'd drummed up enough courage to strike out on her own again with Brian and move to Mirabelle.

"I don't blame you for not wanting to talk about this." Missy reached out and rubbed Sarah's arm. "I would've closed the book on that chapter in my life, too."

"Would've been nice if that chapter had never been written in the first place."

"I wouldn't be so quick to dismiss what happened." Missy smiled, her own experiences lending a quiet wisdom to her gaze. "It's what's gotten you to where you are today."

In fact, she almost hadn't lived through that time in her life. "Brian and I coming here for a long weekend is what got me to where I am today."

That summer five years ago, she'd known almost upon stepping off the ferry that this was where she and Brian needed to live. Mirabelle had been the answer to getting out on her own for which she'd been looking. She'd been living—hiding—at her parents' home long enough. It'd been long past time to strike out on her own again, and Mirabelle felt better than home.

"So much for my walk on the wild side," Sarah said, smiling.

"So I take it Garrett's brother reminds you all too much of Bobby?"

"They have the same smile." Sarah swallowed, remembering Jesse's face, the curve of his lips.

"The one that could charm a rosebud into blooming?"

Sarah laughed. "Exactly."

"You're attracted to him."

"I didn't say that."

Missy raised her eyebrows. "Is that so bad?"

Just looking at him brought back every one of those good-timing men Sarah had lost herself in. There was no way she was going down that path again. "It is when it's coupled with jail time."

"Garrett's brother went to jail? What did he do?"

"I don't know. Garrett's leaving it to his brother to tell people, and when I asked Jesse, he refused to enlighten me."

"Sarah, you know Garrett wouldn't let anyone dangerous work with you on your house. Jesse must have his own reasons for keeping his past to himself. It's hard to say what those reasons might be, but I'm sure they're good ones."

That was Missy. Always ready to give people the benefit of the doubt. Well, that wasn't Sarah's way. "That all depends on what Jesse did to land himself in prison, doesn't it?"

"I suppose," Missy said. "But if you were immune to Jesse as a man that wouldn't be a problem, would it?"

But she wasn't immune. Not even close. One walk on the wild side had almost ruined her life. What kind of damage could a second one do?

THE PHOTOGRAPHS WERE ALWAYS the WORST, the hardest to look at on the entire website. Family positioned around Hank Bowman's hospital bed. Hank forcing out a smile for the camera. His wife holding his hand. His mother looking at him, her eyes bright with unshed tears.

Sitting on the bed with Garrett's laptop in front of him, Jesse made himself face the images head-on. He forced himself to flip through every single photo and every single journal entry that had been loaded onto the website Hank's sister had set up for their family and friends to keep track of Hank's recovery.

Hank had spent not only his birthday in the hospital, but also that first Christmas and New Year's after the accident—assault was more like it. He'd had to go back into the hospital several times over the course of the next couple of years for more surgeries. In every single one of the pictures Hank looked pale and bruised, thin and sickly.

Over the past four years, more than three thousand messages from friends and family expressing their best wishes for Hank's recovery had accumulated and Jesse had read every single one of them at least once. Had even memorized a few.

There were also newspaper articles about the trial, or lack thereof. There was even a picture of Jesse handcuffed and coming out of the county jail. Family members expressed not only their disdain but also outright hostility toward Jesse. He didn't blame them in the slightest.

There was only one bright spot in Hank's entire ordeal. Hank had started a new career as a motivational speaker and already had released two successful self-help-type books. As far as Jesse was concerned the use of a man's legs was too high a price to pay for financial success.

Finally, Jesse closed down the laptop and stood, knowing he wouldn't be able to sleep for a while yet. His throat dry from the winter air, he headed toward the kitchen. The moment the voices registered, quiet and intimate, he stopped and backed up.

"Come here," Garrett whispered.

"Is that an order, Chief Taylor?"

"Damn right it is."

So much for a glass of water. Jesse went to his bedroom and plopped down on the bed. Now they were moving around upstairs. One person went into the master bathroom. Then another. Then the sounds of water running. A shower. Together.

The more Jesse tried not to listen, the more his ears trained to the sounds. Footsteps across the floor. More footsteps in chase. Quiet laughter. Jesse laid on his back in bed, his eyes wide-open, sleep nothing but a pipe dream. He glanced at the clock. Past midnight. He had to get out of this place, but where the hell could he go?

More laughter.

That was it. He couldn't stand another second of it. Pulling a sleeping bag and pad out of the closet in his room, he packed a bag with a few things and quietly walked outside.

Sarah's house was empty. Hell, he spent most of the day there as it was. What difference would seven or eight more hours make whenever Erica and Garrett got a little too frisky upstairs? It's not as if he'd make a regular habit out of sleeping at Sarah's, so she'd never have to know.

CHAPTER SEVEN

"BRIAN, GO GET ME a Philips screwdriver."

Seemed as if no matter what Jesse said or did, the two boys stopped by here almost every day after school. He'd finally decided that if he was going to be stuck with them, he might as well make the most of it. Today Brian had come alone. Apparently, Zach had too much homework and would be by later.

Brian came back with the wrong type of tool.

"That's what you call a standard screwdriver. See the flat head?" Jesse straightened and headed from the bathroom into the hall. "Come on. Let's go have a lesson on tools, so you know what's what."

The boy followed him out into the main living area. One by one, he explained the name of every single tool Garrett had let him leave at Sarah's house and how they were used. Then he explained the difference between the various type of screws and nails. "If you use too small of a screwdriver, you'll strip the head off a screw."

"What does that mean?"

"See these grooves?" Jesse pointed. "You'll tear them right up if your tool doesn't fit properly."

"You know a lot about construction," Brian said. "How did you learn all this stuff?"

"My dad."

"You're lucky. I wish I had a dad to teach me things."

Jesse snorted. "You probably wouldn't be saying that if you'd known my dad."

"Why?"

"He wasn't very nice. If any one of us four boys stepped out of line even the slightest, he'd whack us. He threw a shovel at me once and hit me in the back of the head just because I wasn't moving fast enough after he'd told me to go get a hammer."

Brian's eyes widened. "You're lying."

"No, I'm not." Jesse chuckled. "If we did anything really bad, then we got whipped with his leather belt."

"Where?"

"On our butts. I'm telling you, he was mean." Jesse could honestly say he'd never missed the son of a bitch a single day the man had been gone serving a prison term for manslaughter after he killed another man in a bar fight. It hadn't mattered to Jesse that his father had come out of prison a much calmer, peaceful man. By then the damage to their relationship had been done. Garrett had probably been the only one of the four Taylor boys who'd shed a single tear when their dad died of cancer not long after he'd gotten out of jail.

"Would you ever hit a kid?"

Jesse stopped and glanced into the boy's face. "No, Brian. I've never hit anyone." At least not with his hands. "And I would never hit. Fighting doesn't solve anything."

"That's what Mom says."

The front door opened, letting in a burst of cold air, and Garrett stepped inside. "Brian. What are you sneaking over here for? You're supposed to be up at our house, not bugging Jesse."

"I'm not bugging him," Brian said.

"Well, maybe you are, maybe you aren't. Either way, you're supposed to be where you tell your mom you're going to be."

Brian hung his head. "Yeah, all right."

"So, go on. Head on up to our house." Garrett pointed his thumb behind him. "Now."

Brian glanced up at Jesse, reluctantly shrugged on his coat and, God help him, but he thought he might actually miss the boy's company. "You can come back again," Jesse said. "So can Zach." Had he really just invited them back?

Brian smiled, making Jesse feel marginally better.

"Bye, Jesse," he called out as he ran out the front door.

"Bye, Brian."

The front door closed and Garrett shook his head. "Are those boys bugging you?"

"Not really." Jesse picked up the screwdriver and went back down to the bathroom. "I spend a lot of time here alone, so it's nice to have company every once in a while."

"How's it going?" Garrett poked his head into the room and took a look around.

Jesse finished screwing in a screw, picked up the drill and prepared himself for what would most assuredly be a very thorough big-brother critique. "Things are moving along."

"You haven't been around the house much." Garrett looked under the sink and ran his hands along the pipes, not even bothering to disguise the fact that he was checking for leaks. "You working all those hours or hanging at the Nail?"

"I think you know the answer to that question." Nothing got past Garrett in a town this size. Jesse drilled a small hole in the wall, preparing to mount the mirror over the vanity.

"Yeah, I guess I do." Even so, he ran his fingers along the floor, making sure the tiles were level. "Tongues may be wagging about you, but all I have to do is look around to know you've been working hard."

"So give it a rest, huh? Four years behind bars didn't turn me stupid."

"Don't get all pissy on me. I recommended you to Sarah, so I have a responsibility to make sure you're taking care of things around here."

"And the verdict is?"

Garrett studied the grout lines and shook his head. "That you do a damned good job, little bro. I have to admit you *are* better than me."

Relaxing, Jesse grinned. "That's why boss lady pays me the big bucks."

"Boss lady." Garrett chuckled. "Bet that goes over real well with Sarah."

"Come here a minute and hold this mirror in place."

Garrett grabbed the framed beveled glass. "You put some mounting adhesive on the back of this?"

Once a big brother, always a big brother. "Yes, I did. Keep pressure on that while I finish here." He zipped in a couple screws, stepped back and struck a pose. "There. Now I can check myself out."

"Like what you see?"

"Not as much as Sarah does. My beautiful boss

better be careful, or I just might have to file a sexual-harassment lawsuit against her."

"You're so full of it." Garrett shook his head. "By the way, where did you sleep last night?"

Jesse bristled. "I thought I was out of prison."

"Don't give me that shit." Garrett shook his head. "David was up in the middle of the night. Erica threw in a load of laundry and happened to notice that your coat was gone."

Fair enough. "I slept here." And when Garrett narrowed his eyes, Jesse added, "Alone. Unfortunately."

"Why?"

"Let's just say...it gets a little loud over my head at your house sometimes."

Garrett's confused expression slowly cleared and his probing eyes turned apologetic. "We kept you up, didn't we?"

"It's okay."

"No, it's not. I'm sorry, Jesse—"

"No, Garrett. Do not ever apologize for what you and Erica have." He looked away. "You're living every man's dream."

Garrett smiled. "That I am." Then he sighed and cocked his head toward the front door. "Come on. Why don't you call it a day and take a break from the Nail for a change."

Jesse narrowed his gaze. "What do you got in mind?"

"Wednesday-night b-ball game. We have a standing date for a pickup game. Same night a lot of the younger boys have practice, so it works out well."

"You mean at the community center?" Jesse's stomach flipped at the thought of heading into a building full of people.

"Yep. Believe it or not, we've got a pretty decent facility for an island our size."

"No thanks." Jesse turned away. "I still got some work to do." He started clearing the tools out of the bathroom and carrying them into the kitchen.

"Then you'll head to the Nail." Garrett shook his head. "What the hell are you going there for, anyway? I'd have guessed you'd avoid bars altogether after what happened."

Good question. Except that he wasn't sure he could find the words to explain how hard it was heading back to Garrett's house at the end of a long day. Everything cozy. Warm feelings circulating in the air. It wasn't just Garrett and Erica's healthy marital relations that were a bit too much to bear. It was their entire life, but he sure didn't want Garrett's family making any apologies or compromises for him, even if the Nail was starting to lose a bit of its initial appeal.

"I don't know," Jesse said. "I guess there's something about the dim lights of a bar at night that seem comforting in some way."

"Come on, Jess. Come to the community center with me." Garrett followed him. "You can spare a couple hours away from this place, and it's time for you to meet a few more islanders."

"I want to have this vanity stained and the first coat of varnish applied before the end of the day."

"You're ahead of Sarah's schedule, so that can wait until tomorrow. Besides, you've been here a couple weeks already and you haven't met anyone other than Herman and Renee at the police station. And Sarah."

As well as a couple folks at the Rusty Nail, but they hardly seemed worth mentioning. "Maybe that's the way I want it."

"Bullshit."

"Wanna bet?"

Garrett studied the ceramic-tile work in the shower and ran his hand along the surface. "You do beautiful work, man."

"Yeah, it did turn out pretty nice, didn't it? Those mosaic glass accent tiles were a bitch. Took me a couple hours to get that line right."

"See, that's my point. You're working twelve-hour days. You need to take a break."

"I get breaks. At the Rusty Nail, as you so kindly pointed out. The rest of the time, I don't mind working so many hours. I like what I'm doing."

"I'm sure you do. But you need a change of pace. As it is, you work here, come home, say at best two words to me and Erica if we're still awake and then close yourself up in your room. What kind of existence is that?"

The kind he was shooting for.

"I'm doing fine, Garrett. Don't worry about me. I'm on the outside. That's all I need."

Not to mention the fact that Sarah had paid him for a bunch of hours, and even after replenishing groceries at the Taylor house and ordering some clothes online he still had a nice chunk of change tucked away. It wasn't enough to get him as far south as he wanted, but he was making some headway.

Garrett studied him. "Has Sarah been back here at the house at all?"

"Only once when I was here." Jesse flashed back on the day she'd told him to get the job done and hit the road. He should've been angry at her for the way she'd spoken to him that day, but he couldn't really blame her. If he'd been a parent, he'd have kept his kid away from the likes of him, too.

Since then, she'd been avoiding him. "But she's stopped by a couple times to check on progress. Left me a couple notes on things." She'd been terse and to the point, but Jesse didn't expect anything different. It was the expectation of more that got a man in trouble.

"You two getting along okay?"

"Oh, sure. Like cake and ice cream," he said, a little more sarcastically than he'd planned. He grinned, trying to cover the slip.

"As in she's frosty cold to your gooey and sweet?"

"That's not what I meant."

"Tell me what happened."

"Nothing. Everything's fine."

"That's it. You're coming with me." Garrett took the toolbox out of Jesse's hand and set it on the kitchen floor. "Part of you reintegrating yourself into society involves actually trying to reintegrate."

"I'm doing fine all on my own."

"No, you're not. Big brother here is pulling rank on you." Garrett tapped his own chest. "Now get your coat. We're going."

He supposed this moment had been inevitable. Might as well get it over with. "You might be older, big bro, but these days I could likely take you with one hand tied behind my back."

"I'd like to see you try."

Jesse put on his game face along with his coat and boots, but as they walked down the hill, his heart started racing. He didn't want to meet Garrett's friends. He didn't want to face the questions and comments. The inquisitive or judgmental looks.

Although, now that he thought about it, he had to

admit, he'd been heading to Sarah's before sunrise and heading back to Garrett's well after sunset. Seeing the light of day, even though it was dusky, felt good.

They walked through the residential streets down the hill and into a vast clearing dotted with massive oaks and other hardwoods. The community center was situated between a school and an outdoor ice rink flooded with overhead lighting where a group of teenage boys and girls were playing a fairly loud hockey game. They walked up a cleanly shoveled sidewalk to a two-story redbrick building. It was bigger than Jesse had expected, but no less institutional looking. A green metal roof curved over the entryway, creating the only interesting architectural detail to the otherwise nondescript square structure.

When they stepped inside, he was taken aback. For a cold and seemingly deserted island, this place happened to be loud and crawling with people, although no one was stationed at the front reception desk.

On the way through the building, Jesse managed to get a pretty good idea about the layout of the place. One side of the building was dominated by basketball courts separated by floor-to-ceiling mesh walls. The exterior wall at one end of the courts was covered with a man-made climbing wall, and the other end housed a couple mirrored exercise rooms. On the opposite side of the building was an indoor swimming pool separated from the rest of the facility by a wall of thick glass. There appeared to be swim lanes for adults and waterslides for kids.

"What's upstairs?" Jesse asked.

"An indoor jungle gym for the young kids." He chuckled. "David loves that thing. There's a workout facility with aerobic equipment, weight machines and free weights. A day-care facility, and some meeting rooms for parties and community-ed classes."

A complete state-of-the-art facility. "Do I need to pay a fee or something?"

"Nope." Garrett shook his head. "These facilities are free for residents."

"How can an island as small as Mirabelle afford this place?"

"We live charmed lives. That, and we have a lovely and very wealthy benefactor in our own Missy Abel. She's Sarah's best friend."

"No kidding? How—"

"She's a Camden."

"You mean one of *the* Camdens?"

"Yep."

"Any chance she's one of those single women you warned me away from when I first got to the island?"

Garrett chuckled as he shook his head. "She's married to Jonas Abel. A retired FBI agent, I might add."

"Dang. Guess I'll be steering clear." Jesse glanced around again. "Got a batting cage in this place?"

"Nope." Garrett shook his head. "Zach and Brian have been bugging me for a while on that. It's not likely to happen for a couple years."

They went into the men's locker room, changed and headed back out to the gym. A group of kids, boys and girls, including Zach and Brian, were having basketball practice in the middle gym, and a group of men were warming up on the court nearest the mirrored workout rooms.

A group of women were practicing what looked like yoga next door. Jesse didn't know the pixyish-looking green-eyed blonde teaching the class, but he was surprised to realize he recognized a couple of her students. Erica, Sherri Phillips and...Sarah.

Dressed in black yoga pants that clung to her thighs and butt like no one's business and a tight-fitting red tank top, her thick hair gathered into a messy ponytail, Sarah looked a far cry from the elegantly dressed woman he'd first met. In fact, she looked downright sexy. As if she felt his eyes on her, she glanced up, spotted him and arched an eyebrow. God help him, but a woman on the devilish side always had been his downfall. He was a glutton for punishment, that's for sure.

He nodded at her. She didn't nod back. In all fairness, though, the particular pose she was in—erect, one knee bent, one foot flat against the inside of the other leg and her hands locked above her head—didn't look as if it could stand a loss of concentration. As if to prove his point, she fell out of the pose and glared at him.

So his presence unsettled her, eh? Good. With any luck, he could unsettle her even more.

CHAPTER EIGHT

"That's Missy," Garrett said, following Jesse's gaze. "Teaching the yoga class."

"Are any of those single women I'm supposed to steer clear of in there?"

"Yeah, as a matter of fact. Kelly Moser, our nurse. Hannah Johnson, one of our elementary schoolteachers. Trust me, neither one are your type. Sherri, on the other hand, will no doubt come looking for you."

Jesse smiled and changed the subject. "I saw Zach in practice next door but where's David?"

"At the day care upstairs." Garrett headed toward the group of men warming up in one of the gyms. While his brother introduced each man, Jesse committed each name and face to memory.

"You know Herman and probably Tom."

"Yep." Jesse nodded, shaking hands with Garrett's only other officer and the owner of the Rusty Nail.

Then there was Bob Henderson, a middle-aged fellow in fairly good shape, the drugstore owner. Dan and Mike Newman, father and son owners of the grocery store. Marty Rousseau, manager of the Mirabelle Island Inn. Bud Stall, manager of the golf course and community center. Carl Andersen, owner of the Rock Pointe Lodge. Harry Olson, the island Realtor. Sean Griffin, the island doctor and a man about Garrett's age, and Jonas Abel, the retired FBI agent, were the only people slanting a critical eye in Jesse's direction, but Jesse could deal with two men.

"Guys, this is my brother Jesse."

"Brothers?" Carl said. "No kidding. I see a resemblance, but—"

"I favor my mom," Garrett said with a smile. "Jesse looks like my ugly mug of a dad."

"Yeah, well, who has the gray hair?" Jesse said, grinning. Garrett had a small patch of gray at each of his temples, so it wasn't all that noticeable, but Jesse had to give his nearly perfect brother crap about something. "He is the oldest, you know."

In the hopes of keeping his gaze from straying toward Sarah, Jesse dribbled a couple times and then took a shot from close to the three-point line. The ball swooshed through the net.

"Smart-ass," Garrett muttered as everyone in the gym went for water. "Nice shot, though."

Jesse had played a lot of basketball, too, in prison. "I don't have my calculator handy," he murmured. "But we have twelve guys here."

"Bob and Herman sit out a lot," Garrett whispered back. "Don't worry. You'll get a workout."

"Well, let's get this game going," Jonas said. "I got an hour, tops." He and Missy, he explained, had two kids in the facility day care.

When they finally started the game, Jesse found himself inordinately distracted by the yoga class taking place next door and by Sarah, in particular. It seemed he couldn't shoot a glance to a teammate across the court without finding Sarah directly in his line of vision. He couldn't look up without seeing her face in profile. And those yoga poses. Damn. Some of the positions were downright erotic.

Still, when he could focus, the game that followed was the most fun Jesse had had in a long while. The teams were fairly evenly matched and he loved competing against Garrett. The Taylor siblings had always been competitive, so when Garrett stole the ball from Jesse and broke toward his net, Jesse was hot on his heels. Garrett went up to the hoop. Jesse followed.

"Foul!" Garrett called as he came back down from his layup.

"Because you missed the basket by a mile?" Jesse muttered. "And a half?"

"I only missed that basket," Garrett went on, "because you slapped my arm."

"Like hell," Jesse said, dripping with sweat and his muscles happily alive with the workout. He hadn't been sure he was ready for the camaraderie of men's sports, but he felt relaxed in a way he hadn't felt in...well, at least four years.

"Boys, boys, boys." Marty snatched up the ball from Garrett. "Am I going to have to give you both time-outs?"

"Like to see you try," Garrett said.

"That sounds like a challenge."

"Bring it." Garrett motioned with his fingers, good-naturedly egging Marty on.

"In your dreams," Marty said, laughing even as he tossed the ball back out to Jesse.

"Ready to lose?" Jesse said, snickering.

"Now who's dreaming?"

Jesse slipped around Garrett, charged for the net and missed, but damned if he'd admit it had anything to do with a black-haired beauty just now bent in a downward dog.

"Okay, I need a break," Dan Newman announced.

"Take five," someone said.

Jesse grabbed the ball and started toward the sideline when Jonas stepped in front of him. The man didn't look happy. "I need to get something off my chest," Jonas said softly, narrowing his eyes at Jesse.

"Go for it," Jesse said, bracing himself.

Sean stood only a foot behind Abel, listening, but the rest of the players had taken off for their water bottles on the other side of the court.

"Ex-FBI agents don't get along well with ex-felons," Jonas said. "I'll shoot hoops with you. Talk with you. Hell, I'll even hang out at Duffy's and have a beer with you." His tone of voice and body language wasn't angry or vindictive, only matter-of-fact. "Out of respect for Garrett, I'll put up with you being on this island. But hurt anyone or break any laws, and I'll make your life on this island so miserable you won't even want to wait around for Garrett to ask you to leave. Understand?"

"Yeah," Jesse muttered. "I get it." There was a time he would've hassled the man or joked with him, making light of the situation, but at the moment he wasn't feeling particularly lighthearted.

Jonas walked away, but Sean remained.

"You, too?" Jesse asked, holding the doctor's gaze.

"Yeah, pretty much. Until I know exactly what you did to land in prison, I'm going to assume the worst."

Garrett spun around and glanced from Jonas and Sean to Jesse. "Everything okay over there?"

"Yeah, everything's fine," Jesse said, forcing out a smile. Then he tossed Sean the ball and went for his water. "Just talking strategy. Serious guys. Anyone ever tell them it's just a game?"

But he could tell by the look on Garrett's face that

his brother didn't believe his conversation with Sean and Jonas had been the least bit friendly. Not for a second.

"AGAIN, WE STAND in mountain pose," Missy said, soft instrumental music playing in the background.

Sarah stood, feet together, hands folded in front, and tried to refocus her breathing. Since Jesse had showed up in the gym in shorts and a T-shirt her concentration had gone straight to hell. Those broad shoulders and sculpted arms. Dark curly hair on muscular legs. Not to mention what was likely a large black tattoo, a mass of what looked like Chinese letters peeking out from the edges of his sleeves. She'd never been much of a fan of tattoos, but the severity of the solid black ink against Jesse's skin and the flowing artistry of the design intrigued her.

It was impossible not to sneak a glance at him as he dribbled up and down the court, his skin glistening with the sheen of clean sweat. At least she'd found a way he was nothing like Bobby. Bobby, although naturally lean and fit-looking, had never worked out a day in his life.

"Inhale and back."

Sarah raised her hands and arched backward as far as she could go as Missy walked around correcting positions.

"Exhale and forward," Missy said.

Folding at the hips, Sarah touched her toes.

"Right foot back."

She inhaled and lunged backward.

"Shoulders down and lengthen your spine," Missy whispered in Sarah's ear so no one else could hear.

"What's the matter with you tonight? You're so unfocused, you're going to hurt yourself."

"Left foot back," Sarah said, ignoring her friend. "Into plank position."

"Okay, okay," Missy muttered. "Sweep forward into cobra."

And then the routine of the hundreds of sun salutations she'd done since Missy started teaching classes took over. Lift hips and tailbone into downward dog. Lunge right foot forward. Again bend at the hips, touching toes. Arch backward. Mountain.

"Okay," Missy whispered. "Let's close."

All the women sat on their mats for brief meditation. How was she supposed to relax with Jesse parading back and forth on the basketball court? Of all the attractive, young men in the gym, Sarah found her gaze naturally straying toward Jesse. Sure, Garrett was taken, but she'd never been attracted to him in the first place. Too intense. Marty was too tall and lanky to strike her fancy. Jonas was too serious. Sean too dark. Jesse was the only one out there with a smile that lit up his face. Eyes that sparkled with humor. Just looking at him brought a smile to her insides.

Her smile dampened. Jonas, Sean and Jesse stood on one end of the court, and they didn't appear to be having a friendly exchange. Missy had probably told Jonas about Jesse having been in prison. Rumors were already circulating. What the hell had he expected, coming to this small community?

"Breathe. Slowly. In. Out. That's it, ladies. *Namaste.*"

Most of the women slowly filtered out of the room at about the same time as the basketball game finished.

"I'll catch you guys later," Hannah said, heading toward the door. "Have a phone date in ten minutes."

"With your Madison university professor who was here for a wedding last fall?" Sarah asked.

Hannah grinned and nodded.

"Okay. See ya." Sarah waved as Missy gathered her things.

"So what's with you tonight?" Missy quietly asked.

"Just tired, I guess."

As Missy started toward the door, she caught sight of Jesse. "Tired. Right." She chuckled. "That's him, isn't it?"

"Who?"

"You know who I'm talking about."

"You mean Garrett's brother?" Sarah whispered.

"Mmm-hmm," Missy said. "No wonder you had problems with your tree pose."

They trailed behind the other women. All the men glanced up as Sherri sauntered by. "Hello, boys," she said.

"Sherri," a couple of them murmured.

Although several of the men went directly to the locker rooms, including Jonas after a nod to Missy, a few hung back. With a big smile, Brittany Rousseau jogged toward her husband, Marty. Erica went to Garrett's side. And in typical barracuda fashion, Sherri beelined it toward Sean, the most eligible bachelor on Mirabelle. She seemed more than a little pleased that Jesse was also around.

"Hey, Doc," she said.

"Sherri."

"Hello, Jesse. Good to see you again."

"Hi, Sherri." Jesse grinned as he wiped his face and neck with a white towel.

"Well, Chief." Sherri smiled at Garrett. "'Bout time you talked your brother into coming to the island."

Sarah couldn't help it. She rolled her eyes.

"I take it you two have already met," Garrett said, narrowing his gaze at Jesse.

"At the Nail," Jesse offered, steadily holding his brother's gaze.

"He's a lot more fun than you are, Chief."

At that, Sarah almost snorted out loud.

"That's not saying much," Sean quipped.

"He's more fun than you, too, Doc." Sherri reached up and dragged her finger through Sean's wet hair. "And you are in dire need of a cut. Just stop by the shop for a trim sometime. No appointment necessary. I'm available anytime."

That comment caused a few eyebrows to be raised. If she hadn't been completely fascinated by the strange conversation, she would've headed straight for the locker room.

"You, too, Jesse," Sherri added.

"Well, thanks, Sherri," Jesse said. "I just might take you up on that sometime."

Shaking his head, Sean walked away and headed to the men's locker room. Sherri slipped away from the group in an effort to catch up with Sean.

Jesse slung a towel around his neck. "Thanks for the game, guys. See you around." Then he came straight for Sarah. "Hello, Sarah. Introduce me to your friend?"

"Missy Charms Abel," Missy said before Sarah had the chance.

"Very nice to meet you, Missy."

"She's married," Sarah said, her tone matter-of-fact. "In case you were wondering."

"Darn it." Jesse grinned.

"To Jonas," Sarah added. "An ex-FBI agent who tends toward jealousy."

Missy laughed, but apparently wasn't about to verbally counter the comment. "Glad to have you on the island, Jesse. Hope you'll be around to enjoy some nicer weather."

"You mean it gets better than this?" He tilted his head toward the exterior windows. "That's what I call balmy."

"Then you're in luck, aren't you," Sarah said drily.

"You've been here awhile, haven't you? I'm surprised I haven't seen you around before now."

"Got a slave driver for a boss, you know?" He held Missy's gaze for a long moment. "All I do is eat, sleep and work."

Missy chuckled.

"The regulars at the Nail might disagree with that," Sarah muttered.

"That they might." The smile he threw at Sarah held the slightest tinge of condescension. "Have a nice evening, ladies."

"See you around," Missy said.

Sarah held silent, her thoughts a jumbled mass of contradictions. She both despised Jesse and was fascinated by him, found herself intensely attracted to him, but couldn't seem to bear standing next to him. Clearly, the sooner he got her house done, the better.

CHAPTER NINE

"WHAT'LL IT BE, JESSE?" Tom Bent swiped down the bar with a white towel on his way toward Jesse.

"Ginger ale, please," Jesse said over the rock music blaring from the jukebox and hearty laughter erupting from the group of men playing pool in the far corner of the bar.

"Running a special on a new microbrewery—"

"Thanks, Tom, but the soda's good." He hadn't been to the Nail since the basketball game at the community center more than a week ago, and it was becoming obvious he shouldn't have come here tonight, either. He wasn't in the mood. For some reason laughter, music and the loud conversation and heavy drinking of a group of snowmobiling tourists by the pool table held no appeal these days.

"Hey there, stranger."

Jesse felt a hand smooth across his back a moment before Sherri slid onto the bar stool beside him. "Sherri."

"Haven't seen you around much lately." The smell of hard liquor on her breath wafted toward him.

"Been working some long hours," he said.

"Well, it's just not fair. Sarah monopolizing so much of your time," she said, a syllable or two running together.

"Sarah's house. Not Sarah." That'd be the day his boss would want to personally monopolize his time.

"Well, all I know," she purred, "is that she's one lucky woman."

Tom set the ginger ale in front of Jesse.

Suddenly Sherri hung her arm around Jesse's neck. "Ever had a body shot?"

"Not sure that I have." He chuckled and gently pulled away. "But I'm sure I don't ever want one."

She nodded at Tom, and the bartender set a shot glass in front of her, filled it with tequila, and then set down several wedges of lime and a saltshaker. Sherri proceeded to rub the lime across her chest and sprinkle salt on her skin, very close to her ample cleavage.

"Now," she whispered in his ear. "Shot, lick, lime."

Jesse forced out a smile. "Appreciate the offer, but I don't drink."

"I do." She grabbed a lime and reached toward his neck.

"Whoa, Nelly!" He jumped up and backed away. "I think you've got the wrong idea."

"Do I?"

"Mmm-hmm." When she came toward him, he held her back. "Look. We had fun that first night. But remember? No strings? No ties? Just a good time. I'm not looking for a relationship with you, Sherri."

"Don't get so serious." She laughed. "I just want to have some fun."

"Yeah, well, our fun's over. I'm sorry if I led you on."

"It's Sarah, isn't it? Miss Goody Two-Shoes. Miss High and Mighty." Sherri downed the shot and took a bite of lime. "Good luck with that." She spun away and took off toward the men at the pool table.

Jesse tossed a five spot on the bar and glanced at Tom. "You better cut her off."

"Don't need to. No vehicles here on Mirabelle."

"Will you at least make sure she gets home safely?" He shrugged on his coat.

"That I can do. Will probably end up walking her home myself after closing."

Jesse left the bar, flipped up the collar on his jacket and headed uphill, the occasional patch of ice slowing his progress. It was pitch-black outside. Hell, it was always dark out by the time he'd been leaving Sarah's house, let alone the Nail. It was also chilly, but he didn't mind. The island was quiet and peaceful at night, and the outside air, when there was no wind, felt more crisp than cold. A nearly full moon lit the partly cloudy sky, and warm, golden light spilled from kitchen windows and front porches as he walked down the street. He stopped when he got to the top of the hill and glanced back downtown.

Only the restaurants and bars were open this late at night, and he'd been finding them surprisingly busy since he'd arrived on the island. Even now, a few couples walked the sidewalks. A group of snowmobilers, very likely guests of the Mirabelle Island Inn, zipped into town from Island Drive.

He glanced back down at Main Street and located Sarah's flower shop, now closed and dark. Dim light peeked through the edges of the blinds in her second-floor apartment, but there was no movement. No shadows passing by the windows. Was she home or out? And Brian?

What difference did it make? He caught himself before he went too far down that line of thought. He wasn't a part of her picture-perfect world. Never would be.

Tucking his cold nose into the high collar of his jacket, he continued to Garrett's house. When he turned the last corner he bumped smack-dab into someone rushing down the hill. "Whoa!" *Sarah.* Instinctively, he grabbed her coat as her feet slipped out from under her. "Sorry. Should've been watching where I was going." He held her steady, making sure she wouldn't fall.

When she glanced up into his eyes, he realized how close they were, closer than he'd been to a woman in years. A few inches and the breath puffing out of her beautiful red lips in a light cloud of crystals were all that was between them. Even their coats were touching.

Then her boots slipped again on the ice and she fell into him, her gloved hands landing on his chest, her face pressing against his neck.

"I got you." Tightly, he held her for a moment. He had to admit, he liked the soft feel of her. "You okay?"

Something intense flashed across her face. Quickly, she looked away, gathering herself, and stepped back. "Sorry. These boots are warm, but they don't have much in the way of tread."

Boots? Who cared? He was more interested in figuring out what he'd seen in her eyes. Surprise, for sure. But there'd been something else. Something raw and wild. Something not unlike...desire. That was it. He may have been in prison for almost four years, but a man never forgot what want looked like on a woman's face. No doubt about it. Sarah was attracted to him.

I'll be damned. He wasn't the only one feeling whatever the hell this was passing between them. "On your way home?"

She nodded. "I just walked Brian up to Garrett and Erica's."

"Then I'll walk you the rest of the way."

"Not necessary," Sarah said. "Mirabelle's completely safe."

He glanced behind him, caught sight of those snowmobilers gathering outside Duffy's and said, "I'm sure it is. But it's awfully dark out."

"I'll be fine. I walk home from Garrett and Erica's all the time at night." She started down the hill and slipped again.

Jesse grabbed her arm. "Mirabelle might be safe, but her sidewalks aren't. You want to break a leg, fine, but if I have to start doing your painting up at the house just 'cause you're laid up, it's going to cost you extra."

"Oh, all right." She sighed and then said quietly, "And thank you."

"Don't mention it."

They walked side by side in complete silence for several long moments while they made their way down the hill. Sarah ended up grabbing Jesse's coat once or twice, but quickly released him once she'd regained her balance.

"Have you lived on Mirabelle all your life?" he asked, trying to break the awkwardness.

"No. Only for the last few years. I'm originally from Indiana."

"Didn't end up very far from home, huh?"

"I lived in Miami for a while. Turns out the big city's not my thing."

"Makes two of us."

They hit Main and headed toward her flower shop. As they neared the group of snowmobilers standing outside of Duffy's, laughing and talking loudly as they recounted their escapades on the trails, he felt more so than noticed Sarah tensing. A few men glanced their way as they walked by, but no one paid much attention to them.

On passing the group, they headed behind the building and she stopped at the base of the stairs leading to the second floor. "Well, here I am." She went up several steps and then turned. "Good night, Jesse, and thank you."

"No problem." He waited while she entered her apartment. The lights flicked on, the lock sounded on the door, and he turned back the way they'd come.

Surprising himself, he passed the snowmobilers without a word, but then he hadn't wanted to hang at the Nail, either. Talking to Sarah, on the other hand, had somehow felt right. All the way to Garrett's, he fought the urge to head back to her building, knock on her door and ask her to, if nothing else, just talk, connect. What the hell was the matter with him? Must be all the solitary work at Sarah's house was finally getting to him.

Jesse reached Garrett's yard, quietly let himself into the house and then snuck into the mudroom to remove his boots and coat. The TV was on, but based on the sounds coming from the family room no one was paying any attention to the show.

"Now you're all going to get it!" Garrett said, his voice carrying a mock-stern tone.

David squealed.

Dammit. They were all still awake. What was that all about?

"That's what you said last time," Zach said, taunting Garrett.

"Just try and catch me!" That last was Brian's voice.

Jesse peeked out of the mudroom. Garrett was wrestling with the boys in the family room. A kid Jesse had seen at Zach and Brian's basketball practice up at the community center was here, too.

"Garrett, if a lamp gets broken," Erica said from where she was folding clothes in the kitchen, "it's going to be your fault."

"Don't worry, honey," Garrett said. "I won't break anything. Except little boy *bones*."

That met with more squeals. Even Zach and Brian yelled and ran as Garrett lunged toward him.

Jesse couldn't suppress the smile spreading across his face and he watched his brother. Their father hadn't played one minute with them as they'd been growing up, but they'd wrestled with each other. Jesse, as the youngest, had always gotten more bumps and bruises than the older three boys, but he'd still had fun. It warmed his heart to see Garrett doing everything their father should've done.

Jesse walked into the kitchen. "Hello, Erica," he said quietly, hoping he wouldn't disturb the activity in the family room.

"Hi." Erica glanced up at him. "You're home early tonight."

"Yeah, I'm bushed."

"Hungry?"

"Starving."

"There's some leftover chicken, sweet potatoes and broccoli in the refrigerator there."

"You sure you don't mind?" he said, opening the door.

"I made extra for you. Just in case."

"What's with Brian being here this late?" Jesse loaded up a plate and stuck it in the microwave.

"They have a sleepover almost every Friday night."

"It's Friday?"

"Yeah." Erica chuckled. "But then, how can you keep track when you work seven days a week?"

"Who's the other boy?"

"Alex Andersen, Carl and Carol's boy. He's older, but they still hang out together."

"Hey, Jesse," Garrett said, glancing into the kitchen. "Come and join us."

"That's okay. I'm pretty tired. I think I'll call it a night." The microwave dinged and he took out his plate of hot food. "I'll just take this back to my room."

Erica studied him, as if she were debating what to say. "You know, Jesse, you've been here almost a month," she whispered. "And you haven't once sat down for dinner with our family."

"Sorry 'bout that. I've been working a lot."

"Right."

She didn't buy it. Not for one second, but, apparently, she wasn't going to call him on it, not directly, anyway.

"I want you to know," Jesse said, "I appreciate you letting me stay here, but I've noticed there are several places I could rent. I don't need to be bothering your family—"

"You're not bothering us. We—I—want you stay here. It's not good for a person to be alone as long as you have."

"You're never alone in prison."

"Yes. You are." She gave him a small smile. "I'll give you a little more time to get settled, but if you don't show up at our table for dinner soon," she added, snapping out a T-shirt before folding it, "dinner's going to come to you whether you want it to or not."

Garrett had married a very smart and loving woman. And she didn't pull any punches, either.

She cocked her head at him and smiled softly. "Understand?"

Reconnect on your own, or we'll reconnect for you. "Yeah. I get it." Even so, he took his plate down the hall to his bedroom. Before he could close the door, Garrett appeared in the hall. "You okay?"

"Sure. I'm good." He smiled. "I'm always good."

The boys came up behind Garrett. David grabbed his dad's legs and peered up at Jesse with a smile on his face. "Hi, Unc Jess."

"Hey, David."

"Jesse, you want to play some video games?" Zach asked.

"Or some other game?" Brian added.

"Another night, maybe."

"Okay." Brian and Zach went back down the hall with David toddling after them.

Garrett held back, studying Jesse. "You sure you're okay?"

"Really, Garrett, I'm fine. A little tired tonight."

A look of frustration passed over his brother's features. "All right, then." He turned and went back into the family room.

Jesse sat back on his bed, propped up his feet and took a bite of chicken and sweet potatoes, savoring the homemade flavors. A moment later the ruckus resumed out in the family room, the voices carrying down the hall as clear as bells. Jesse had inadvertently left his bedroom door ajar.

He moved to close the door and then stopped, falling back against the pillow. The sounds, innocent and homey, comforted him in some small way. He might not be a part of their lives, but there was no harm in listening.

CHAPTER TEN

"READY TO PAINT THIS WALL?" Sarah asked Brian as she finished trimming out a large section of the main bathroom.

It was Sunday, her favorite day of the week. Normally, she would take off work from both her flower-shop and wedding-planning businesses and spend the entire day with Brian watching movies, playing video games—which was getting harder and harder for her to do as he got more and more proficient—or messing around up at the community center shooting hoops, swimming or using the climbing wall. For the next couple of months, though, she'd be spending her Sundays working at the house, hopefully with Brian. Already, she could feel the place taking shape.

"Do I have to keep painting?" Brian moaned.

So maybe Brian wouldn't be spending as much time here as she'd hoped. "It's your bathroom, dude, and you picked out the color. I thought you'd be excited."

"It's paint, Mom. How excited can I get?"

"Yeah, well, you're the one who'll be using the main bathroom most often." She'd have her own—her own lovely bathroom—off the master bedroom. The idea of luxuriating in a bubble bath without the worry of young boys pounding on the door with urgent bathroom needs sounded nothing short of heavenly.

"I'd rather play with Zach."

"You two are practically glued at the hip, seeing each other every day after school. Sleepovers practically every weekend."

"I spend less time with Zach than you spend working. Besides, he's my best friend."

She let the comment about her work slide. As the kid of one of the only single parents on Mirabelle, Brian had no other frame of reference. "I'm glad you've got Zach, but can't you spare a few hours for your mom?"

"I suppose so. Sure," he said, sounding as if she was punishing him.

"I'll make a deal with you. Spend an hour helping me paint this bathroom and then you can hang with Zach."

"Deal."

She showed him how to use the paint roller and watched him do a small section. Her plan was to trim the room and let Brian roll the paint out on the larger, easier sections.

"Good job," she said. "Soak up some more paint on that roller and do another section."

She went back to trimming another area, taking her time, making sure she didn't get any paint on the ceiling. At first, she hadn't been sure about Brian's choice of paint color, Brownie Parfait, but now she realized the deep chocolate would contrast nicely with the white enameled woodwork and hide the fingerprints that would invariably make their way onto the walls.

Although she'd been resistant to the idea of replacing Garrett with his brother Jesse, she had to give credit where credit was due. This bathroom with its decorative ceramic tile, new light fixtures, not to mention a new tub, toilet and sink, didn't bear the slightest resemblance to the old room with its peeling gold linoleum floor, chipped and stained counter and moldy shower stall. He was already working on the master bathroom, making amazing progress, and was several days ahead of Garrett's plan.

She hadn't seen Jesse since that night when he'd walked her home. Oddly enough, during all that time, she kept expecting to bump into him. Maybe expectant hadn't been exactly the way she'd been feeling. Hopeful, maybe.

She wanted to bump into him again, talk to him, at least catch a glimpse of him. And it had a lot to do with him walking her home. At first, she really hadn't wanted him to bother. She had, in fact, been surprised he'd offered after the way she'd spoken to him about staying away from Brian. But the moment she'd seen those snowmobilers gathered outside Duffy's, she had been thankful he was there.

She should've been afraid of Jesse. He was such an unknown. Instead, his presence had been surprisingly comforting. What it meant, she hadn't a clue.

As she and Brian worked together trimming and painting, they talked about, among other things, school and the upcoming baseball season. A couple times she hazarded a glance at his painting. The dark color wasn't covering the light undersurface very well. She was definitely going to have to redo every section, but at least they were together and talking.

"A little excited to move into this place?"

Sarah spun around at the sound of the man's voice. Jesse was leaning against the doorjamb, his arms folded over his chest, his feet crossed. He looked awfully comfortable. How long had he been standing there watching them?

Not expecting him to be here today, she'd dressed in

old jeans and a faded T-shirt. She also hadn't bothered with makeup and had quickly braided her hair in two pigtails. Suddenly, she felt exposed, almost vulnerable without at least the veneer of professionalism that work clothes and lipstick provided.

"Hi, Jesse." Brian waved his roller, dribbling brown paint that looked an awful lot like milk-chocolate syrup onto the drop cloth.

"Hey, Brian." Jesse tipped his head toward Brian and then glanced at Sarah. "I know you want to keep this ball rolling, but you're jumping ahead of yourself."

"You said you were finished with the main bathroom."

"Yes, boss, I did, but those walls you're working on now should've been primed before you started in painting."

She hated the way he called her boss, drawing the word out long and slow with a touch of sarcasm, but she was not going to stoop to his level. What was he doing here on a Sunday, anyway? She'd been hoping to work here without him butting in. "What does that mean, priming?"

"You've never worked on new drywall before, have you?"

"No."

He glanced around the bathroom. "Well, it's too late now. Don't worry about it." He turned and went down the hall.

"Wait a minute." She jumped down from the step stool and, brush in hand, followed him. "If I'm doing something wrong, I need to know. I want the walls to look perfect."

He raised his eyebrows and a slight smile tugged

at the corner of his mouth. "There is no such thing as perfect in the construction business."

"Tell me what I should've done."

"Prime first." He brushed past her and into the living area and pointed to a large five-gallon pail. "Primer soaks into the drywall, leaves a more even surface and it's cheaper than regular paint. Without primer and as dark as that color is, you'll have to do two to three coats."

"Oh."

"So your wall can still look *perfect*. It'll just cost a little more to get it there and it won't be particularly... *efficient*."

The man was insufferable. But sexy. Dressed in faded blue jeans and a plaid, flannel shirt, the sleeves rolled up to show muscled forearms and a mass of dark hair. She couldn't really blame him for being slightly antagonistic toward her. When it came down to it, he had every reason to be outright angry with her. She hadn't exactly put out a welcome mat for him.

"I'll keep your tips in mind for the next room," she said, spinning around and heading back into the bathroom. Good thing efficient wasn't her objective as she glanced at Brian tracking paint all over the drop cloth when he walked to another section of bare wall.

"Did we do something wrong?" he asked.

"We're doing fine, Bri."

"Jesse knows more about this than you do, Mom. You should listen to him."

Listen to him, indeed. She went back to trimming. About the time she completed outlining the room Brian finished rolling the last big section.

"Has it been an hour yet?" he asked hopefully.

Only about fifty minutes had passed, but she'd call it good. "You're done. Thanks for your help."

"I'm going over to Zach's." He dropped the roller in the paint pan.

"Be home by five-thirty for dinner. It's movie night tonight, remember?"

"Bye, Mom!" He zipped through the door. "Bye, Jesse!"

"Bye," Jesse called, his voice muffled by the walls.

The front door had no sooner closed than rock music blared from the back of the house. Jesse must've turned on the radio. Although she wasn't crazy about his choice of stations, she was glad for the distraction as she picked up Brian's paint roller and went to work finishing up the bathroom.

In no time, she'd finished the first coat. Jesse had been right on. The walls were going to need at least one more coat of brown, possibly two, but first the initial layer needed to dry. Her right arm, shoulder and hand were already aching. She was going to be hurting by the time this room was finished.

"Son of a bitch!" Jesse's epithet sounded through the wall followed by sawing, pounding and grunting. Whatever he was doing was not going smoothly.

Curiosity got the better of her. She walked quietly—possible only because the new flooring Jesse had installed didn't squeak—down the hall and through her bedroom. Peeking into the bathroom, she found him bent over attempting to lift away the old toilet. It didn't seem to be budging.

He tapped something down low with a rubber mallet, and then seemed to be getting ready for another try. A moment later, his quads tensed and the muscles in his back and on his arms bulged with the effort. He was a lot stronger than he looked in relaxed mode.

He'd taken off his flannel shirt, leaving on a gray cotton undershirt. The short sleeves had ridden high up on his arms, revealing the edges of his tattoo, and she couldn't seem to stop thinking about the design. Did it mean something? Were those letters? Did the tat cover his shoulder? His entire chest? What she would've given in that moment for him to take off his shirt so she could see the whole thing. Would he look as good as she imagined? Would he feel as—

"Need something, *boss?*"

"What?" She started, feeling her skin flush with embarrassment. "Stop calling me that," she said, recovering quickly.

"Why?" He was watching her, his gaze intense as he clearly tried to figure out what was going through her mind. "You are my boss, aren't you?"

"Well…yes, technically, but…" She crossed her arms. "Do you need some help there?"

He stared at her for a moment as if he were deciding whether or not to let her off the hook. Then, almost as if she wasn't worth the effort, he turned back to his task. "The bolts are badly rusted. I can manage."

"I'm sure you can, but it looks like another hand might make that process more…*efficient.*"

"Whatever you say." He glanced up at her. "After all, you are the boss."

She narrowed her gaze.

"All right, come here," he ordered. "When I say *go,* whale on the bottom of the toilet with that mallet. Hit that sucker as hard as you can to dislodge some of that rust." He glanced at her. "Ready."

She picked up the mallet and nodded.

"Set." His muscles tensed again. "Go."

She hit the porcelain.

"Harder!"

Winding up, she smacked it as hard as she could, breaking things free. Jesse jerked the unit up and off the floor, spilling some clean water out of the tank and onto his chest, but all she seemed to be able to focus on were his bulging biceps.

"Open the front door for me, would you?" he grunted.

She took off ahead of him as he carried the toilet outside and threw it in the Dumpster. He came back inside and then, as if it was the most natural thing in the world, he pulled off his wet shirt.

On some level, Sarah knew she was gawking, but he was truly beautiful. His muscles were defined, but not overwhelming, and there was just enough black hair curling between his pecs and running down a set of six-packs to make him look real. And that tattoo. The look of it sent her over the edge. The black symbols swept up onto his shoulder and down onto part of his chest, swirling and looping in a design that was at once bold and fluid, artistic and wild.

She couldn't remember the last time she'd wanted a man. Couldn't remember what it felt like to need something this badly. But want and need were suddenly all she could think about. She wanted to reach out and touch. She needed to feel smooth skin, hard muscle. Man.

Oh, no. No, no. Snap out of it!

She glanced up and found him watching her.

His eyes smoldered as if he knew exactly what she was thinking. "You know…it's interesting," he said softly. "But one of the things I was worried about when

I walked out of prison was people judging me before knowing the facts. They'd take one look at me and all they'd see was a criminal. So far on Mirabelle the person who's done that more than anyone else is you, Sarah."

She didn't know what to say.

"You think you're justified, don't you? You think you know me. You think you know who I am."

"Oh, I know you, all right."

"Oh, yeah? Then who am I?"

"A man who couldn't make a commitment to save his soul. The life of the party. The ladies' man. Just ask Sherri Phillips."

"Sherri, huh?"

Sarah nodded.

"Jealous?"

"Not on your life. You can screw around with whoever you want whenever you want."

"Well, for what it's worth, Sherri and I had a onetime fling my first night here on Mirabelle. She was more than happy with a no-strings-attached arrangement. And she's fun. Which is more than I can say about some of the inhabitants of this island." He narrowed his gaze. "But then, it's not really me you're mad at, is it?"

She didn't trust herself to speak.

"No, Sarah. You're mad at yourself. Because you can't decide whether to tell me to hit the road or…strip me naked."

"That's ridiculous."

"Is it?" He smiled as he stepped toward her. "You've got a thing for bad boys, don't you, boss lady?"

She held her ground, lifting her gaze to meet his. He was so close she could feel the heat of him on her face. If he reached out to touch her she had a feeling she just might let him touch anywhere he wanted.

Instead, he leaned in, his hands still at his sides, but his face closing in, his lips only inches from her cheek. If he'd pressed her, if he'd shown an ounce of force, she'd have pulled away in an instant. Instead, his slow, smooth movements disarmed her. She couldn't move. She could only breathe. His lips hovered over her mouth. She closed her eyes. Waiting. Waiting.

Kiss me. Kiss me, dammit!

As if reading her mind, he moved infinitesimally closer. The touch of his lips against hers was unexpectedly as soft as a feather, so light it was almost as if she imagined his touch. She wasn't even sure she could technically call it a kiss. She tilted her head, hoping to feel the pressure of his lips, or—God help her—the heat of his tongue.

That's when he chuckled, soft and low, the sound vibrating through her. "You know what you are, Sarah?" he whispered against her lips. "You're a very beautiful...very seductive...*hypocrite.*"

As he pulled back, shame swept through her. The look of smug satisfaction on his face was enough to make her want to haul off and hit him. "I could fire you for that."

"Go ahead. I dare you."

He was right and she was so, so out of line. An apology was on the tip of her tongue, but she couldn't seem to open her mouth.

"Yeah. That's what I thought." He spun around, stalked back down the hall and into the bedroom. A moment after the door closed, the volume on the radio pumped up. His message was loud and clear. He'd not only shut her out of the room, but out of his head.

She couldn't blame him. She *was* a hypocrite. She wanted Jesse Taylor with a need that threatened to consume her, but he was as wrong for her as wrong got. She'd worked too hard building a life here on Mirabelle to let a man, any man, ruin it. "I won't let me ruin it, either," she whispered.

JESSE LEANED BACK against the wall in the bathroom and let the beat of the bass guitar pounding over the radio thrum through him. With any luck, the waves of sound would dispel the white-hot need burning him up from the inside out.

When he'd first come into the house and found her painting the bathroom, dressed in faded jeans and a tight T-shirt, his heart had started pounding so hard, he'd had to stand there for a long moment before attempting to speak. It was the first time he'd seen her looking so...natural, so relaxed, so approachable, and his reaction to her, more than anything, had pissed him off.

Then when he'd been so close to her that he could smell her very skin, paint mixed with a light powdery scent of flowers, he'd almost lost it. Flowers. Always, she smelled like blooming flowers. Roses, lilies, carnations, fuchsia, all mixed together. It was the femininity of the scent that had got to him, snuck right in and grabbed him by the groin.

Not to mention the way her lips had parted, oh, so expectantly. The air had moved in and out of her chest in great gulps, drawing her paint-spattered T-shirt tight across her chest. She'd practically panted. Then when the tip of her sweet tongue had touched his mouth, he'd gone nearly insane.

But he'd wanted to break her control, unleash that

raw sexual power he could practically see boiling beneath the surface of her skin, and in the process he almost lost his own control. One more second in front of Sarah, and as close as he'd been to her, there was no telling what might've happened between them. Spontaneous combustion. Or something damned close to it. Even now, he felt as if he might explode.

He pushed against his groin, adjusting the erection pressing uncomfortably against his jeans. What the hell was the matter with him? Four years ago, he wouldn't have hesitated for a split second. If a woman had looked at him with half the want in Sarah's eyes, he'd have had her naked and under him within minutes.

And now? Now he was a felon. Prison had changed him. He might be able to fool the rest of the world into thinking he was the same old Jesse as before, but he couldn't lie to himself. He wasn't footloose and fancy-free. Not anymore.

Leave. Get your ass off this island before you do something really, really stupid.

He couldn't leave. Not yet. Sarah had paid him for his work to date, but it wasn't enough. One more month. Tough it out four more weeks. *Whatever you do, do not touch Sarah.*

CHAPTER ELEVEN

"UNCLE JESSE?" Like clockwork, Zach knocked on Jesse's bedroom door.

It'd only been a little more than a month since Jesse had arrived on Mirabelle, but already a new routine had established itself in the Taylor household. Daytimes were pretty much the same as before his arrival, given Jesse was generally gone off to work before the kids were awake, but after Erica's admonishment, he'd started coming back to the house for dinner most nights. Afterward, he'd take a shower to wash away the day's construction grime, and invariably the boys would come down to knock on his bedroom door.

"Unc Jess?" David's chubby hands landed flat against the wood with a sticky slap.

Those boys were as persistent as a jackhammer. Still dripping from his shower, Jesse ran the towel through his wet hair and silently hoped they'd go away.

"He dare?" David said, presumably asking his brother.

"Yeah, he's there," Zach said, sounding discouraged. "But he doesn't want to play with us. Come on, Davie. I'll play with you."

Dammit. He stared at himself in the mirror and ran his fingertips along the dramatic lines of his tattoo. *You may have gotten out of prison, but how long are you going to live as though you're still behind bars?*

"Gimme a minute, boys!" Jesse called, wondering how long it would take to end up eventually regretting this decision.

"Were you talking to us?" Zach asked, surprise registering.

"Yeah. I gotta get dressed." He pulled on a pair of clean jeans and then opened the door.

Tentatively, Zach came to stand in the threshold, but David barreled right in, climbed onto the bed and started jumping up and down. The kid was having so much fun he didn't have the heart to tell him to stop. "How you doing, Zach?"

"Okay."

The kid didn't look okay. "Hey, I'm sorry I've been a little distant since I got here, but…it doesn't have anything to do with you. It's me. Takes me a while to settle in places, you know?"

"It's cool."

"Brian's not coming over tonight for a sleepover?" Jesse could've been wrong, but it seemed as though the two had spent almost every weekend together since Jesse had gotten on the island.

"Nope," Brian said. "Can you play video games with us?" he asked, his voice brightening. "Garrett and Erica are going out."

Suddenly, spending a quiet night at home with the two boys was sounding awfully nice. "Sure. How 'bout we play some cards first?"

"David doesn't know how."

"That's okay. He and I can beat—er play you." Jesse winked at Zach. Jesse ruffled his nephew's hair, then he grabbed a heavy cable-knit sweater out of a dresser drawer and dragged it over his head. "You guys already eat dinner?"

"Yep."

"So what did Erica make tonight?" Jesse's stomach growled at the thought of his sister-in-law's cooking.

"Lasagna. Garlic bread." Zach shrugged. "I didn't eat the salad."

"I don't like zaniah," David said, his voice jiggling as he continued to jump.

"Good. That leaves more for me." He'd been in the middle of texturing one of the ceilings in Sarah's house, so he hadn't been able to make it home in time for dinner, but he'd been counting on leftovers. "Let's go." He snatched David off the bed, stepped into the hallway and headed toward the kitchen with Zach trailing behind him.

"Mmm," a feminine voice purred from the general vicinity of the kitchen. "Do that again."

Jesse stopped in his tracks and Zach bumped into him.

"This?" That was Garrett's voice. "Or this?"

Damn. He couldn't see them, but there was no mistaking those two were at it again. They never seemed to let up. If they weren't looking at each other, they were touching. Holding hands. Lightly running fingertips along the other's forearms. Arms wrapping around waists at the stove or sink. Lying next to each other on the couch while watching TV. It didn't seem to matter who was or wasn't around.

"They're kissing again," Zach whispered, rolling his eyes.

"Ewww." David scrunched up his nose.

"Yuck is right." Jesse made a face, but he really couldn't fault either Garrett or Erica. If Jesse ever got lucky enough to fall in love with a woman and vice versa, he'd probably be worse than Garrett. That didn't make the attention they gave one another easy to live with. Every time he heard or saw them getting the slightest bit intimate, his thoughts immediately tracked to Sarah.

Which didn't make a damned bit of sense as far as he was concerned. He doubted that opinionated, judgmental woman had even an ounce of Erica's tenderness. Too bad, too. To waste all that female hotness Sarah exuded in an uptight, perfectionist personality.

Without warning, Jesse's stomach growled and the sound echoed loudly in the narrow hall. Zach hid a laugh behind his hand. No heading back into his bedroom now. Jesse cleared his throat and continued toward the kitchen. By the time they emerged from the shadows, Garrett and Erica had put a respectable distance between them.

"Were you guys spying on us?" Erica asked, tilting her head to one side.

"Like I want to see you two kissing," Zach said, heading off into the family room and flipping on the TV.

"Absolutely not." Jesse set David down to toddle after his brother.

"Any chance there are leftovers?" Jesse asked, opening the refrigerator door.

"Of course," Erica said. "I made sure there was extra for you."

"Erica, if you weren't taken," Jesse said, setting a few containers on the center aisle, "I'd snap you up so fast this island would be spinning where it sits."

"Well, she is taken," Garrett growled. "So don't even think about it."

Erica smiled slyly. "There's nothing wrong with keeping him on his toes, though, is there, Jesse?"

"Nope. You ever tire of my brother, you let me know."

Garrett shook his head. "That'd be the day."

"You never know." Erica ran her finger down Garrett's cheek. "Someday I might just trade you in for this younger model."

Jesse laughed.

Garrett grabbed her around the waist and pulled her tight. "Never gonna happen." Then he kissed her, deeply, and Jesse regretted ever joking around with them. He put the leftovers on a plate, heated them in the microwave and cleared his throat, hoping to break them up.

A moment later, Erica pulled back. "I have to go change before heading to work." She spun around, handed David a sippy cup, planted a kiss on her son's head and climbed the stairs.

Garrett moved to the dishwasher and started putting away the clean dishes. "I'm planning on keeping Erica company tonight down at Duffy's," he said. "You up for joining us?"

"Naw, that's okay. I'm pretty tired. Want to get up bright and early in the morning to finish the knockdown ceilings at Sarah's. Besides, the boys asked if I could play some games with them tonight."

"Did I hear that right? You and the boys are going to play games?"

"Sure. Why not?"

Garrett nodded. "Good. That's good. Except for one thing," he said, his voice lowered. "You've been working twelve-hour days, seven days a week since you got here. You don't let down a little bit, you're going to explode."

"Yeah, well, I've decided bars aren't the kind of places I let down anymore."

Garrett glanced at him. "Duffy's is a little different than the Nail. I'll be there. Erica. A couple of the guys you met at the community center. And Sarah."

Sarah. Reason enough not to go. "No thanks, bro. I'll be happy to keep an eye on Zach and the baby for you and Erica, though." Now that he thought about it, built-in babysitter was the only benefit of his presence to Garrett and Erica. He might as well help out when he could.

"Renee's daughter, Teresa, is babysitting tonight."

"All right." Jesse sat down at the center island counter with his plate of food. "I'm still not going out."

"Not a good answer."

A moment later, the babysitter arrived. She looked to be only a few years older than Zach, but the boys seemed to like her. Garrett gave her directions, Erica came downstairs and the two said their goodbyes. They had their coats on and were about to head out the door when Garrett glanced at Jesse. "Think about it, Jesse." Garrett opened the door, letting in a burst of cold air. "You can't hide forever."

Like hell I can't.

Jesse finished eating and made sure the kitchen was clean. Teresa was playing with David so Jesse glanced at Zach. "How 'bout I beat you in chess?"

"You can try." Grinning, Zach jumped up and sat down in front of the chessboard.

After Zach beat him two out of three games it was obvious Zach knew more about chess than Jesse had expected. "You didn't tell me you could play."

"You didn't ask. Garrett taught me."

"That explains it, then." Jesse laughed. "So why didn't Brian come over tonight?" It had seemed to Jesse as though they'd had a routine. Fridays they slept at Zach's and Saturdays at Brian's.

"I don't know." Zach's gaze dodged Jesse's, belying his words.

"You guys get into a fight or something?"

"No."

"Zach, what's going on?"

"I don't know." The boy shrugged. "He said his mom won't let him play over here unless Garrett or Erica are home."

"What?" Jesse glanced up. "Why? Teresa's baby-sitting."

"I told you. I don't know."

Jesse knew. It was because of him. That wasn't right.

"Checkmate!" Zach grinned. "Wanna play again?"

"Maybe later."

Jesse stood and paced. Finally, he walked to the picture window to glance out through the woods. If he focused hard enough he could almost kid himself into thinking he could see the lights from Main Street flickering through the bare trees.

Garrett was right. He couldn't hide forever. He had to tell Zach the truth, but there was one thing he had to do first. "Zach, I need to go out."

"But you said you were going to play cards."

"Can I catch you tomorrow?"

"Yeah, all right."

Before he could think better of it, Jesse said goodbye to both boys, grabbed his coat and marched off down the hill toward Duffy's. As he reached the door, the sounds of people enjoying life fell over him and he hesitated. Things had been going good. Well, maybe not good, but all right. Why rock the boat?

You're not ready for this. Go back.

No. No.

Time to face your demons, Jesse. Face 'em head-on.

He opened the door and went inside.

"WHAT IN THE WORLD are they celebrating?" Sarah nodded toward the group of men, Garrett, Carl, Sean, Bud Stall and Mike Newman, clanking glasses together up at the bar in Duffy's Pub.

Missy glanced backward from where she, Hannah Johnson and Sarah were all sitting in their regular booth for their once-a-week happy hour at Duffy's Pub. During the summer months, they usually met to catch up on a weekday evening, but during the winter it was Friday nights.

"You didn't hear?" Missy said, turning back around. "Sean bought Arlo Duffy's carriage and stable operations today."

"Our Doctor Sean?" Hannah said, openmouthed.

"Mmm-hmm." Missy nodded. "Sean's been boarding his horse with Arlo since he moved here and helping Arlo out with this and that. He said he's been loving taking care of the horses while Lynn and Arlo spend the winter in Florida, and the whole carriage operation was getting to be too much for Arlo. So…"

"Is Sean still going to run the medical clinic?" Hannah asked.

"I think so. He said there shouldn't be a problem doing both. As it is he said his clinic office hours are part-time, at most, even over the summer, and Arlo's going to be running some of the operations. He insisted on driving the main carriage over the summers."

"That's good," Sarah said, nursing a glass of wine. Mirabelle wouldn't be Mirabelle without old Arlo, the single most photographed man on Mirabelle, sitting atop a carriage and holding a set of reins. "Sounds like a perfect arrangement for both of them."

"Look at all those attractive men," Hannah mused as she stared at the bar. "And they're all taken, except for Sean."

"You said you were going to ask him out." Missy took a sip from her beer bottle. "Did you?"

"Yep." Hannah sighed. "He turned me down. Said he wasn't looking to date."

"Oddly enough, that makes sense." Missy shook her head. "I think what he's looking for is a wife."

Sarah laughed. "How's he going to find a wife if he doesn't date?"

"He'll know," Missy said softly.

She and Sean were good friends. There'd even been some conjecture that the two might become a couple until Jonas had shown up on the island, squashing any possibility of that ever happening.

"Honestly, he's been awfully grouchy lately," Hannah said. "Sometimes I wish Doc Welinski had never retired."

"I guess this island starts to feel small sometimes," Sarah said, patting Hannah's hand. "Especially in the winter."

"At least in the summer, there are men coming and going," Hannah grumbled. "But in the winter, the flow of available men slows to, at best, a trickle."

"I love our winters," Missy said, smiling dreamily. "All the peace and quiet. The long, dark nights."

"Easy for you to say." Sarah laughed. "You've got a husband."

"And two kids," Hannah added.

"First it was Sophie Rousseau. Then Erica. Then you." Sarah sighed. "Mirabelle's young single women are getting snapped up one by one."

"Except for you and me," Hannah murmured.

"What about your professor?" Sarah asked. "I thought you two had really hit it off."

"Oh, I don't know." Hannah groaned. "He's nice and all, but…"

"Nice? He drove all the way up here in a blizzard just to be with you on New Year's," Missy said.

"He asked me to come to Madison for Valentine's Day."

Sarah laughed. "That sounds serious to me."

"Long-distance relationships suck," Hannah said. "And it's not likely he'll move here anytime soon. Do you see any colleges on the island?"

"All right. All right." Missy set her white wine down. "There are several single guys here on Mirabelle. Even in the winter. What are you two looking for?"

"Oh, oh, oh!" Hannah said, pulling a small notebook from her purse. "A list. The everything-I-want-in-a-man list."

"That's easy," Sarah said. "Financially secure, good listener, responsible, consistent." She ticked the attributes off on her fingers. "A man who wants to be a father, doesn't drink or do drugs, has never had a one-night stand, has never been to prison, doesn't own a sports car—or a yacht—and above all else, is absolutely no fun."

"You've thought about this before," Missy said, chuckling.

"Only a few times." Sarah glanced up and froze the moment she caught sight of a man coming into Duffy's. Although his features were shadowed, she instantly knew him. Already the shape of Jesse—his short haircut, the breadth of his shoulders, the way he carried himself—was familiar.

As he moved into the dim light of the pub, she saw his features more clearly. He might've been smiling as he headed toward the group of men by the bar, but that jovial expression didn't come close to making it to his eyes. This was not good.

Garrett slapped Jesse on the back and pulled him into the midst of the group, introducing him to a couple of islanders who didn't often venture out to socialize. Among the men was Al Richter, the new postmaster, who was twice as grumpy and half as lovable as his predecessor, Sally McGregor.

All the while he seemed to be chatting it up, Jesse seemed to be surveying the Duffy's crowd, looking for something. Or someone. He certainly couldn't have missed the new bank manager and his wife sitting near him at the bar, eyeing him warily. When the man threw a twenty down on the bar and they got up and left, Sarah couldn't help but feel a certain amount of satisfaction. But then Jesse's gaze landed on her, and she knew he'd been looking for her. He was angry. At her. His gaze seemed to travel all over her at once as if he couldn't decide what to do with her.

Then he shrugged out of his winter coat, dragging the collar of his sweater down his shoulder and baring another edge of that mysterious, very large black tattoo, and all Sarah could think about was the other day at her house when he'd gotten his shirt wet. His bare chest.

That tattoo. She took a gulp of white wine and willed her breathing to remain steady.

"What's the matter?" Missy said, following Sarah's gaze. "Oh. Garrett's brother is here."

"Is he?" Hannah spun around. "Is that him? Next to Garrett?"

"Yeah," Sarah whispered, her throat suddenly dry.

"I thought you said he wasn't at all attractive," Hannah muttered.

"I guess dark and rugged isn't my cup of tea." Sarah took a sip of wine.

"Oh, sure." Missy laughed, turning back around. "And I don't go for FBI agents."

"He's not as handsome as Garrett, but he's okay. So what?"

"So you have first dibs is what," Hannah said. "With him working on your house 24/7, the other single women on this island don't stand a chance."

"Jesse fails every item on my list but one," Sarah said. "He doesn't own a sports car."

"That's a little harsh, don't you think?" Missy took a sip of her drink.

"Why?"

"For starters," Missy said, "you said yourself that he's been doing a great job on your house."

"All right, I'll give him consistent."

"And responsible," Missy added, clearly defending Jesse.

"That remains to be seen."

"He doesn't drink or do drugs."

"Not anymore, but I'll bet he used to," Sarah said. "You want him, Hannah, you can have him."

"Seriously?"

"Yup."

"Wait a minute." Hannah glanced from Sarah to Missy and back again. "You two have talked about this before, haven't you?"

Jesse took a swig from a bottle of water and chuckled at something Garrett said. Then he made a comment that got the whole group of guys bellowing with laughter. There he was. The life of the party. The man everyone wanted to be with. Even her.

"Sarah?" Hannah looked confused. "What's going on?"

In for a penny, in for a pound. Sarah had told Missy about a big chunk of her past. She might as well spill an abbreviated version to Hannah. After she'd finished, she took another big gulp of wine and glanced at her friends.

"Now I get your list," Hannah said.

"I could be wrong," Missy said. "But from everything I've heard and seen there's not a lot about that story that sounds like Jesse."

Jesse had set down his bottle of water and, with hands moving this way and that, he was clearly telling a story. The men beside him seemed spellbound. She knew the feeling.

"Bobby and Jesse are more alike than you know."

"Maybe. But he sure has an interesting aura," Missy said. "There's a lot of red."

Normally, Sarah would've found Missy's woo-woo mumbo jumbo interesting, but this time she wasn't buying it.

"Red is emotion," Missy went on. "Raw passion. Determination. He's very sexual."

"Ooooh," Hannah murmured.

"Missy—"

"The best of man, the worst of man."

That piqued Sarah's curiosity. "What does that mean?"

"He has amazing abilities inside him. As long as he puts his efforts to good use, he can do incredible things."

"But there's a dark side, isn't there?" Sarah asked.

"There usually is," Hannah muttered.

"I don't see one, Sarah. His color is clear."

His color could be perfect and he would still scare the hell out of her. That smile. That voice. Those eyes, looking at her as if he was thinking of undressing her. "I thought I was all over bad boys," she said, groaning. "After all the things Bobby said and did. I thought I was finished with them."

"We've all lived here for years," Hannah said, her voice laced with more than a little disappointment. "It's not as if Mirabelle offers much in the way of temptation."

"You got that right." Until Jesse.

"Maybe the man isn't as bad as you think."

Sarah shook her head. "He's the epitome of a bad boy."

She glanced up and saw Jonas coming into the bar, one bundled-up baby boy in each arm. He nodded to the men at the bar and proceeded toward their table. Before Sarah could tell Missy that her husband had arrived, Missy spun around as if she could sense his presence.

"There are my boys," she said with a smile.

"And there's Mommy," Jonas said, bending to let Missy plant a kiss on each child's cheek. "Sarah. Hannah," Jonas said, nodding to each of them in turn.

"Are you hungry?" Missy asked.

"That can wait." Jonas grinned at her. "First, I want a dance."

"I'll watch the babies," Sarah offered.

"Thanks, Sarah, but there's no need," Jonas said. "I hold the boys and...Missy can hold me. *Real* close." Then he bent down to kiss his wife's head before whispering something in her ear. Her face beaming with a satisfied smile, Missy stood, threw her arms around Jonas's waist and tugged them all out onto the dance floor, where they proceeded to dance much too slowly to the beat of the fast rock song.

"That's it," Hannah muttered, turning back toward Sarah. "I'm going to Madison for Valentine's Day."

Sarah laughed out loud, and then immediately sobered when she noticed Jesse had broken away from the group of men at the bar and was coming right toward their table. "Hello, ladies." He smiled at Hannah. "You must be Hannah Johnson, the best teacher in the world if what Brian and Zach say is true."

Hannah actually blushed. Blushed. "Well, on an island as small as Mirabelle," she said, "the kids don't have much by way of comparison."

"I'm sure you'd hold your own in any big city." He turned to Sarah. "Can I talk to you?" His grin belied the intensity in his eyes. "Alone."

CHAPTER TWELVE

HANNAH RAISED HER EYEBROWS in surprise at Jesse's request, but a slight smile tugged at her lips. "Go ahead. I'll watch your wine for you."

Sarah glared at her friend. She was oblivious to Jesse's true mood. Was Sarah the only one who could see there was a boiling tempest beneath his jovial exterior?

Then again, this was a small island. You could try running from conflict, but sooner or later it was bound to catch up to you. Except that maybe conflict wasn't what she was worried about in this situation. The last time Sarah had been alone with Jesse, the attraction she'd felt toward him had been worse than an argument could ever be. Still, she'd confronted him and he'd taken it. Felon or not, didn't he deserve the same from her? She stood and followed him.

A few steps away from Hannah, he asked, "Is there somewhere we can go that's quiet?"

She hesitated. Being with him here in the bar surrounded by other islanders was one thing. Being alone with him was an entirely different matter.

"Don't get your hopes up," he murmured. "I just want to talk."

"The restaurant. It's closed this time of night." She led him across the bar and through a large set of double doors. He closed the doors behind him and leaned against the wall.

The long, narrow room that looked out over Mirabelle's empty marina was relatively quiet and dark but for the moon shining through the large windows facing the white expanse of a frozen Lake Superior. There was a distinct chill in the air.

She wrapped her arms around herself. "Is there something wrong at the hous—"

"You got a problem with me, that's fine." Jesse spun around and glared at her. "Don't take your issues with me out on Zach."

She stiffened. "I'm not sure I know what you mean."

"Like hell. You wouldn't let Brian have a sleepover at Zach's house tonight. Why?"

She wished she could say she'd labored over the decision, that she'd spent hours pondering the implications of the influence Jesse might have or not have on Brian. The fact was her decision tonight had been a knee-jerk reaction to what had happened in her house the other day. Jesse had frightened her.

"I don't know much about you," she said. "And what I do know makes me wonder what kind of influence you'd have on Brian."

Silent, he walked toward the windows. Stood there, looking out.

"Tell me," she whispered, "why you went to prison."

JESSE'S THROAT WENT DRY and he couldn't seem to push out a single word. He'd known this moment would eventually come. He'd known that at some point he was going to have to spill his guts to someone on this island. He just hadn't wanted that first someone to be Sarah.

"I need to know," she whispered.

"I'm no threat to Brian. Or you. Isn't knowing that enough?"

"Going to prison...had to have a big impact on you. I need to know what you did. I need to know who you are before I can let my son be alone with you."

"You said you know who I am. Remember?" He turned away, anger building inside him. What right did she have to intrude? What right—

But the truth was that his shame wasn't her problem. He'd been working for her for weeks now and, for the most part, she'd let it lie. She was Brian's mother and she had a right to limit his involvement with a felon. She was being a good mother. She deserved to know the truth.

"Jesse, tell m—"

"I've always worked construction," he said, not really sure how to begin. "Usually followed the weather. In the winters I went south. In the summers I came north. Late one summer, I was working outside of Milwaukee. A housing development. I was in charge of two of the projects. This was years back. During a peak in new building."

He started pacing in front of the windows and refused to look at her, knowing that the mere sight of Sarah's eyes might cause him to freeze up.

"We'd all been working God-awful hours," he went on. "Trying to complete the houses before the snow started flying. Seventy-hour weeks for more than a month. Finally, we got to a point where we could relax. It was a Saturday night. The heat was off and all the crews were celebrating."

"You mean at a bar?" she asked.

Jesse nodded. He could almost hear the music playing in the background, the voices in his head as if it was yesterday.

Come on, Jesse. Bottoms up.

Happy hour ain't happy without the life of the party.

You're empty, man. That's no good.

One more. It's just beer. It's not like you're doing shots, right?

On and on and on, that night's dialogue had been running through his mind for years. Though the lines might change from one time to the next, one thing remained constant. He was always left with the desperate longing to go back in time and do it all over again. Do it right this time.

"The bottom line is that I drank one beer too many and then got behind the wheel of my truck." He stopped and stared out into the bitterly cold night. There was no way he could look at Sarah. "I was on my way home when I fell asleep. Next thing I knew, my horn was blaring and the air bag had smacked me in the face. I don't know how long it took to get that thing out of the way, but by the time I climbed out of the truck, sirens were wailing toward me. I'd run my truck right up onto the sidewalk and smashed into the corner of a drugstore."

"So you got a DWI. That doesn't explain—"

"I hit a man, Sarah." His hands trembled and his heart raced. He turned then, knowing he had to face her. He had to face what he'd done.

She stared at him, her eyes wide.

"I ran into a human being with my truck," he whispered, the truth spilling from him like bile. "One minute the man was at one of those video machines outside a drugstore picking out a movie. And the next minute he was pinned between the front of my truck and the brick building."

"Oh, my God," she whispered. "Was he still alive?"

"Unconscious, but alive." Jesse nodded, forcing himself to hold her gaze. "I ran back to the truck, threw her in Reverse, but she wouldn't budge." He swallowed. "My truck had somehow gotten wedged between that building and a corner streetlight."

She put her hand to her mouth and her eyes watered, but she didn't turn away from him as he'd expected. She didn't look away as if she couldn't stand the sight of him. The way he often couldn't stand the sight of himself.

"Seconds later, an ambulance arrived and the EMTs pushed me aside. Then the cops came."

"How did they get the man free?"

"The cops drove gently into the side of my truck, dislodging it."

"Did the man die?"

"No. And the man's name is Hank Bowman." A husband, son and brother. "He ended up with head injuries and internal bruising. He was in a coma for about a month. But the worst thing…" he said, pausing. "He's now paralyzed from the waist down. Hank hadn't even turned thirty years old yet when I ruined his life. He may never walk again."

For Jesse, one of the worst parts about it all was that he couldn't remember a thing about hitting Hank with his truck. Jesse had been asleep at the time he'd gone off the road and that wasn't right, that he had no memory of the moment of impact. By rights, he should be haunted by that instant every day, day in and day out for the rest of his life. The look of Hank's face as the grille of Jesse's truck hit the man's body should cause restless nights and plague his nightmares. Nothing else seemed like justice.

"And don't go off saying things like at least he didn't die. At least you didn't kill him. At least he didn't…" Jesse groaned and spun away from her. Jesse's family, his mother and brothers and sister-in-law had tried to help him cope, tried to help him feel better. "There's no way to make this okay. No way to diminish the wrong I did."

He'd had almost four years to think about this. Justify. Minimize. Rationalize. Hell, all he'd had were a couple of beers that night. His only problem had been drinking on an empty stomach. People drove drunk all the time and never got caught. Never caused an accident. Here he was, with his first DWI, and this is what happened. All he'd done was fall asleep. Such a simple thing. It wasn't his fault the guy had been in the wrong place at the wrong time. But, in the end, he knew in his heart. There was no excuse for what he'd done. No excuse.

"So you went to trial and were convicted—"

"I waived my right to a trial and pled guilty. With my clean record, Garrett said that a good attorney could've gotten me off without any prison time, but that didn't seem right. Hank lost his ability to walk as a direct result of me slamming my truck into him," Jesse whispered. "I broke the law and deserved to go to jail."

Sarah looked back at him, but he couldn't for the life of him venture a guess as to what she was thinking.

"That's the only time. The only time I've ever hurt anyone," he offered. "There are no cars on Mirabelle, and I won't ever touch a drop of alcohol so long as I live. So you go ahead and hate me all you want, Sarah. I won't blame you. But don't punish Zach, or Brian, because of what I did. I would never, ever hurt either one of those boys."

There. It was done.

Jesse spun away from the look on Sarah's face and stalked through the double door and out of Duffy's dining room. Keeping his head down, he went directly toward the pub's side exit, effectively evading anyone he might've met in the short time he'd been on the island. Then he ran down the alley, crossed Main and took off up the hill to Garrett's house as fast as his legs would carry him.

Now that it was out of him, now that Sarah knew, he should've felt relieved, free. Instead, shame overwhelmed him. The freezing air numbed his cheeks and stung his lungs, but still he couldn't erase the look on Sarah's face from his mind. Part anger, part sympathy, part pity, and all disgust. He couldn't take it anymore.

On reaching the house, he nodded at the boys and their babysitter watching a movie in the family room and headed directly back to the spare bedroom, grabbed his duffel bag from under the bed and started throwing things inside. The new clothing he'd bought. The books. A few new toiletries. If he had to cross Chequamegon Bay's ice pack on foot, he was getting the hell off this island tonight.

The front door opened and closed. A moment later footsteps pounded down the hall and a big shadow appeared in the doorway. Garrett. "What happened?"

"Nothing," Jesse said. "I've overstayed my welcome. That's all."

"I saw you leaving Duffy's. I saw the look on your face. And I saw Sarah coming out of the dining room a moment later."

Jesse continued throwing things in his pack.

"You told her, didn't you?"

Jesse paused, but he kept his back to his brother and his mouth closed, not trusting himself to speak in that instant.

"Jesse, listen to me," Garrett said. "I know I played a bit of a hard-ass when you first got to Mirabelle, but I was worried you might slip back into some old bad patterns. You haven't. You've changed. You've grown. You've done your time. You deserve to move on."

"Do I?"

"You paid your debt to society."

"What about my debt to Hank? He's in a wheelchair, for God's sake. May never walk again. He had to sell his house and move because he couldn't go up stairs. He can only enter buildings that are handicapped accessible. He lost his job because of me. His life. Even his marriage is on the rocks."

"You've kept in touch with him?"

"He's kept in touch with me. God only knows why, but he visited me a couple times in prison. Sent emails." Jesse put his head down. "I took everything away from Hank. He won't ever be able to move on, Garrett. Why should I have that luxury?"

"So that's it?" Garrett said. "One sign of trouble and it's hit the road again."

Garrett paced behind him. "Dammit, Jesse! I thought things would be different this time. Maybe I was wrong. Maybe you haven't changed."

Jesse spun around ready to defend himself. "You don't understand—"

"You can't face what you did."

"That's not entirely true," he murmured. "I can't face...Sarah."

Garrett held his gaze.

"People I don't know. I can stand their disapproval. Jonas. Sean. That couple at the pub tonight. They don't know me. They don't know what's inside. They don't know what I've been through. But there's something about Sarah." He threw a balled-up T-shirt into his pack. "I don't know how to live with the way she looked at me."

"You live with it by staying and fighting it. You follow through on a job you committed to finishing. Sarah doesn't need to like you for you to get the job done. And you don't need to like her. She's your boss."

Garrett didn't understand.

"Maybe...just maybe...if you show Sarah the man you've become, she'll come around. With any luck, she'll eventually accept and possibly even respect the brother I know regrets with his whole heart and soul what happened that night four years ago. Stay, Jesse. Face it."

Zach appeared in the doorway. He glanced down at the bag on the bed and pushed his way into the room. "You're not leaving, are you, Uncle Jesse? You can't leave. You just got to Mirabelle."

Everything in Jesse was ready to bolt and run. He wanted to be anyplace but here. Someplace he wouldn't know anyone. Someplace no one knew him. Someplace—

Then what? Some other town? Some other job? If not Sarah, it'd be someone else he was starting to care about who would look at him the way she had tonight.

That was the real problem. He'd started to care for Sarah. Zach, Brian and Erica, too. Jesse glanced from the boy's face to his brother's. He'd missed Garrett much more than he'd realized all these years.

"Uncle Jesse? Are you really leaving?"

He'd planned on staying on the island only long enough to stash away some traveling cash, but is that really what he wanted? Was the man who'd walked out of prison really no different than the man they'd locked up four years ago?

Maybe it was time this rolling stone settled for a while, at least until this frozen rock of an island thawed a bit. Maybe it was time to prove to himself he'd changed, regardless of Sarah. "No, Zach, I'm not going anywhere," Jesse said, giving his nephew a half smile. "Had some dirty clothes to carry down to the washing machine." He glanced at Garrett. "I'll be staying on Mirabelle for a little while yet."

CHAPTER THIRTEEN

"I HAVE IN MY NOTES that you wanted a buffet," Sarah said, trying hard to keep the frustration from her voice as she paced up and down the living room of her house. It'd taken her less than fifteen minutes to confirm the menus for her other June weddings. In contrast, she'd already been on the phone with Megan for more than half an hour.

"Absolutely not," Megan said. "I ended up deciding on a sit-down dinner for the wedding reception, remember? I know I emailed you."

Megan had definitely not emailed that change to Sarah, and this was exactly why she made it a point to, without exception, reconfirm everything months ahead of time.

Taking a deep breath and glancing up in an effort to clear her head, Sarah immediately noticed that Jesse had finished what he'd called knockdown texturing on all the ceilings. She studied several edges and corners and couldn't pick out a single flaw. The man was nothing if not meticulous. And he was right, too. She'd been reluctant to spend the extra money renting a spraying machine, but the new ceilings gave the house an updated, contemporary look and feel. She loved it.

"All right, Megan," she said, feeling suddenly renewed. "A sit-down dinner it is. I've got you down for marinated chicken with olive tapenade and filet mignon with béarnaise."

Megan sighed. "What do you think about adding some Lake Superior flavor? Maybe whitefish with a white-wine cream sauce?"

"I think you should stick with chicken and beef. If you want fish, we can add that to the groom's dinner buffet."

"This is a destination wedding. I want more Mirabelle flavor—"

"I get that, Megan," Sarah interrupted, needing to shut this bride down. "But a lot of people don't like fish. Remember that Mirabelle's flavor comes into play the moment your guests step onto the ferry. The island charm is solidified when they're whisked away on horse-drawn carriages to the Mirabelle Island Inn. Then there are the historic rooms. The rose gardens. The breezes coming in off the lake. The view. The gazebo. That's what Mirabelle Island is all about."

Megan sighed. "You're right. You're right. Just like the gold calla lilies. Beef and chicken it is. But I want the vegetables steamed, not boiled. And I want pasta, not potatoes…"

Sarah closed her eyes and kept her mouth shut, hoping Megan would soon run out of steam. Several minutes later, the bride took a breath and Sarah seized the opportunity. "Megan, I must run. I've got everything under control, okay?"

"You're sure?"

"Positive. See you soon."

Sarah clicked off her cell phone and glanced around, taking in the status of her house. As picky as she could be, she couldn't fault Jesse's work. As for his admission at Duffy's the other night as to why he'd gone to prison, she was at a loss. She hadn't seen him since then and had no clue as to how to proceed in this strange relationship.

Picking up a broom, she walked toward the back and started sweeping up the bathrooms. She and Jesse had an unwritten, unspoken agreement. He made messes. She cleaned them up.

When the front door opened and closed, her stomach clenched.

"Hello? Sarah?" Close but no cigar. It was Garrett.

She stepped out into the hall. "Jesse's not here."

"Actually, I was looking for you." He came toward her, examining every angle and line of Sheetrock and trim with a critical eye. "My brother might not be able to design furniture to save his soul," he murmured. "But he does damn good remodeling work."

"You were right." Sarah finished sweeping the floor. "He *was* the best man for this job."

"The only person likely to satisfy a perfectionist is another perfectionist." Garrett smiled. "How are things going between you two?"

Avoiding his gaze, she dumped the full dustpan into the garbage. "All right." It'd been several days since Jesse had come to Duffy's, and since then, she had to admit, she'd been avoiding him, coming to the house late in the day and hoping Jesse would already be gone. The time or two that lights had still been on inside she'd left to come back later.

"You sure about that?"

Silently, she glanced up at Garrett.

"The other night at Duffy's," he said. "I know he told you about his DWI. Hitting a pedestrian."

She didn't know what to say. Since then, Jesse's admission had been all she'd thought about. What he had done was wrong. There was no way around that. But Sarah would've been lying to herself to not admit she'd made her share of mistakes.

While she empathized with the man Jesse had hit and his family, people made mistakes every day, and sometimes those mistakes impacted other's lives. Sometimes people even died. During her stint down in Miami, there were a number of times she could've been the one who'd ended up in prison for any number of infractions.

"I think there might be a few other things about Jesse that might help you understand," Garrett said softly.

"I won't say anything to any of the other islanders," Sarah said, putting the broom and dustpan in the closet. "If that's what you're worried about."

"I hadn't even considered that, to be honest."

"Then what?"

"I'm worried about Jesse. Guess it's the big-brother thing. What he's been through has hit him pretty hard," Garrett said. "Sometimes I'm surprised he still has a sense of humor." He chuckled. "When we were kids he was always the comic relief. Bet that doesn't come as a surprise, huh?"

"No."

"Something that might surprise you is that for whatever reason—and I'm trying hard not to read anything into this—your opinion has become important to Jesse."

Amidst the emotions rolling off him in waves the other night, she'd sensed that. She didn't understand it, but she'd felt it.

"The truth is that Jesse is one of the most misunderstood people I know. It wasn't until I became an adult that I realized what a stand-up guy he was compared to the rest of us. He might've been the baby in the family, but he had more balls than me."

Knowing Garrett, that seemed hard to believe.

"I remember time and time again," Garrett said, "my dad would come home in a bad mood looking for a fight. The rest of us would hightail it outside, or hide in our rooms. Not Jesse. He'd get right in front of Dad and try to make the man laugh. Sometimes it'd work and defuse things, and sometimes it didn't. Sometimes my dad would lighten up, but more often than not Jesse would get the back of a hand. You'd think a split lip would be enough to shut a kid down. Hell, it always shut me right up. Not Jesse."

"What would he do?"

"He'd change tactics. If humor didn't work, he'd purposefully antagonize my dad. Egg him on. Get him mad."

"Why? Why wouldn't he just leave your dad alone?"

"I think he was afraid that if he left my dad alone when he was in those gnarly moods, then Dad would take his anger out on someone else. Like one of us other boys. Or Mom. That was completely unacceptable as far as Jesse was concerned."

Emotion clogged Sarah's throat.

"Jess would step in front of a speeding truck to save someone else. That's one of the things that's so sad about what happened that night in Milwaukee four years ago." He held Sarah's gaze. "I'm not sure he'll ever forgive himself for *being* the truck."

Once upon a time, she could've been in Jesse's shoes. The fact that she hadn't gotten caught didn't make it right. The fact that she'd hurt no one but herself in the process had been sheer luck. She didn't have a right to judge him, and it had been unfair of her to assume he'd be a bad influence on Brian. It was time she apologized to Jesse, and the best way she knew how to do that was to share with him everything she hadn't been able to share with Missy about her past. Sooner rather than later.

"By the way," Garrett said. "Did you hear the bad news?"

"No, what happened?"

"Carl's mom died."

"Jean Andersen died?" Sarah murmured. "Oh, my God, no."

Mirabelle Island's retired pastor John Andersen and his wife, Jean, had been wintering in Arizona for years. She hadn't known Jean very well, but she'd worked with John on many weddings before he'd retired, and even a few afterward. He was a kind-hearted, quiet man, and this would definitely be hard for him.

"What happened?" she asked.

"Massive heart attack. Apparently, John found her outside, near her garden. There was nothing he could do."

"BRIAN, ARE YOU SURE your mom said it's okay for you to be here helping out?" Jesse asked from his crouched position in front of the old kitchen cabinets at Sarah's house.

Brian and Zach were completely inside the empty cupboards helping to detach the backs from the kitchen wall.

"Positive. I swear," Brian said. "She told me it was okay."

"All right. Just checking." Jesse may have spilled his guts to Sarah at Duffy's, but a part of him completely understood Sarah's reservations. Now that the truth was out, though, he had to tell the boys. He'd delayed long enough.

"She treats me like a baby," Brian complained before Jesse could formulate any kind of way to broach the subject. "I'm sick of it."

"Maybe if you acted more grown-up," Jesse said, "she'd treat you more like a grown-up."

"What do you mean?" Brian asked, poking his head out from the cabinet.

"When's the last time you helped out without being asked?"

Brian frowned.

"Try doing the dishes on your own sometime." With four boys in the house and him being the youngest, Jesse had always gotten stuck with the worst of the household chores. "Getting your homework done before your mom asks about it."

"Whatever." Brian grunted, as if he were dismissing Jesse, and slid back inside the old cabinet.

"Hey, wait a minute. Come on back out here. Both of you. I need to talk with you guys about something."

They scrambled out from inside the cabinets, tools in hand, and sat there on the floor, both of them looking at him so innocently. So expectantly. And for what?

He could deal with Jonas and Sean saying it like it is. He told himself he couldn't care less about the judgments of the other people on Mirabelle that he didn't even know, but somehow, someway, he'd come to care about what these young boys thought of him almost as much as Sarah.

He sat down on the floor. "There's something I haven't told you about myself." There was no easy way to do this. He just had to say spit it out. "Right before I came here to Mirabelle, I spent four years in prison."

Zach's gaze slid away.

"Yeah, we know," Brian said.

"You already know?"

"I heard Garrett and Erica talking about it one night when they thought I was asleep," Zach said.

"Kids were talking about it at recess," Brian added.

"They said you probably killed someone." Zach jerked his head back up and his cheeks got red. "We told them it wasn't true."

Brian clenched his jaw. "I swear, I almost punched Alex."

"Nobody needs to punch anybody." Jesse sighed. "I should've told you sooner, but I…I guess I was embarrassed."

"What did you do?" Brian asked.

Zach cringed. "Was it bad?"

"No one goes to prison without doing something bad." Jesse looked into their faces and the urge to sugar-coat the situation shot through him. They were kids, he reasoned. He could paint any picture he wanted and they'd believe him. They'd want to believe him. But he couldn't do that to them. To himself.

"I was at a bar," Jesse said. "I drank too much beer and then I drove my truck. I went off the road and I hit a man. Almost killed him."

For a moment, neither boy said anything. Then they looked at each other.

"Yeah, that's bad," Zach said.

"But at least he didn't kill anyone," Brian said.

Zach nodded. "Everyone makes mistakes."

"No, listen." Jesse shook his head. "Don't make this

seem like it's no big deal. Just because I didn't kill him doesn't make it okay."

"But we like you, Jesse."

"And you'd never hurt us."

"No," Jesse whispered. "I'd never hurt anyone. Not on purpose."

"See? You're not a bad man."

"No, I'm not a bad man. Good people sometimes make bad decisions. You're right. Everyone makes mistakes. Some of us, like me, make big ones. That's why I had to go to prison. Just because I went to prison, though, doesn't make everything okay." He glanced from one to the other, hoping this was sinking in. "So if anyone says anything bad about me, you let it go. Understand?"

Zach's shoulders dropped.

Brian frowned. "But—"

"I mean it, boys. I don't want anyone defending me, and I sure as hell don't want anyone fighting for me. I did something very wrong. There's no way around that. That means everyone on Mirabelle has a right to make up their own minds about me. So you just let them say and think what they want. And you walk away."

"Fine," Brian muttered.

"All right," Zach agreed.

"I have to learn from my mistakes. *You two* can learn from my mistake. We'll all be better in the end." If only Jesse could believe that. "Well, that's that." He smiled, feeling surprisingly relieved for the first time in a very long while. "Now, let's get back to work!"

The boys climbed back inside the lower kitchen cabinets as if nothing earth-shattering had happened. Jesse wasn't fool enough to think this conversation was over, but at least he'd broached the subject, opened the door for them to talk with him. With any luck, they would.

"Don't worry about breaking anything, Zach," Jesse said, keeping the cabinet doors wide-open and shining a large flashlight into the darkness so the boys could see what they were doing. "Put some muscle into it, Brian. You two can get those screws out."

"These screws are really hard to turn," Brian said.

"You'll get them," Jesse said, keeping the tone of his voice as encouraging as possible. "Keep working on it. Only about fifty more screws to go."

"Fifty!" Brian groaned. "Oh, man!"

"That's too many!" Zach complained.

"Ah, come on." Jesse grinned. "Work together to zap those suckers out of there."

"You hold up the screwdriver, Zach," Brian said. "And I'll push it onto the screw."

"Now you're talking," Jesse said.

The motor on the battery-operated tool sounded briefly. "We got it!" Zach exclaimed.

"Good job. Keep going."

"Hello, there." Sarah's voice sounded from the front door. "How's it going?"

Jesse glanced up above the counter. She was taking off her coat and boots, looking as if she might stay awhile. This was the first time he'd seen her since Duffy's and he wasn't exactly sure how to be around her.

Her boss. You lackey. Seemed best, all things considered, to keep things on that level.

"Things are clipping along," he answered. "Your bathrooms are finished, so the kitchen is next. First thing we have to do is to remove the old cabinets and counters."

She walked into the kitchen, and he immediately backed up, putting distance between them. Bending over, she glanced inside the cabinets. "What are you two doing in there?"

"Helping," Zach said.

"Jesse needed the screws out of these cabinets, so he can install the new ones."

She straightened and smiled. "Looks like the boys have come in handy."

"You know it." Jesse chuckled. "I'd be a little on the contorted side trying to fit inside there to unscrew the cabinets from the wall. They're doing a good job."

In truth, they were barely strong enough to hold up the cordless screwdriver, and she knew it. But it was nice of them to help, and Jesse, surprisingly, enjoyed their company.

"So what's next after you dismantle the kitchen cabinets and counters?"

"I'll put in the floor." He nodded toward the wide-width wood planks stacked against the wall in the living room. "Once that's in, then I can install the new cupboards and counter."

Sarah's expression turned soft. "Once you finish with the kitchen, the house will start looking like a home."

"Kitchens are the focal point for a lot of people." Jesse looked away. The moment turned awkward, and he wracked his brain for something to say. "How—"

"I—"

They both talked at the same time.

"You go first," she said.

"I was wondering if you wanted to salvage the old kitchen counter and cabinets. They're outdated, but they're still in good shape. They'd make for a nice workbench and storage."

"Where would you suggest putting them?"

"Well, since you don't have a garage, in the basement. I'll show you." He headed toward the stairs just off the side door into the kitchen. "Boys, we'll be right back. You guys keep at it, okay?"

"Okay," they both said in unison.

He flipped on the light at the top of the basement steps. It flickered for a moment before holding steady. "That's a bad ballast. I can replace this one, but there's more rewiring that needs to be done here and there, and I don't do electricity." He could, in reality, manage it, but it'd likely take him twice as long as an experienced electrician. "I recommend hiring someone to do the rewiring."

"Do you know anyone?"

"No, but Garrett might."

She followed him down the steps and he crossed to the far corner.

"I didn't know you'd cleaned out the cellar," she said. The basement had been filled with junk, broken screens, old dehumidifiers, discarded small appliances and the like.

"On the first day," he said. "Thought I'd better take advantage of the Dumpster."

"No wonder things seemed to be going a little slow initially. Why didn't you say something?"

He only slanted his head at her. They hadn't exactly been on cordial terms back then.

"Never mind," she said, seeming to remember. "Thank you for clearing the mess out."

"Not a big deal." He pointed to the corner. "The

counter and cabinets would fit right here. Makes for a good work area."

"I was only planning on using the basement for storage, so that'll work."

"I'll make it happen." He turned toward the stairs.

"Jesse?"

He paused, but he wasn't sure he wanted to look at her. In fact, he was sure he didn't.

"About the other night," she said. "At Duffy's. I have something I need to say."

CHAPTER FOURTEEN

"YOU DON'T NEED TO SAY anything, Sarah." He shrugged. "You were protecting Brian. You're his mom. It's your job."

"I need to explain why I've been so…"

"Antagonistic toward me?" He cocked his head. "That's okay. I figured I'd get that a lot just getting out of prison and all."

"I guess that was part of it." She lightly touched his arm, holding him back. "Not knowing what you'd done… I have to admit, I got on the internet and tried to find out why you'd been sent to prison. But I couldn't find any—"

He laughed as he imagined her searching for him online. "That's because my first name is really James. Jesse is a nickname. Been stuck with it ever since a game of cops and robbers when I was about Brian's age. And, yes, in case you're wondering…I was a robber, not a cop. Get it? Jesse James?"

"Well, that explains it. I couldn't find anything, so all kinds of horrific crimes went through my head. I imagined the worst."

"Sarah, it's okay."

"No. It's not. I—"

The light flickered again, and then it went completely out. The narrow, belowground windows were caked with dirt and very little light filtered down from upstairs.

Jesse wasn't sure if it was his imagination or not, but it seemed as if Sarah had stepped closer to him. "You okay?" he whispered, reaching out to steady her.

"I'm fine." She leaned into his touch, belying her words. Something was happening here between them and that was definitely not his imagination. "I just don't like... This cellar is a little creepy, isn't it?"

"It's old, but it'd sure come in handy if a tornado ever hit the island."

The light flickered on.

"Uncle Jesse!" Zach called from upstairs.

"Coming!" Jesse turned, thankful for the reprieve.

"But I wanted to apologize," Sarah said quickly.

"Don't sweat it." Feeling as if a fire was at his heels, Jesse took the steps two at a time. "Gotta get back to work, or there'll be hell to pay with boss lady."

Sarah followed. When they reached the kitchen, the boys were taking large gulps from a couple cans of sodas.

"What's up?" Jesse asked.

"I can't do any more," Zach said, shaking his head.

"Me neither," Brian added. "My arms are shot."

"Well, you guys have been working pretty hard since you got out of school. I'll do the rest."

"Let's go back to my house," Zach said. "And get something to eat."

"I'm starving."

"Leave room for dinner," Sarah cautioned. "Be home by six, okay?"

Within minutes, the boys were dashing out the door, leaving Jesse alone with Sarah. Again. Attempting to avoid her, he slid halfway into the lower cabinets and was working to remove the rest of the screws holding the cabinets to the wall.

"Jesse, can I talk—"

"Now's not a good time, Sarah. I'd like—"

"I'm not going away. I need to say something. Please."

Jesse took his finger off the power button on the battery-operated screwdriver. There was something in her voice that didn't seem right. "Okay, fine." He slid out of the cupboard to face her and leaned back against the counter. "We might as well get this over with. Shoot."

"I have a confession to make."

"Oh, no." *Hell, no!* "I don't take confessions—"

"I need you to listen."

"Sarah—"

"There was a time in my life when what happened to you that night in Milwaukee could've happened to me."

That stopped him. What she'd just admitted was about as honest as confessions got.

"I could've been driving a truck that caused a man to be paralyzed." She had a hard time holding his gaze. "There was a time in my life when I could've hurt, or killed, someone. I'm not very proud of it."

"Don't we all have some history we'd rather forget?"

"Not like this." She shook her head. "There are some things I did back then that make the hair stand up on the back of my neck."

"Sarah, you don't need to tell me—"

"Yes, I do." She paused. "But maybe if you understand... I grew up in a small town in Indiana. I hit my teenage years and went just about out of my mind with boredom. I couldn't get out of Indiana fast enough after I finished high school. Ended up in Florida. Started working for the wedding planner of Miami's wealthiest. I couldn't wait to start living. And, trust me, I crammed a lot of living into a few short years. Fell in with a bad crowd. Started partying, and…well, let's say that I had more than the average person's wild oats to sow and I sowed them but good." Out of the blue, tears welled in her eyes. "Dipped my toes into a little more than top-shelf tequila."

"Drugs?"

"Mostly cocaine. Some ecstasy. The truth is, if there was a drug available, I pretty much did it. If there was a man available, I did him, too. As long as he was fun, footloose and fancy-free. The badder the bad boy, the better."

Wow. This, I never expected. Not from the likes of Sarah. "But you broke the cycle, right?"

"If you can call hitting rock bottom breaking the cycle, then yeah. The truth is…I'm lucky to be alive."

"What happened?"

"I woke up one morning in a stranger's bed. I didn't know who he was, how I'd met him, how I'd gotten on his yacht. We were in the Bahamas. I'd lost two days of my life drugged up on God knows what."

"Yeah, that's a doozy. I've done a lot of crazy things, but I can honestly say I knew every single bed I ever woke up in."

"I'm not proud of it. Safe to say, I'm ashamed of it, actually. It was the lowest point in my life, but it was also a turning point." She sighed and seemed to be gathering herself. "Everything was different for me after that day. I knew my life had to change. *I* had to change. I went straight. At least I did for a few weeks. Just when I slipped back into one more binge, the real turning point hit me."

"You found out you were pregnant. With Brian."

Sarah nodded. "Knowing I was carrying a baby. Knowing I was going to be responsible for a little one made me do the right thing." She held Jesse's gaze. "So that was it. The end of the parties. No more clubs. No more of my old friends. I quit my job, moved into a new apartment to get away from that old crowd and started up my own wedding-planning business. Things were actually going okay."

"Who's the father?" As he held her gaze, he could see the shame virtually sweep through her.

"See that's the thing. I don't know," she whispered. "At the time, I narrowed it down to one of three men. One was married at the time. One wouldn't take my calls. But the other man…Bobby…asked me to marry him."

"Were you straight with him? Did you tell him you didn't know who the father was?"

"No." She couldn't hold his gaze and looked away. "I was scared. Didn't have any savings. Didn't know how I could support a baby all on my own. I convinced myself that I wasn't really lying because I really didn't know the truth."

"Did you marry him?"

She shook her head. "Got engaged to him, though. Went through all the plans. For a while, the prospect of a wedding seemed to help him clean up, too, so that was another reason how I justified keeping the truth from him. I would've gone through with it, I think."

"But?"

"He OD'd not long after Brian was born."

"I'm sorry."

"Don't be. At least not for me. Me getting away from Bobby, from that lifestyle, was very likely the best thing for me and Brian. Bobby's mother, though, was in a lot of pain over losing her only son. She blamed me for his death and threatened to take Brian away. Like a pit bull, she just wouldn't let go. The court ordered a blood test and it turned out Bobby wasn't the father."

Turning her justifications into outright lies.

"A part of me has always felt responsible for Bobby's death."

"Sounds to me like the writing was on the wall for that man even before he met you, Sarah."

"Maybe. Maybe not. Either way, I left Florida and never looked back. Since then, it's been nothing but the straight and narrow for me. Almost ten years."

He held silent, absorbing what she was saying.

"So now you know. You're the only one who knows every sordid detail of my past."

"You've never told anyone?"

"Missy knows bits and pieces. That's all."

It'd taken a lot for her to admit this to him, and he wished he could say that she looked relieved. She didn't.

"So...I guess what I'm trying to say is that...I'm sorry. I know it's not fair, but you...reminded me of my old life. Of all the mistakes I'd made."

She was so serious. Too serious. Everyone made mistakes. Hers were a long time in the past, way past time to let it all go. "So am I hearing this right?" He chuckled, trying to lighten things up. "It's my fault you're attracted to me?"

"I didn't say that."

He continued smiling.

"I'm trying to be honest, here, Jesse. I'm trying to tell you I'm sorry for holding my own past against you."

Oddly enough, her admissions only served to make her even more attractive to him. Bad girls were sexy. Bad girls masquerading as good girls were damned near irresistible. He was going to have to watch his Ps and Qs even more now. "Apology accepted, Sarah."

"Can we start over?"

"Hmm. I'm not sure about that. I have a feeling there's already too much water over the dam between the two of us for that to work."

"We can try. There's no harm in that, is there?"

Starting over. Sounded harmless enough. So why did it feel as if this change in their relationship didn't bode well for him?

"You never know," she said, raising her dark eyebrows. "We might even become friends."

Now that, he knew, was never going to happen. Sarah's friendship was the last thing he wanted from her, but things between them probably did need to change. "Okay, sure. Let's start over." He held out his hand. "Jesse Taylor."

"Sarah Marshik." She grinned as she shook his hand. "Pleased to meet you."

In that moment, he knew. He should've never come to Mirabelle.

THERE WAS A REASON Sarah planned happy things like weddings. She hated funerals, even more than thunderstorms, and chose a seat near the rear of Mirabelle's small church. About a week had passed since she'd heard the news through Garrett of Jean Andersen's death. Apparently, Jean and John's daughter, Grace, a model who lived in L.A. and Mirabelle's biggest celebrity, hadn't been able to make it to the island any sooner for a more timely service. The rumor-mill speculation, never particularly kind to begin with, was that the daughter had refused to miss some big fashion show in Paris. It made more sense to Sarah that it had taken a while to make preparations, considering Jean had died in Arizona.

In any case, the delay had given relatives and friends a chance to travel from far and wide to Mirabelle. Arlo and Lynn Duffy, as well as Jan and Ron Setterberg, both snowbird couples, had returned to pay their respects. Before retiring, the Duffys had owned both Duffy's Pub and Mirabelle Stable and Livery. Although the Setterbergs were also retired, they still owned the building from which Sarah rented both her flower shop and apartment. Despite the circumstances, it was nice to see both couples midwinter.

Not long after Sarah had arrived at the church, Hannah came to the door. She spotted Sarah and made a beeline for the seat next to her. Missy and Jonas came in and sat beside Hannah. Much to Sarah's surprise, Jesse appeared next in the doorway.

"What's he doing here?" Hannah said.

"He knows Carl," Missy whispered. "I think it's nice that he came."

Jesse headed toward the outside of a pew on the other side of the church. He nodded at Jan and Ron Setterberg, who were already sitting toward the middle of that same pew, and sat down. Jan said something to Ron. He shook his head, but then Jan got up and moved to the other side of the aisle. Ron sighed and followed.

"Ouch," Hannah whispered. "But then Jesse's probably used to that kind of cold shoulder."

No one ever got used to that kind of obvious scorn.

Jesse, clearly aware of what had just happened, looked down for a moment, as if to gather himself, and then kept his gaze focused toward the center of the church as if he hadn't noticed Jan's rudeness. Sarah might've expected that kind of reaction from Jan, but Ron acquiescing to Jan's judgmental behavior surprised her.

A few moments later, Shirley Gilbert came down the center aisle, was about to move into Jesse's pew until she saw him and kept moving on to the next open seat. No surprise in the reaction toward Jesse that time, either.

Sarah was about to get up and go sit by him when Garrett and Erica entered the church. They saw Jesse and immediately joined him. Sarah took a deep breath and relaxed, but she couldn't help feeling a little more compassion for Jesse. Possibly even respect. He could've gone to a town where no one was aware of his past. Instead, he'd come to little Mirabelle, where everyone knew everything about everybody and faced outright censure.

Sarah glanced back at the door and saw Sean coming into the church. He went up to Carl and Carol, who were standing in the entryway with their two kids, Nikki and Alex, and gave them both hugs. They talked for a few moments and then Sean took a seat next to Erica.

Little by little the tiny church filled to capacity. People were standing in the rear and along the wall. Not long after Jesse gave up his seat for Delores Kowalski to stand in the aisle, the organist began playing somber funeral music and the family walked in to be seated at the front of the church.

John came in first with Carl on one side and Carol on the other. She'd read in the obituary that John and Jean had been married for more than forty years, so there was no surprise he didn't look as if he was handling the loss well.

Carl and Carol looked only marginally better. Sarah didn't know Carol well, but she knew Carl both personally and in her business dealings. Most of the weddings she planned were held at the Mirabelle Island Inn, but occasionally a bride and groom opted for the more rustic setting of the Rock Pointe Lodge. Carl, and sometimes both Carl and Carol, came to Duffy's for happy hour.

The moment Carl's sister, Grace, appeared at the door, the church erupted in quiet whispers.

"Skinny ugly duckling turned into a skinny swan..."

"...looks terrible...never was as pretty as my Gail."

"...that designer, Jeremy Kahill..."

"...thought they were divorced."

"Separated is what I heard."

"...after the accident..."

"...said she might move back to Mirabelle."

On and on and on, the whispered speculation continued. Sarah shook her head and glanced at Hannah. "Oh, for crying out loud, so she's a famous model. So what?"

"You'd think she was a princess."

The woman was wearing a black turtleneck dress and small black hat with netting that came down over her face. Large, dark sunglasses completely hid her eyes, and her long, curly blond hair, the model's trademark, came forward to hide her neck and cheeks. She looked far too secretive to Sarah. And sad.

Her husband, a world-famous designer in a beautifully cut black suit, walked next to her. They couldn't be divorced, or separated, not as attentive as he appeared. Grace had hooked her hand through the crook of one of his arms and seemed to be almost leaning into him.

"She's beautiful," Missy whispered. "Much prettier in person than in her photos."

"How can you tell?" Sarah murmured. "You can barely see any part of her."

"Just look at her profile," Missy whispered. "No wonder she's one of the highest-paid models."

"God, I wish I had her posture," Hannah mumbled. "So regal and confident."

"I wonder how Carl's doing," Sarah said.

"I think he's holding it together," Jonas whispered. "But John isn't doing very well."

"Is he staying here the rest of the winter?"

"I think so."

The service began and a hush fell over the crowd. Sarah felt her gaze, more often than not, settling on Jesse. He was easy to spot, standing as he was on the other side of the church. More than once, she found him watching her. Before she knew it, the service had ended and everyone was filing out of the church. She and Jesse ended up meeting at the door.

"Hi," he whispered.

She smiled. "It was nice that you came even though you don't know the family well."

"Carl's a good guy, but it's been a while since I've been to a funeral." As they walked outside, he pulled a hat over his head and tugged on his gloves.

She slipped on the ice and he grabbed her arm.

He glanced down at her high-heeled black leather boots and grinned. "Pretty, but what happened to your mukluks?"

She chuckled. "Are you coming to the cemetery?"

"No. Don't feel like I know the family well enough. You?"

"Yeah." For some reason, she felt she needed to apologize for the way a few people had snubbed him before the service started. "Hey, um, you know...the Setterbergs—Jan, I should say—can be a bit..."

"Who?"

"The people who got up and...then Shirley Gilbert—"

"Not sure what you're talking about. Say, have you found an electrician yet?"

He didn't want to talk about it. Could she blame him? "No, but I've made a few calls."

"You want me to—"

"I'll find one. Promise."

"Okay. See ya." He headed down the sidewalk toward Garrett and Erica's house, and Sarah found herself wishing she could go with him.

CHAPTER FIFTEEN

"A THOUSAND DOLLARS A DAY?" Sarah said, frustrated. "Just because the job is on Mirabelle?"

She was on the phone with the fifth and last electrician Garrett had recommended for the work needed to be done on her house, and all of their stories and costs were similar. They were busy with other construction projects and her job was too small for any kind of price negotiation.

"You gotta remember almost half the first and last days are taken up by travel time," the electrician from Ashland said. "Which means I'll have to stay overnight on the island, and I'll have to hire a helicopter to get me there and back. I'm not crossing that ice this time of year. Too risky."

The ice had already started softening, but Garrett maintained it was still safe.

"I'm sorry, ma'am. If you can wait until June when my father-in-law gets back from Texas, he'll be able to take care of this for a more reasonable price."

"I can't wait until June."

"Well, then," the man said, sighing. "There is someone else."

"Who?"

The electrician hesitated before giving her another man's name and number. "He might be more in your price range."

"Thank you." She called the other number.

The phone rang several times before a man's raspy voice finally sounded over the line. "Yeah."

She explained the situation and was happy to settle on a price within her budget and timing that worked for Jesse. She'd no sooner hung up the phone than the doorbell rang.

Brian dropped his gaming controller to run across the room. "That's gotta be Zach!"

"Is he coming for dinner?" Sarah asked as she ground fresh black peppercorns into the bubbling pot on the stove.

"Can he?"

"Sure."

As good of a cook as Erica was, Zach surprisingly wound up eating at their house more often than not. Apparently, from a kid's perspective, Sarah's plain cooking of things like macaroni and cheese, hamburgers and hot dogs, beat out the likes of grilled sea bass and prosciutto-wrapped scallops any day of the week. There was no understanding a kid's palate.

Sarah glanced up as Brian opened the door. Zach stood on the landing, but it was the tall frame of his uncle standing behind him that sent an immediate shock of awareness to her gut.

She wasn't prepared for this. Dressed in an old thermal Henley and her rattiest pair of jeans, not to mention her hair up in a haphazardly gathered ponytail, she'd been expecting to go up to the house after dinner to paint. Entertaining a visitor, especially Jesse, hadn't been on the agenda.

The boys ran into the family room and immediately immersed themselves in some video game, leaving her and Jesse in her entryway.

"Hi." She wiped her hands on her jeans as she walked toward the door. "What's up?"

His gaze seemed to travel all over her in an instant, and he cleared his throat. "Did you get the note I left you up at the house about painting the kitchen?"

"Um, no." The part of her that couldn't help but want him couldn't help but be disappointed that he hadn't simply come to see her.

"Yeah, I didn't think so. The kitchen will be easier to paint if you do it before I install the cabinets. The cabinet installation is a two-man job and I have Garrett lined up to help me next week."

"Then I'll make sure and get the walls painted this weekend."

"One more thing—"

"Why don't you come in?" It was freezing outside. The wind was whipping in off the lake, blowing the light snow that had fallen during the day into small drifts on her deck.

"That's okay. I—"

"Come on. It's too cold to stand out there with the door open." She tugged him inside and closed the door.

"Can Jesse stay for dinner, too, Mom?" Brian called.

"Um...I'm not sure we'll have enough."

"You always make extra," Brian said.

She did, given she was never sure whether or not Zach might show up at the last minute, but then she was used to boy-size portions, and a man the size of Jesse could likely pack it away.

"Besides, I'm not that hungry," Brian said.

"Neither am I," Zach added.

"That's okay, boys." Jesse shook his head. "Thanks anyway. I've got—"

"Please stay." If they were truly starting over, it was up to her to extend the first olive branch. "The least I can do is feed you to thank you for going above and beyond on our house."

"Yeah, well, you're paying me for that. Remember?"

"We're supposed to be friends. Remember that?" She held his gaze, smiling slightly. "But then I don't want to force you to do anything you really don't want to do. This isn't prison, you know."

At that he chuckled. "Dinner sounds great. Thank you."

"It isn't anything special. Knowing Erica, she's whipped up something absolutely divine tonight. This is just some homemade chicken noodle soup."

"Sounds great." His eyes brightened and he slipped off his jacket. "No wonder it smells so good in here."

"Right." She put her hands on her hips. "Erica's not cooking tonight, is she?"

"Nope." He grinned. "She's at the pub."

Sarah laughed. "Well, we wouldn't want you to have to make something yourself."

She quickly glanced around, wondering what he'd think of her apartment. Although the space was small, she'd used the areas well, partitioning off the family room from the kitchen with a large sectional sofa. Since she rarely had guests other than Zach, she'd never bothered with a kitchen table, preferring to have the boys eat at the counter instead.

The moment Jesse came into her small kitchen, the room seemed to shrink to half its size. He didn't seem to mind being in such close proximity to her, but his nearness was making it a little difficult for Sarah to catch her breath.

"I think this is the brightest apartment I've ever seen," he said. "I like it."

"Comes in handy during the dreary days of winter," she said, pulling four heavy red bowls from the cabinet. "Missy always teases me that the place looks like a Mexican restaurant."

Jesse laughed.

A couple years ago, sick of the various hues of tan she'd chosen when she'd first moved to Mirabelle and this apartment, she'd redecorated with bright, cheery colors. She'd painted the walls a combination of red and white and accented with royal blue and apple green. Orange and yellow.

"I'm ready for a change." For the house she was sticking with more neutral, muted browns, greens and coral tones and accenting with deeper, bolder colors.

"I think I like the choices you've made on your house better, but you definitely have an eye for color."

"Good attribute for a flower-shop owner and wedding planner."

"Can I help with anything?"

"Everything's under control. If you want something to drink, help yourself to whatever is in the fridge."

He opened the door, peered inside and pulled out a cola. Despite the initial awkwardness, there was something surprisingly comforting about having Jesse here. Something homey and right-feeling. Aside from Ron Setterberg making repairs as her landlord, Sarah couldn't remember ever having had a man in her apartment. It wasn't as if she ever dated.

Hannah dated all the time, especially in the summer months when school was out and the island was crawling with tourists and fishermen. Missy had dated occasionally before Jonas had shown up on Mirabelle out of the blue. Erica had been married to Garrett within several months of coming to Mirabelle. And Natalie? Their summer friend who ran the camp for disadvantaged kids on the remote side of the island had apparently dated more men than she'd been able to count before falling head over heels in love with Jamis, the island's resident hermit. Sarah, on the other hand, hadn't been out with a man since Bobby.

Almost ten years ago.

Too long.

But then that's what happened, she supposed, when a woman didn't trust herself, didn't trust her judgment in men.

"Jesse, come and play with us," Brian called.

"Yeah," Zach said. "You always say you'll play video games and then you never do."

He glanced at Sarah.

"Go ahead. The soup's not ready yet. And I really should make another client call."

"She's always on the phone with clients," Brian muttered, keeping his head focused on the TV.

Jesse frowned. "Yeah, okay, I'll play. As long as you quit giving your mom a hard time." He walked into the family room and grabbed a controller.

As she picked up the phone and made her last call of the day, she heard Jesse say, "Being a single parent is hard. Your mom's on her own, taking care of you, running her own business. Cut her some slack, man. Better yet, help out without being asked. If you did more around here, she'd have more time to spend with you."

Although she couldn't hear Brian's mumbled response, she smiled as she wrapped up the conversation and hung up the phone. "Soup's on," she called.

"Okay, we're saving the game," Jesse replied.

Then he came into the kitchen and sat down at the counter. She set a bowl of soup in front of him. "Want some bread? Salad?"

"No, thank you," he murmured, dipping his spoon into the steaming broth. "This is going to be perfect all by itself."

"Zach and Brian, you guys coming?"

The boys joined Jesse at the counter and a light conversation ensued revolving around the boys. Soon the discussion turned to Jesse's progress on the house. In no time, the boys finished eating, hopped down from their chairs and headed toward the family room.

"Hey, boys," Jesse said.

They turned.

He glanced down at their dirty dishes. "Didn't you forget something?"

Brian shook his head and grinned, then he came back to rinse out his bowl and put it in the dishwasher. Zach followed suit. "Anything else we can help with, Mom?" Brian asked, surprisingly sincere.

"Thank you, but I'll get the rest. You two go back to your game." They took off and she smiled at Jesse. It was nice having someone at her back. "Thank you."

"No problem. It's easy for me. I'm not mom."

"So what are you doing tomorrow night, the night after that, and so on?"

He chuckled as he scooped out the last of his third bowlful. "That was really good." Then suddenly he was next to her, rinsing out his bowl in the sink.

Close enough that she could feel his heat. Too close. "Um…was there something else about the house?"

"Yeah, I almost forgot." He stepped back, as if he, too, was uncomfortable. "I need you to decide on a fixture for over the island in your kitchen."

"I didn't do that with Garrett?" She'd picked out so many things during the preparations for this remodeling project that she couldn't remember.

He shook his head. "I'm going into Duluth with Garrett tomorrow for some supplies. You want to come along and pick something out?"

"Can't." She grimaced. "I have three conference calls lined up with brides."

"Want me to pick up a light fixture for you?"

She held her breath. She'd labored over the house decisions. Stain and paint colors, cabinet pulls. Carpet. Window treatments. On, and on, and on. She'd painstakingly chosen everything herself. Garrett might design and build beautiful furniture, but she'd found he was terrible in pulling together all the pieces that went into home decor. Did she want to take a chance on Jesse being any better? "Can the kitchen go without a fixture until I can get to Duluth?"

"Sure. Or you could order something online. Or... you could trust me to pick something out."

Trust him. With something as important as her house.

"If you don't like it, I'll take it back. No harm done."

Of course, he was right, and, to a degree, she was already trusting him with her house. "Sure. What the heck? Pick something out and surprise me."

"Do you have any pictures of what you might be looking for? A brochure you might've picked up from the home-supply store?"

"Now that you mention it, I do. Downstairs in my flower shop. I've got a home file."

She told the boys they'd be back in a few minutes and opened the door to the stairs leading down to her shop. Jesse followed her through the back entrance to her flower shop. She flicked on a light to reveal a tightly arranged back workroom and storage area.

"So this is it?" he said. "Your business."

She glanced around. "Yep. This is it."

One wall of shelving was packed with supplies, there were several coolers for the extra flower stock she'd have in the summer months that were empty and turned off. A work island sat in the center of the room with a couple of stools around it. It wasn't anything fancy, but it was organized and clean.

"That file is in my desk out front."

He followed her out into the retail part of her shop. "You should be proud of yourself, Sarah. A single mom, building her own business. Supporting yourself and Brian. Even buying a house."

She was proud, but it was still nice of him to make the comment. "Thank you." She pulled the file out of her desk and quickly flipped through all the invoices and brochures she'd gathered these past few months.

"Nice place."

The front was as different from the back room as night from day. This was where she visited with wedding clients and made sales to the public. With dark woods and granite, she hoped the area felt updated and classy.

"Your store looks like you," he said.

"Does it?"

He nodded.

There was a counter with a register for flower sales,

but it was the desk and workspace occupying about a third of the front area that seemed to capture his eye. The trappings of a wedding planner. Wedding magazines and books on floral arrangements filled a small bookcase. There were three-ring binders filled with wedding invitations, cake designs, place settings and menu selections.

"So with all this wedding planning you do, what will your wedding be like?"

"Who says I'm ever getting married?" She found the brochure on lighting fixtures, pulled it out and tucked the rest of the house file back into her desk.

"Okay, so if you ever get married, what would your wedding be like?"

"Simple. About as simple as it gets. I'd elope."

"A wedding planner eloping." He shook his head. "Doesn't sound quite right."

"Then I'd have a big outside barbecue to celebrate with friends. That's it."

"Interesting." Jesse took a deep breath and smiled.

"What's so funny?" she asked, coming back around her desk.

"Nothing."

"What? Tell me."

"All right," he said quietly, studying her, all humor disappearing from his face. "This shop smells like you. And you always smell like flowers. Your hair. Your skin. I just figured out why."

She swallowed. "No one's ever told me... I didn't realize... I..."

"That you smell as sweet as those lilies over there?" He nodded toward the stargazers in the cooler. Then he leaned toward her, closed his eyes and inhaled a long slow breath. "Nope. You smell better."

Suddenly, almost paralyzed, she couldn't take her eyes off his face. When he opened his eyes, the expression on his face was as intense as if he were drilling a hole through her. "Sarah," he whispered, moving toward her.

She couldn't—didn't want to—step back. Instead, she glanced up at him, felt her mouth part and her head tilt back.

"Here we are again," he whispered, his gaze heavy-lidded.

Only this time, as he tucked her close and kissed her, she could tell he wasn't angry, and he wasn't trying to prove a point. And this time she wanted more. She wanted skin. Heat. Her hands on him. His on her. She wanted to see his tattoo. Reaching under his shirt, she splayed her hands over the springy hair on his chest and Jesse stilled even as his nipples turned pebble-hard. "I haven't been kissed like that in so long," she whispered, leaning into him.

"How long?"

"Too long."

"Sarah?"

"I want to see your tattoo," she whispered. Drawing his shirt up, she traced her hands along the dark lines. "It's beautiful. Did you get it in prison?"

"Yes, and I don't want to talk about it." He drew her hands down, and his shirt fell back into place. "How long has it been since you've been kissed like that?"

"Almost ten years."

He put his hands on her shoulders and set her back, as if a glass of ice-cold water had been tossed in his face. "So it's been a decade since you've…"

She nodded.

Shaking his head, he looked away.

"It's not that I haven't wanted to, if that's what you're thinking," she said, feeling defensive.

"That's not what I was thinking."

"I'm as hot-blooded as any woman."

"Trust me, I know. I can feel it."

"You can?"

"Uh-huh." He ran his hands through his hair. "But this is all because you see me as a bad boy, isn't it? A ladies' man. Exciting. Dangerous. Nothing but trouble."

She didn't say anything, didn't know what to say. Maybe that was partly true.

"What if I told you I'm none of those things?" he said, glaring back at her. "What if I told you I've had sex with only four women? My first serious girlfriend when I was seventeen. A one-night stand at a bar in Nashville. And, no, I wasn't too drunk to use a condom. A short relationship with a woman in L.A. when I lived there for a few months before I came back north. Just before…Milwaukee."

"And Sherri. That's it?"

"That's it." Then he chuckled. "Based on what you've told me about your past, I'm thinking you have me beat."

She looked away. "And you'd be right." The time she'd spent in Miami, before meeting Bobby, had been one man after another. She frowned.

"Ah, Sarah. It's a joke."

"Not to me."

"All you did was sow a few wild oats. To be honest, it's kind of sexy. Me, on the other hand…"

"Jesse."

He grabbed the brochure out of her hand. "Maybe this truce wasn't such a good idea, after all." Then he climbed the steps two at a time. By the time she made it back up to her apartment, he was gone and she was left thinking that he might be right.

"DAVID," GARRETT SAID, patiently. "Put the hammer down, please."

Ignoring his father, David sat in his car seat in back, pounding a plastic hammer against the window.

"Well, there's another benefit to living on Mirabelle," Jesse muttered. "No driving with kids in the car."

"David. It's too loud, buckaroo. Put that hammer down."

Jesse opened up the diaper bag on the car seat between him and Garrett and found a juice box. "Here, Davie." He reached back, took the pacifier from the little boy's mouth and handed him the juice.

The hammering immediately stopped as David hungrily sucked on the straw.

"You're getting pretty good at that." Garrett grinned. "I'd even go so far as to say you're a natural."

"Yeah, right."

Erica was busy giving the men's bathroom at Duffy's a new paint job after a group of snowmobilers got overly rambunctious the prior weekend and accidentally bashed in a chunk of drywall. So Garrett had brought David along on their road trip into civilization.

With a population of less than one hundred thousand, the city of Duluth didn't come close to qualifying as big as far as Jesse was concerned. Having grown up in Chicago, there was nothing in the entire states of Minnesota and Wisconsin that could top the Windy City. Still, he felt strange being off Mirabelle the day after he'd had dinner at Sarah and Brian's apartment. He'd gotten surprisingly used to, comfortable with, even, the island's slow, quiet pace, peaceful environs and, more often than not, friendly faces. Sitting in Garrett's truck cruising down a six-lane freeway felt like being on another planet.

"You ever miss Chicago?" Jesse asked his brother as they zipped by cars, passed billboards and crossed over the bridge spanning the Duluth harbor.

"No." Garrett firmly shook his head. "Well, every once in a while I miss a couple old friends, but they all come to Mirabelle over the summer, so I get a chance to catch up. What about you?"

"Naw. It'd be nice to see Christian and Drew more often, but I never miss the city."

"Don't you think you're ever going to settle down in one place?"

"What the hell for?"

"Oh, I don't know. A job. Sense of community. God forbid, a wife and kids."

Jesse's palms started sweating at the thought of his own family and he inhaled deeply. "Not my thing."

"I see you with Zach and David." Garrett exited the freeway. "I think it might be more your thing than you think, Jesse. And I think there's a certain woman on Mirabelle who's thinking so, too."

Jesse kept his mouth shut.

"Erica sees a lot more than I do. She said Sarah—"

"I seem to recall you warning me to steer clear of Mirabelle's princesses."

"That was then. This is now." Garrett pulled his truck into the parking lot of the home-supply store. "You've grown up a lot in the last four years. I think you're ready—"

"I don't want to talk about it." What he was ready

for was something hot and heavy with Sarah, but that didn't mean it was ever, ever going to happen.

"Have it your way."

Jesse climbed out of the truck and waited while Garrett got David out from the back. His brother slammed the other door, and they headed toward the entrance.

"We might as well split up," Garrett said, putting David in a cart. "We'll get out of here quicker." The moment Garrett started walking away, though, David fussed.

"Unc Jess," he cried, reaching his arms out toward Jesse.

Garrett laughed.

"I can't help it if the kid's sick of you." Jesse nudged Garrett out of the way and pushed the cart into the store. "I'll catch up with you when I'm finished." Jesse walked up and down the aisles, dropping drywall tape, a couple switch plates, some lightbulbs and a towel rack for the master bath into the cart as he went.

David started trying to get out of his seat in the cart.

"Hey, dude, you gotta stay in the cart." Poor kid. He'd been stuck in the car the entire way here. Now he was stuck in the cart. No wonder he was getting crabby. "When's the last time you ate?"

"Cackers." He pointed to the front of the store.

"Okay. Let's go see what they got." He found some snacks at the front registers.

David reached for some sugar candies.

"Oh, no. Your mother would kill me if I gave you those." Jesse grabbed a box of animal crackers, opened them up and handed them to David.

On his way back through the aisles, he passed a section dedicated to fireplaces and mantels and glanced at the various shapes and sizes of stone and brick. They were gorgeous, but too expensive, so he wandered away, crossing into an aisle with closet organizers. Sarah didn't know it yet, but a shelving unit in her laundry room would come in handy, so he threw one of those in the cart, planning to pay for it himself.

One thing he couldn't afford to pay for himself, though, was prefabricated gingerbread to replace the old, damaged trim on Sarah's front porch. She'd love it, though. He knew she would. He stood in front of the store display and mentally calculated what it would cost. Too much. And it wasn't in Sarah's budget.

For the hell of it, he went to the lumber section and asked a bunch of questions. David had finished his crackers, and when he fussed again, Jesse picked him up.

As he finished questioning the guy in the lumber department, David laid his head on Jesse's shoulder. Before he knew it, the little guy's fingers were working at the neckline of Jesse's T-shirt as if he was fingering the edges of a blanket. He was so trusting and so comfortable in Jesse's arms, and it was nice having some one-on-one time with his nephew.

In the end, Jesse threw a few more supplies onto his cart. It wouldn't cost that much to give the gingerbread a shot. Garrett had all the detail tools and the worst thing that could happen is Jesse would be out some time.

He'd managed to find everything on his lists, except for the fixture for Sarah's kitchen, and was walking through the lighting area for the second time when Garrett found him. "I'm ready to hit it anytime you are," Garrett said, glancing into David's face. "He looks pretty damned content."

"He's getting tired."

"I see that." Garrett held out his hands. "You want me to take him?"

"No, he's okay." Jesse pulled back. He couldn't remember ever having held a kid in his arms like this, and he suddenly felt quite reluctant to give David up.

"Are you finished yet?" Garrett asked.

"I still need a light fixture, but I don't think any of the styles they've got here will work." Jesse didn't even need to look at the brochure Sarah had found for him to know that. "Sarah won't like any of these."

"Pick something close. What difference does it make?"

It was for Sarah and her house. That was the difference. "I wrote down directions to a specialty store just in case." He handed the address to Garrett. "Know where this is?"

Garrett glanced at the addresses and frowned. "Yeah, I can find it, but this is going to add almost an hour onto our trip."

"Let's go."

It took close to twenty minutes to drive to the store and once again David wanted Jesse to hold him. Slowly but surely, Jesse felt the boy's body get heavier and heavier. Soon, he was sound asleep. It felt peaceful, holding the little guy while he slept so soundly. A short time later, Jesse found what he was looking for.

"That's it." With his free hand, he pointed to a light fixture in antique bronze. It hung from an adjustable-length chain and featured hand-painted glass shades.

"A little on the spendy side, don't you think?"

More than her budget, that's for sure. "I'll pay the difference myself."

"See?" Garrett raised his eyebrows. "That's what I'm talking about."

"Just because I care about her, Garrett, doesn't mean anything's ever going to happen between us."

Jesse paid for the fixture, and then they walked out of the lighting store and headed toward the car.

Garrett glanced into his son's face. "How long's he been asleep?"

"Heck, I don't know. Half an hour." As they passed a small, locally owned hardware shop, Jesse glanced through the window and stopped at the sight of the piece of equipment shoved in the corner of the display with a For Sale, As Is sign propped against it.

Garrett pulled up short. "What is it?" He followed Jesse's gaze.

"That what I think it is?"

"Sure as hell looks like it."

The machine was clearly going to need some major TLC, but it'd be worth it. "Do you think you can talk the community-center manager into making room for it?"

"Might take a six-pack, but Bud will eventually cave."

Still holding sleeping David, Jesse went into the store and came out a few minutes later with a paid receipt. "Let's get it in the back of your truck."

"First, you're going to have to extricate yourself from your new appendage." Garrett nodded at David.

"Will he stay asleep if I put him in the car seat?"

"Doubtful. He wakes up every time I try moving him."

Jesse opened the back door of the pickup and very gently hoisted David into the seat. When he stirred, Jesse whispered into his ear, "Shhh." Then he gave the boy his pacifier, hooked up the straps and quietly closed the door. "Start up the engine, would you? That'll keep him asleep."

Garrett fired up the truck and hopped out.

David never opened his eyes.

"Kids are not your thing," Garrett said, glancing into the back of his truck. "Right."

CHAPTER SIXTEEN

"I'M BORED," Zach said as he finished washing the kitchen table.

"Bored, huh?" Jesse said from his position at the kitchen sink. It was several days after he'd made the trip into Duluth with Garrett and he'd yet to run into Sarah. Unfortunately, the distance hadn't helped clear his mind. "You could finish these dishes if you can't think of anything else to do."

It was a Saturday night, and one of the rare occasions when Erica took the night off from Duffy's, so Jesse had taken off from work early and fixed dinner for Garrett's family. After they'd eaten his meat loaf, mashed potatoes and green beans, he'd forced Erica into the family room to relax while Zach and Jesse cleaned the kitchen. She had her feet up on the couch and was reading a magazine while Garrett was playing with David on the floor.

"I don't want to do dishes," Zach said. "I want to do something. And I'm sick of video games."

Jesse gripped his chest, pretending to have a heart attack. "Did I hear that right? You've had enough of video games?"

Zach shook his head. "I want spring to come. I wanna play baseball." There was no doubt this long winter was starting to wear on everyone.

Jesse had just finished draining the sink when he

felt a tug on his jeans, little hands probably sticky with all kinds of goop, but who cared? "Is that a bug I feel climbing up my leg?" Without looking down, he shook his foot a bit. "If I get hold of it, I'm going to squash it flat as a pancake!" Growling, he reached down.

David squealed, showing a mouthful of baby teeth, and ran to hide behind Zach's legs.

"Oh, no, that little bug's not getting away that easily." Jesse snatched the boy and tossed him in the air. David laughed, a full belly laugh that resonated all the way down Jesse's arms. He tossed his littlest nephew again, turned to Zach and the grin on Zach's face gripped his heart. He was really going to miss these boys, but his traveling cash was just about where he needed it. Another month and he'd have all he'd need to head as far south as he wanted.

A loud knock sounded on the front door.

"I'll get it!" Zach ran to open the door.

Sarah and Brian stood on the porch all bundled up in hats, scarves and snowpants. They stepped inside. "Hey," Jesse said, drying his hands on a towel. "What's up?"

"We're going sledding," Brian said, the excitement in his voice nearly tangible. "You guys want to come with us?"

"I do!" Zach ran to the family-room couch. "Can I go, Erica?"

"I don't know." Erica sat up from the couch and glanced at Sarah. "David's bedtime is in half an hour."

"No problem," Sarah said. "I can take Zach. You and Garrett can chill with David."

"Can Zach come over to my house afterward for a sleepover?" Brian asked.

"Fine by me." Erica glanced at Zach. "But you have to get your own stuff together."

In a flash, Zach disappeared upstairs and then reappeared with a backpack. He raced to the mudroom and immediately pulled on snowpants.

Sarah glanced Jesse's way. "You want to join us, Jesse?"

She wanted him to come out and play. He glanced into her eyes. Not good. Not good at all. "Naw, I was just settling—"

"Come on, Jesse," Brian urged. "We just got six inches of new powder and our sledding hill rocks."

"Winter's almost over," Sarah said. "This will likely be the last chance you have to go sledding before the snow is all gone."

Jesse hadn't been sledding since he'd been about ten years old. "It's too cold out. The windchill's below zero."

"Crybaby," Zach muttered under his breath, the challenge clear.

"What did you call me?" Jesse glared good-naturedly at his nephew.

"What?" Zach put his hands out. "I didn't say anything."

"There's no wind tonight." Sarah smiled. "So that means no windchill."

"I was about to start a movie."

"Yeah, I think he should stay," Garrett said, grinning at Jesse. "That way he can get the downstairs to himself for a little while. Erica and I were about to head upstairs and get David to bed. Then head to bed ourselves."

Jesse glared at his brother, the message coming through loud and clear. Anything would be better than being forced to listen to Garrett and Erica getting amorous. Again. "All right. Fine. I'll go. The minute I start getting cold, I'm coming home."

He put on Garrett's snowsuit and his own hat and mitts and the four of them walked down Mirabelle's residential back streets, dragging sleds and snow tubes behind them. The night was still and quiet, the only sound the crunching of the snow beneath their boots. A brilliant moon hung in the black early-evening sky, lighting their way. As the boys raced ahead, leaving him and Sarah to walk alone, the night turned decidedly intimate.

"So where's this hill?" Jesse asked, trying to keep things light.

"Past the abandoned Draeger Mansion and the Hendersons' orchard. On the way to Full Moon Bay."

"Didn't know the island had any bays other than the marina in town."

"We have a couple. Full Moon Bay's on the northeast side of the island, but the sledding hill—the biggest hill on the island—is just before the lighthouse," Sarah explained. "Marty Rousseau installed some floodlights a couple years back. It's become popular with young kids during the day and older kids at night."

They followed a path through a line of white pines and broke into a small clearing to find a bonfire blazing at the top of the hill. Several people sat on tree stumps sipping hot drinks in front of a fire pit made from Lake Superior stone.

A crowd. Good. He wouldn't be alone with Sarah.

Brian immediately set out for the hill. "Woo hoo!"

"Race you down!" Zach yelled, hot on his trail.

They hopped onto their sleds and slid down faster than anything Jesse had ever seen. Jesse went to stand next to Sarah, watching them. It was a steep hill and the boys were flying. "That looks like fun," he murmured.

"Let's go." Sarah lined up her snow tube and settled on top of it, shoving her thickly mitted hands into the snow as brakes. "Last one to the bottom carries up both tubes." She pushed off.

"Hey, that's not fair!" Jesse hopped onto his tube and raced after her. He was a good fifteen feet behind her but gaining fast. Then his boot caught a chunk of hard-packed snow, spinning his tube. Before he knew it, he was careening backward down the hill.

"Whoa, Nelly," he yelled. "These tubes are fast!"

Sarah, of course, beat him down, so he carried her tube back up the hill.

"Race you, Jesse!" Brian called once he'd gotten to the top.

"Let's *all* race," Zach said.

"You're on!" Jesse lined himself up. "Sarah, you in?"

"Of course."

Jesse glanced at the other three and put his hands down in preparation for pushing off. "Ready, set." He pushed off before saying *go.*

"No fair!" Brian yelled.

"Cheater!" Zach called.

Sarah's laughter followed him all the way down the hill. He got to the bottom and hopped off his tube. "I won!"

A split second later, Brian purposefully ran into him, toppling him onto his side.

"You didn't say *go,*" Brian said. "It doesn't count."

"Oh, I'm sorry," he said as innocently as he could manage.

"Let's get him," Zach said.

The boys hopped on top of him, throwing snow into his face. "Hey, I think I deserve a handicap." The moment he wiped the melting snow off his cheeks, the boys flicked more at him. "That's cold!" he yelled.

"That's what cheaters get," Sarah said, joining in by pushing a handful of snow down the back of his jacket.

"Okay, that's it! You boys are dead meat now!" He pushed the boys off. "And you—" he pointed to Sarah "—I'm saving for later."

"Oh, now I'm really scared."

He chased after the boys. They made the critical mistake of running together, making tackling them together all the easier. He roughhoused with them, got them full of snow and ran after them up the hill. By the time he got to the top, he was almost out of gas, but he was having so much fun he didn't want to stop. This night reminded him so much of the simpler times he'd spent with his brothers. Laughing, fighting, playing hard. After several runs down the hill, everyone was ready for a break, even the boys.

"Anyone for some hot cocoa?" Sarah asked.

"Me!"

"And me!"

She'd stuffed a thermos into a backpack. After pulling it out, she poured some cocoa into cups and passed them around, then sat on a stump by the fire. "Glad you came out with us?" She handed him a cup.

"Yeah," he whispered. "I haven't had this much good, clean fun in…well, a long time." He took a sip of steaming hot cocoa and the taste took him back.

Not since he was a kid, that's for sure, had he experienced this kind of simple, uncomplicated joy. When he smiled at Sarah it felt honest and from the heart. He was happy. And it was just getting outside and sledding. It was hanging with Zach and Brian. It was simply being with Sarah. Jesse glanced at her across the fire. The glow of the flames cast her features in warm gold light. That's when he realized the other families who'd already been there when they'd arrived earlier had all gone home. Brian and Zach were somewhere down the hillside. He and Sarah were alone.

Their gazes caught. He looked away. The silence only made him more aware of the attraction between them, so he cleared his throat. "How long have you been on Mirabelle?"

"A little more than four years."

About the time he'd gone to prison, she'd settled here. "Do you ever miss Indiana?"

"Never."

"Winters must be colder here. Don't they ever get too long?"

"February and March can drag. That's why it's important to get out like this and enjoy this kind of idyllic night." As she sipped her cocoa a few plump snowflakes fell lazily from the dark sky. One landed on her cheek and as Jesse imagined licking it off, she brushed it away. "It doesn't get any better than this." She smiled.

No, he imagined, it didn't. Women didn't get much prettier, either. He swallowed down the last of his cocoa and then he tapped the stone surrounding the fire with the tip of his boot. "These stones come from the shoreline?"

She nodded. "Most likely from Full Moon Bay. Why?"

"Come springtime, if we can gather enough decent-size rocks, I could cover that old brick fireplace in your house."

"A rock fireplace would look amazing," she said. "I never thought to collect rocks from the Mirabelle shore."

"We'd need to collect a lot, roughly the same size. Getting them up to your house would be an issue."

"Mirabelle has some utility vehicles. Maybe the town council will let us use one for a day."

"Then let's do it. As soon as the snow melts." They fell quiet again. This was dangerous, sitting alone around a fire with Sarah. "Ready to hit the hill again?"

"Absolutely."

The boys were having the most fun Jesse had seen them having since he'd come to the island. They raced him and Sarah, even tried knocking them off their tubes. This last time down, they'd gotten quite a head start on Jesse and Sarah and were already heading up the hill before he and Sarah were ready to sail down.

She went first.

Jesse took a running jump at his tube and caught up with her in seconds. He'd miscalculated and was going too fast. "Watch out, Sarah!" he called, laughing.

It was too late. His tube crashed into hers, flipping them both. An instant later, they were rolling the rest of the way down the hill, a mass of bodies and inner tubes. When they stopped and the snow settled, he was flat on his back with Sarah spread out on top of him and inner tubes were skimming their way down the rest of the hill.

Instinctively, he put his arms around her, and their gazes locked. "You all right?"

"Fine," she breathed, the air slipping past her lips in visible puffs.

God, she was beautiful. Moonlight sparkled in her

eyes, and her cheeks were pink with cold. Snowflakes melted on her skin. Her lips. Oh, man, her lips.

He was pretty sure Garrett's insistence that Jesse show Sarah the man he'd become and prove to her that he wasn't the same man who'd driven drunk four years ago didn't involve persuasion of a physical kind. But the hell with it.

He quickly glanced back to find the boys halfway up the hill. Before giving himself the chance to think better of it, Jesse rolled over and reversed their positions. "I still owe you for pushing snow down my back." He bent his head to kiss her. The moment his cool lips touched her warm mouth he touched the tip of his tongue to the inside of her upper lip. Sweet cocoa and Sarah.

She stiffened for a moment as if taken by surprise before wrapping her arms around him and kissing him back. Her mouth opened, her tongue tangled with his and she moaned. "I've been wanting to do that all night," she whispered.

"Then why didn't you?" he said, kissing her again. And again.

"Because...I don't...I don't know what we're doing." Her breath left her mouth in quick bursts of frozen air.

"Does it matter?"

She put her hands on his chest and held him back. "Maybe not to you, but it does to me."

"Don't get so serious, Sarah. What's wrong with a lighthearted fling? We're adults. We can handle that." No one could rationalize better than a man with a hard-on. "I won't ask for anything you don't want to give."

"That's the problem. I'm not sure there's anything I'd hold back from you."

"Sarah—"

"No, Jesse." She stood and brushed the snow from her pants. "I'm a single parent, and Brian is starting to like you. Maybe too much. Things like this…matter a lot. You don't want to hurt anyone, I know. But a man like you leaves nothing but a mess in his wake."

She was right. Still, it stung. He got to his feet. "Maybe you should fire me."

"I should've never said that. I'm sorry." She shook her head and looked away. "The truth is that as soon as my house is done you're gone as quickly as you came, right? It's what you do, isn't it? Leave?"

That fact he couldn't argue, or reason away.

"Well, Mirabelle's my home. It's where I plan on staying for the rest of my life," she said. "We have no future, so there's no point in creating a present."

CHAPTER SEVENTEEN

SPRING, IT SEEMED, had come to Mirabelle almost overnight. One day, high-school basketball state championships were on TV and a blizzard had popped up out of nowhere to blanket Mirabelle in several inches of sticky wet snow and the next day the sounds of trickling and dripping water could be heard around every corner.

As the weeks passed, the days got longer and the sun got stronger. Before Sarah knew it, Main Street was clear of ice and snow from curb to curb, every speck of white was gone from the rooftops and had started to recede from yards to expose little patches of grass struggling to turn green. The ice cover on Chequamegon Bay broke into pieces and melted. Trees leafed out and perennial gardens burst from the ground. And her first wedding of the season was around the corner.

"Sarah?" It was bridezilla Megan on the phone and she sounded stressed.

"Hi, Megan," Sarah answered, making sure her voice stayed calm and soothing. "How are you?"

"Not good." A muffled sob sounded over the line. For a moment, Megan didn't—probably couldn't—speak.

Oh, no. What was it this time? Engagement off? Groom broke his leg in a car accident? Parents bailed on promises to pay for everything? Sarah had worked through all of the above and more. "What happened? What's wrong?"

"Brandon's deployment date…was moved up." She paused, sniffling and taking in a shaky breath.

"By how much?" Sarah crossed her fingers.

"He's leaving for Afghanistan…a month ahead of schedule."

Uh-oh. "Kind of upsets all the wedding plans, doesn't it?"

"Yeeesss," the young woman wailed.

"Did you still want to get married before he leaves?"

"Are you kidding? I'm marrying that man. Come hell or high water."

"Well, you could always scrap your plans for a wedding here on Mirabelle and get married by a judge. Right now. Be able to enjoy the time with Brandon before he goes, rather than worrying about the wedding. All you'd be out is a few deposits."

"Oh, no!" Megan said. "Remember my dream since I was eight? This is happening. On Mirabelle. Reception, food, dancing, champagne. The whole nine yards. Or else."

If the vows and Brandon were really what counted, rather than all the pomp and circumstance, then the *I do* part was all that mattered. "You sure about that?"

"Positive."

"If it's that important, you could always have a big party when he comes home on his first leave."

"And give up my dream? There's got to be another option. Do you ever have weddings on Mirabelle in May?"

"Occasionally, we have weddings here during the off-season. The problem is that most of our summer staff are college students and they generally don't get here until just before Memorial Day weekend."

"I've already checked with our parents. The third weekend in May will work. Is that late enough?"

The third weekend in May. The weekend Sarah had been planning on moving into her house. Sarah paced behind her front counter. If she agreed to move up Megan's wedding she could say goodbye to getting her home settled and organized before she basically put her life on hold for all the brides and grooms who had chosen Mirabelle for their wedding destination.

"Um, Megan, I'm not sure that weekend works for m—"

"Please, Sarah. Daddy said he'd make it worth your while. Double your fee. Tell the inn we'll double the staff wages. Whatever it takes to make it work."

Sarah could use the extra money. She glanced at the calendar, hoping a few extra days would miraculously appear in her schedule. It wasn't going to happen.

"Sarah?"

Sarah closed her eyes. "All right. I can't promise anything, but I'll try. I'll contact the Mirabelle Island Inn and all the other vendors and find out if they can move your wedding up. You'll probably have to have both the ceremony and the reception at the inn."

"That, I can deal with. Do it. Please."

"Okay. I'll call you as soon as I know."

Sarah hung up and immediately called the Mirabelle Island Inn. Brittany Rousseau answered and Sarah explained the situation.

"Oh, heck, yes, we can make that happen," Brittany said, her voice as bubbly as ever. "Most of the college kids we've hired will already be out of school by then. We'll call a few and get them here early."

That took care of the catering, the reception location and the rooms for the guests. That left calls to the photographer, the band and the cake decorator. Sarah took a deep breath. "Okay, Brittany, plan on the date change. I've got a few more calls to make."

"Good luck."

The back door to her shop opened. "Mom?"

"In here, Brian."

"Jesse said we're supposed to meet him at the house at five-thirty," he said. "What's taking you so long?"

Sarah had completely forgotten about the surprise Jesse had waiting for the boys the moment she'd heard Megan's voice on the phone. "I have a wedding crisis. Call Jesse and tell him we'll be half an hour late."

"But Mom," Brian groaned.

"I have to do this. After you talk to Jesse, call Zach and tell him to meet us here."

An hour, two chewed nails and a broken pencil later Sarah had contacted every key player in Megan and Brandon's wedding. She'd had to find a new photographer, but everyone else had been pleased to reschedule as it would lighten their respective June loads. She called Megan back.

"Sarah?" Megan sounded hopeful, yet worried.

"It's done. You're rescheduled."

Megan screamed. "Yes! You're the best."

In Megan's eyes. Now to repair the damage with her son.

She went upstairs and found the boys playing video games. "I'm ready anytime you boys are."

"It's about time," Brian mumbled, shutting off his gaming unit and the TV. He barely glanced at Sarah. "All you do is work."

"Hey." His attitude was starting to bother her. "My work is what puts food on our table, remember, Brian?"

"Yeah, whatever."

She cocked her head at him. This discussion had been a long time in coming. "Zach, could you wait for us outside?"

"Sure." Zach hopped up and, clearly uncomfortable, put on his jacket and left the apartment.

"You got a problem with me, spit it out," Sarah said.

Brian glared at her, but he truly looked as if he was formulating his argument. "You work all the time and you treat me like a little kid."

Couldn't get much more straightforward than that. "I work all the time because I own my own business. Unfortunately, that business is busiest when you're out of school."

His shoulders slumped. "I know."

"Do you really think I don't spend enough time with you?"

"No. You do."

"Then what do we do to fix this?"

"I'm ten, Mom. Let me grow up."

"Okay. I'll try." She resisted the urge to hug him, exactly what she would've done ten minutes ago. "You, though, have to start acting more grown-up."

"That's what Jesse says."

"Take on more responsibilities and you get more freedom."

"What do you want me to do?"

"Pick some chores around here and make them yours. All the time. Sound like a plan?"

He nodded.

"Now should we go see Jesse?"

"Yes!" He bolted outside.

Zach grinned the moment he saw Brian. "I wonder what the surprise is."

"I don't know," Brian said. "But if Jesse's involved, you know it'll be fun."

Sarah pulled on her jacket and tried to keep up with them. Though the snow was all gone, it was still a bit chilly outside. The nasty weather of January, February and March were nothing but a bad memory. The coming of April and more consistent days of clear sunshine had brought along with it the hope of summer, and nothing but confusion for Sarah.

This issue with Brian was a cakewalk compared to her relationship with Jesse. She felt like a ping-pong ball. As the tight lock she'd had on her heart cracked slowly but surely open, her emotions flip-flopped between euphoria and fear. Mostly fear. She couldn't let herself fall in love with Jesse. That was the surest way to a broken heart. As soon as her house was done, he'd be leaving Mirabelle.

They reached her yard and let themselves inside the house. Voices from the basement emanated up the stairs off the kitchen.

"Let me see your electrician's license," Jesse said.

A male voice mumbled something indiscernible.

"Don't mess with me," Jesse said. "I know what you're doing isn't code."

Another mumble as Sarah made her way to the top of the stairs. The boys, wide-eyed over the raised voices, stood back and away.

"You don't know what you're doing," Jesse said, his voice angry.

More loud grumbles.

"Like hell. I'm the main contractor here, and what I say goes. You're fired."

That met with the slamming of toolboxes and feet pounding up the steps. This electrician had been her last option, the only one who would make the trip to Mirabelle for a price within her budget. If this man walked away, she'd be out of luck until June.

"What's going on?" she asked as Jesse and the electrician arrived in the kitchen.

"Nothing," Jesse murmured.

Wearing a navy blue company uniform, the electrician looked competent enough.

"I wouldn't work for you if you paid me double time." The man pounded across the porch. "Good luck finding another electrician."

"We'll take our chances." Jesse closed the door and turned to Sarah.

"You can't fire him. There is no one else to do the job."

"You want code violations? Shoddy workmanship?"

"No."

"Then you don't want this guy working on your house."

"But Jesse—"

"Sarah, do you trust me?"

Her heart seemed to skip a beat as the question reverberated in her head. The light fixture he'd picked out for her in Duluth, now hanging in her kitchen, caught her eye. The first time she'd seen it, she'd known it was perfect for her house.

"I only want the best for you and Brian. Do you believe that?"

A lump formed in her throat as she realized she did believe him. "I know," she whispered. "I do trust you."

He held her gaze as if he seemed to understand the import of her admission. "Electrical work is tricky. So I kept a close eye on him as he was working."

"We'll find someone else. You don't need to explain."

"I want to, though," he said softly. "The guy seemed to do an okay job rewiring the switches at the top and bottom of the stairs, but when he started working on updating your circuit breakers, I could tell he was taking shortcuts. I'll do the work."

"But I thought you couldn't—"

"It'll take me longer than a *qualified* electrician, but I'll figure it out. After that guy, I don't want anyone except for me and Garrett working on your home."

His obvious show of protectiveness astounded her. There was more going on inside him than physical attraction.

"Okay, that's enough of that," Jesse said, smiling as he glanced at the boys. "I have a surprise for you two."

"Where are we going?" Brian asked.

"The community center."

Zach groaned. "Why? We've done everything there is to do there a gazillion times."

"That place is totally lame."

"There've been a few changes. Trust me. This you guys are going to want to see." He glanced at Sarah. "You want to come?"

"I don't know." She smiled, wondering what he had up his sleeve. "Do I?"

"Yeah." He nodded. "You want to come."

"You going to give us a hint?" she asked.

"Nope. You're just going to have to see it for yourselves."

Sarah's interest definitely piqued, they all walked the couple of blocks to the two-story brick building. She dashed through the front door, following Jesse, but the boys, on the other hand, were dragging their feet the entire way.

She and Jesse both nodded to Bud Stall, the community-center manager, and walked toward the far corner of the building. "Okay, guys. Close your eyes."

Zach and Brian rolled their eyes at each other, but complied.

"You, too," Jesse said, grinning at her.

Suspicious, she raised her eyebrows at him, but did as he said. When his warm hand wrapped around her arm, she sucked in a breath. When his other hand settled at her lower back, directing her forward, it was all she could do not to lean into him.

"Okay, stand right here," he whispered, "until I get the boys. Don't open your eyes."

She heard him bringing Zach and Brian next to her.

"Okay. Take a look."

Sarah opened her eyes. For a moment, she wasn't sure what she was seeing. The boys, though, knew right way.

"Sweet!" Zach cried.

"A batting cage!" Brian yelled. "Dude!"

"Oh, my," Sarah whispered.

"Looks like spring training to me," Jesse said, grinning.

The boys ran off, grabbed helmets and bats and, after fighting over who would go first, finally settled on taking ten-hit turns. They flipped the machine on and Brian stepped into the cage. Like a little kid, Jesse was grinning from ear to ear as he adjusted the pitch setting to slow until they warmed up. He came to stand next to her.

"How did you do this?" she asked.

"Found an old pitching machine at a hardware store when Garrett and I were in Duluth a while back. It wasn't working, so I bought it for a song and talked Bud Stall into giving a batting cage a shot. He said if I could get the machine working, he'd think about it. Took me some time, but I eventually figured it out. So Bud ordered the heavy-duty netting and I set up the temporary wall here in the gym. That was that. Gotta keep 'em out of trouble, right?"

There was more to it than that. She knew it. She felt it. His protectiveness over that electrician. His wanting to make a new fireplace. Now this. The boys had been getting attached to Jesse for a long while now. It was too late to do anything about that, but she didn't understand. "Jesse, what are you doing?"

He seemed to recognize her concern and turned instantly wary. "Can't I do something nice for the boys?"

"Of course you can, but what does it mean?"

"Nothing, Sarah."

"Jesse—"

"Not a big deal, Sarah. Don't make too much of any of it, okay?" He stepped back, putting more distance between them, and called to the boys. "You guys ready for me to speed up those pitches?"

"Oh, yeah!" Brian said.

"You know it," Zach agreed.

He glanced at her. "Just because I found a pitching machine and fixed it up doesn't mean I'm not still leaving Mirabelle." Abruptly, he turned away, flipped the machine to a new setting and focused on giving the boys a few pointers, effectively shutting her out.

CHAPTER EIGHTEEN

SARAH WALKED Brian up to Zach's, where he'd be spending the day. By the time she arrived at her house to paint the living room, it was already midmorning. Oddly enough, she found the front door still locked, so Jesse mostly likely hadn't yet arrived. She let herself in and took off her shoes and coat.

Jesse had said he'd have the kitchen finished by the end of next week. After that, the only inside work left to be done would be the family room and carpeting the entire house. Then he could start on the outside, by which time, hopefully, the weather would have improved. It looked as if he was going to have her house finished on time. Too bad she wasn't going to be able to move in before Megan's wedding.

Slowly, she walked through each room, admiring Jesse's handiwork. Jesse had clearly been the right man for this job. Wondering how far he'd gotten in the bedroom, she walked down the hall and pulled up short at the sight of a figure lying on the floor wrapped up in a sleeping bag. That dark head of hair looked famil—

Jesse?

She tiptoed closer. It *was* him. Lying on his back and his head tilted to one side, he was sleeping like the dead. What was he doing here? She should sneak out and make some noise in the living area to wake him, but what could be the harm in admiring him for a moment?

He wasn't wearing a shirt and his arms hung outside the sleeping bag, baring a large part of his upper body. Dark, springy hair splashed the middle of his chest and ran the length of his forearms. His biceps and shoulders were perfectly contoured, and he looked so strong, but it was his tattoo that held her mesmerized. The bold flowing Chinese script ran in a line from his left pec, down what she could see of his abs, only to disappear beneath the edge of the sleeping bag.

How far down his torso did that tat go? It was all she could do not to inch the sleeping bag lower—

"Morning, Sarah."

Jesse's voice startled her and she jumped.

"Like what you see?"

Oh, hell. Sarah straightened and glanced into Jesse's very open and smiling eyes.

"If not, I can pull the sleeping bag down a little farther?" he said, grinning.

"I was looking at your tattoo," she said, trying to cover for her lapse in judgment.

"Sure you were." Lazily, he threw his hands up behind his head to reveal a smattering of dark hair under each chiseled arm.

He looked warm and relaxed and all Sarah wanted to do was strip naked and climb inside that bag with him. She cleared her throat and backed away. "Seriously, what does it mean?"

For a moment, he looked as if he wasn't going to tell her. Then softly, he said, "There is no wave without wind."

"That's it? All that drama for that simple saying?"

Still smiling, he nodded. "The guy who did it was a

tattoo artist. Fond of drama. My cellmate. He was constantly working on other guys, but he never mentioned a tat to me. Then one day, he showed me a design he'd been working on. When I saw it and he told me what it meant, I knew."

"What does it mean?"

His expression turned serious. "If you want a calm pool, no waves, don't cause a wind."

"And what if you surf and happen to like waves? Big ones."

"That's good." He held her gaze. "The point is that I won't ever go back to prison, but I don't ever want to forget, either." Then, as if the moment had gotten too serious, he grinned. "Want to see the rest?" He pushed the sleeping bag down to reveal that the script did, indeed, continue over the nicely defined muscles of his abdomen.

But, now, instead of the tattoo holding her attention, it was the line of dark hair that traveled from his belly button and down that had her swallowing back a sudden surge of desire.

He slowly pushed the sleeping bag lower. Lower still.

"Don't," she whispered. "Don't do that."

"Just getting up to put on some clothes," he said. "So if you don't want an eyeful—"

"I'm going, I'm going." She spun around, closing the door on her way out.

A moment later, he came out of the room wearing a pair of low-slung jeans that barely hung on his hips and pulling a black T-shirt over his head.

"What are you doing here, anyway?" she asked.

The moment his head poked through the neck of the

T-shirt, his smile disappeared. "I was having a hard time sleeping at Garrett's. Hope you don't mind."

"No. That's fine. Did you two argue or something?"

"Or something." He went into the kitchen and filled the coffeepot with water. "It's nothing. Really."

"Then there's no reason not to tell me."

He seemed to be debating as he went about prepping the coffeemaker. "Let's just say Garrett and Erica have...a...*very* healthy relationship."

"A healthy rel—?" Sex. He was talking about sex. "Oh."

"Sometimes they're pretty verbal about it." He glanced back at her, his eyes dark. "Enough said?"

She nodded. "Feel free to stay here whenever you'd like."

"Thank you." He flipped the lid down on the coffeepot, pressed his hands on the countertop as if to hold himself up and stared out the window. "I'm happy for him, you know. That he's found someone he loves. Someone who loves him back. Not many people are lucky enough to find that."

"No. Not many." For the first time in a very long while, she wondered if she'd been wrong to close the possibility of love so firmly out of her life. Maybe love wasn't such a bad thing. Falling in love with Jesse, though, that was a problem.

A FEW HOURS LATER, with an upbeat, light rock song playing softly on the radio, Jesse watched Sarah painting Brian's bedroom navy blue. Dark colors were much harder to work with than light, but she was nothing if not methodical and meticulous. The roller went into the paint. Swinging her hips a bit to the music, she evened out the layer of color on the roller. One, two, three rolls, every time. Then up the roller went diagonally across the top half of a small section of wall. Up and down, over and over, she covered the wall efficiently. Beautifully. Even managed to teach him a thing or two with her technique.

As she finished out the last section, something in her every stroke resonated deep within him. At first, he couldn't put his finger on it, but the more he watched, the more he understood. There was life and feeling in her every motion. As if this house was alive to her and instead of merely painting a wall, she was petting a favored pet or brushing a child's hair.

She took her last stroke and, as if sensing his eyes on her, glanced back. "What?" She looked over the section she'd just painted. "Did I miss something?"

"No."

"Then what?" She put her roller down.

"This house is pretty important to you, isn't it?"

"It's my first house." She smiled, wiping her hands on the rag sticking out of her pocket. "That's a big deal for anyone."

"I don't think that's all there is to it. This means so much more to you. Why?"

"Brian and I have been in an apartment since we moved here. Don't get me wrong. The rent was reasonable and we've managed, but I want a yard. A porch. A garden. Know what I mean?"

"I know those are all the surface reasons, but this is deeper for you."

The smile disappeared from her face and she looked away. "You're right, I suppose."

"Your parents ever own a house?"

"No. Poor, remember?" Glancing at him, she shook

her head. "We lived in an apartment, but my parents always dreamed of buying this old place outside of town with some acreage. The house had been abandoned for years so the paint was peeling and the roof needed work. It was two stories and there was a barn and some equipment. Us kids used to ride our bikes out there and pretend it was ours. If you moved the knob on the back door just right it would open. I remember going through the rooms and picking out my bedroom." She paused. "But it never happened."

"How are they doing now?"

"My dad died when I was about Brian's age."

"I didn't know that. I'm sorry."

"It's okay. My mom remarried a couple years later and we moved into my stepdad's house."

"How did you end up on Mirabelle?"

"Fate." She laughed, soft and low. "That's the only answer."

"Come on."

"All right, then what would you call it? I opened a bride magazine and found an advertisement for destination weddings at the Mirabelle Island Inn. It looked like the perfect place to raise a child. When I called and found out there was no wedding planner on the island that was it. Brian and I came up here for a long weekend to check it out. I knew from the moment I stepped off the ferry that I wanted to live here. I couldn't afford a down payment on a house, so we rented the apartment above my shop from the Setterbergs.

"When this house went up for sale, I knew it was meant to be mine. I used to come up here sometimes, lie in the grass in the backyard and dream of owning this place."

She crossed over to the window and pointed. "In no

time, those two big, beautiful bridal-veil spirea bushes will bloom so gorgeous and full they'll put any of the wedding bouquets I design to shame. Same with the lilacs along the side yard. Soon the irises will be blooming in the front yard. And on the north side of the house, around the corner, is a long patch of lilies of the valley growing by the downspout.

"The maple in front and the old oak in the back don't look all that special now, but just wait until they're all leafed out. They're nothing short of majestic. And when I got sick of looking at the plants, I'd look up at the house and I'd imagine it with all new paint."

That's when she closed her eyes and he felt himself right there with her. He could see the picture she began to paint as clear as day.

"A pale gray home," she softly said. "With black shutters and trim and a red front door. Full, lush Boston ferns hanging from the porch. Flower boxes filled with petunias and vinca vines. Pots of geraniums lining the steps. White gingerbread trim glistening in the sunlight." She paused. "Gingerbread is atrociously expensive, so I can't afford it."

"Yet, you mean. It'll come." He smiled, so glad he'd already started work on the intricate trim. He realized then that no matter how much cash he'd accumulated, he wouldn't be leaving Mirabelle until he was finished with Sarah's house. "How 'bout a swing? On the porch."

"Yes," she whispered. "Perfect."

"It's almost yours."

She opened her eyes. "Thanks to you."

"No." He shook his head and brushed at a spot of paint on her forehead. "You did the hard stuff before

I ever got here, saving the down payment and making up the plans. It's yours. All yours."

As a slow country song about a broken road leading two lovers to each other sifted through the air, her eyes were filled with dreams, her smile with hope, and Jesse knew right then and there that he was falling in love with this woman. He was already slipping down that devastating slope.

He'd never felt this way before, had never believed he would, and maybe that's how these feelings had blindsided him so easily. Before he'd known to try and fight the emotions, there they were, full-blown and rooted as deeply inside him as the roots of an old oak spread into the earth. How had he ever lived without Sarah?

"Come here," he murmured, stepping toward her.

Looking slightly dazed, she glanced up into his face, but she came to him easily and he drew her into his arms. Inevitably, they began moving slowly in time with the soft guitar sounding over the radio.

The moment he felt her warmth, Jesse realized his mistake. It'd been years since he'd held a woman in his arms. Several long years since he'd held a woman's hands. Or buried his face in a woman's hair. Years since he'd sensed a woman's want.

And Sarah did want him. He could almost taste the subtle change in her body as she'd stepped in closer and rested her cheek against his shoulder. Then her lips were at his throat, her quiet breath in his ear.

"Sarah—"

She wrapped a hand around his neck and kissed him, slanted her mouth over his, dipped her eager tongue inside his mouth. Warm woman. Sweet and wet. As if he was fourteen all over again and this was the first time he'd ever kissed a girl, Jesse's knees nearly buckled. He backed up against the door for support, drawing her with him, kissing her.

Groaning, she ran her hands through his hair, down his chest and then under his shirt and up along his sides, her touch licking over his skin like fire. He slid to the floor, taking her with him. She grabbed his shirt and dragged it over his head. Then she was straddling him, her hands on his chest, tugging at his hair. Her mouth was on his nipple, her tongue licking back and forth. She looked drugged as if she didn't know what she was doing, but what she was doing was driving him crazy.

"I want to see you," he whispered, slowly drawing her T-shirt up, giving her every chance to stop him. Instead, she took the shirt out of his hands and yanked it off herself. Reaching up, he cupped her beautifully rounded breasts, ran his fingers over the pink lace of her bra and felt her nipples harden under his hand.

God help him, but he couldn't help reacting it'd been so long. Need tightened in his groin and he had to feel her against him. Cupping her backside, he pulled her to him, kissed her deeply and pulsed against her. For a moment, she was right there with him, moving with him, turning him rock-hard with need.

Then suddenly she tensed. Before she'd uttered a sound, he knew they'd gone too far.

"This can't happen," she whispered against his lips.

"I know," he groaned.

"You are the worst thing in the world for me."

"I know that, too."

She scrambled back, looking as dazed and devastated as he felt. Her lips were swollen and kiss-reddened, her neck marked by his rough cheeks, as if she belonged to him. But she didn't. Never would.

She stood and balled her shirt up in front of her. "All you want from me is a good time. A party. A little romp under the sheets. Fun. And then you'll move on as if I never existed."

Now there she was wrong, as wrong as a woman could ever be, but he sure as hell wasn't going to enlighten her. "I'm falling in love with you" wasn't exactly something she was going to want to hear. Not from him.

Still, a small part of him, the part that still held a scrap of self-respect, came to life. He dragged his shirt back over his head and stood. "You kissed me first, remember?"

"I know. I did." She glanced away as if she couldn't bear to hold his gaze. "But every time you look at me, it's as if you're touching me. Your eyes skate over my face, my lips, my skin like a featherlight touch. Whether you're inches away or across a room, I can...feel you. Undressing me. Wanting me."

The way he wanted her now.

"Just finish my house, Jesse, okay? That's all I need from you," she whispered as she walked out the door. "All I will ever let myself want from you."

CHAPTER NINETEEN

ONE OF THE BENEFITS to living in the Midwest as far as Jesse was concerned was the change of the season, and spring had long been his favorite. The island had completely come back to life after the long, cold winter, and Jesse finally understood why the residents so loved this little chunk of rock, as he'd once thought of it.

The scent of lilacs and Russian olive trees in the air. Cool breezes coming in off Lake Superior. The quaintness of horse-drawn carriages clip-clopping over cobblestone. Most importantly, there was a certain comfort in knowing—not necessarily liking—every person he met on the street. Somehow the judgmental glares from people like Shirley Gilbert and Mary Miller were easier to tolerate given the welcoming conversation of the likes of Bob and Marsha Henderson and Charlotte Day.

As soon as it got warm enough, Jesse enlisted Garrett's help and they replaced Sarah's roof before the spring rains had a chance to set in. Then, given the interior of Sarah's house was nearly finished, he helped Garrett put in a large deck spanning the entire lakeshore side of Duffy's Pub.

One increasingly warmer day flowed into the next and before Jesse knew it, all he had left to do was the fireplace and finish the drywall and molding in one of the bedrooms before he could move on to the exterior, replacing a few windows and painting.

As his stash of traveling cash grew, he realized he'd reached the point that he could leave Mirabelle and never look back. He had enough money banked to get far, far away from this island and start a new life someplace else. As soon as he finished Sarah's house, that's exactly what he was going to do.

Oddly enough, Sarah had taken to bringing him dinner at her house on a relatively regular basis. It wasn't Erica fare, by any means, but it meant something to him, something he wasn't sure he wanted to understand. He had no clue what was going on between the two of them, but he was doing his utmost best to keep a distance.

Sarah, on the other hand, seemed confused. One minute she could be as cold as ice and the next as warm as sunshine. One minute she'd be standing next to him, talking and laughing as they worked together, and the next she wouldn't come within three feet of him.

Today was one of those good nights, one of those times when sharing her company was as easy as slipping off to sleep after a fifteen-hour workday. They'd been taping the drywall in the last bedroom and sanding to finish.

"That's pretty good," Jesse said, reaching over her shoulder and running his hand across the surface. "But you need to remember that a coat of paint has a way of bringing out every imperfection in the surface of a wall. You want it as smooth as a baby's bottom."

Sarah laughed as she turned to look up at him. "You touch that wall as if it was alive."

"Maybe it is, in a way." He looked down at her and wasn't sure he'd ever seen a more beautiful sight.

Her hair. Her cheeks. Her shoulders. She was covered in drywall dust and he wanted nothing more in that moment than to lay her back and make love to her. "Like a woman."

"Oh, no, you don't." Laughing, she spun away from him. "We still have a lot of work to—"

A knock sounded on the front door.

"I wonder who that is," she said, walking down the hall. "Brian's at Zach's."

Jesse got ready to sand the next sections. He heard Sarah's footsteps come back down the hall.

"Jesse?" she said. "There's someone here to see you."

"I'm right in the middle of this." Not to mention covered head to toe in plaster dust. "Who is it?"

"I think you just need to come."

At the odd sound of her voice, he turned. A shadow of concern had passed over her features. "What's the matter?" He shut off the sander and climbed down the ladder. Then he removed his mask and walked into the hall. Garrett was at the front door, standing next to—

Jesse stopped in his tracks. He swallowed, then felt the back of his neck twinge with foreboding.

"Hello, Jesse."

Jesse took a couple steps, his feet feeling weighted in concrete. "Hello, Hank."

Hank Bowman, the man Jesse had just about killed that night he'd driven drunk and fallen asleep at the wheel of his truck, reached out from where he sat in his wheelchair to shake Jesse's hand.

Jesse hesitated. Quickly, he rubbed his dirty palm down the front of his pants, trying to remove as much grime as he could before shaking the other man's hand. "Sorry. Been drywalling. Did you meet Sarah?"

"I did." Hank smiled at her. "This is your house, Sarah?"

She nodded.

"And Jesse's helping to remodel it?"

"He's doing it all. I just help out here and there. Painting. Sanding."

Hank glanced around. "Looks pretty good."

"The interior is almost finished, but there's still a lot to do outside," Jesse said. "How did you—"

"I stopped at the police station, thinking someone there would be able to help me find you." He glanced back at Garrett. "Didn't know your brother was the chief of police. He pushed me up the hill. I hope that's okay."

"That's fine. Thanks, Garrett."

"Well, I've got a meeting in a few minutes at my office," Garrett said. "So I've got to head back. Call me if you need anything."

Jesse nodded as Garrett disappeared back through the front door.

"Maybe I should…go, too," Sarah offered.

"It's all right with me if you stay," Hank said. "But that's really up to Jesse."

Jesse glanced at Sarah. He had no clue why Hank was here or what he might want from Jesse, but like it or not, he and Sarah had become friends. He was surprised by how much he wanted her to stay. "I have no secrets from Sarah."

Hank smiled at her. "That's good. Everyone needs someone."

Jesse pulled a chair from the kitchen out into the living area for Sarah. "Would you like something to drink, Hank?"

"Water's fine."

"I'll get it," Sarah said as Jesse brought a step stool over for himself.

He sat down and held Hank's gaze, waiting, wondering.

"So…how have you been?" Hank asked.

"Good. I've been living here with my brother, working on Sarah's house since I got out in January."

"That's what I've heard. I'm glad."

"And you?"

"Doing good. Really, really good."

Not exactly what Jesse had expected to hear and relief momentarily flooded his senses. Hank did look healthy. Natural color had returned to his cheeks. Although his legs looked as if they'd atrophied a bit, his arms and chest looked strong. Those muscles hadn't come from pushing himself around in that chair. He'd clearly been lifting weights.

"In fact," Hank went on, smiling, "I got some great news last week. There's a specialist out at John Hopkins that agreed to take a look at my records. He's not making any guarantees, but there's a very slight possibility I might walk again."

"That's wonderful."

"Well, I'm not going to hold my breath, but I'm not giving up, either."

Sarah set a glass of ice water on a toolbox sitting next to Hank.

"Thank you, Sarah."

"No problem. We've got some cookies. Or some fruit."

"No, thank you." He smiled at Sarah and then glanced back at Jesse. "My third book will be out in a couple months."

"Another self-help-type book?"

"Yeah. Sales have been going well, creating a lot of speaking engagements." He paused and smiled. "It's funny, although I sometimes miss my old life, I'm enjoying this new venture. It's been an interesting challenge."

"You've made lemonade out of some very sour lemons."

"Guess you could say that." He looked away. "I'm not going to lie to you. Some days are better than others. Then there are some days when I'm not sure I want to get out of bed."

Jesse swallowed, but he forced himself to hold Hank's gaze. A part of him desperately wanted to reach out for Sarah's hand. Instead, he crossed his arms and braced himself for what would most assuredly be an onslaught of blame and anger. Resentment. He deserved no less. The least he could do was sit here and take it. "I'm sorry, Han—"

"No, Jesse. No. That's not why I came here. You've apologized in every possible way. There's nothing more you can say. I am sorry for showing up unannounced today. I would've called to let you know I was coming, but I figured it best to just show up and say what I have to say face-to-face." Hank took a sip of water. "I know this is going to seem rather sudden, but I have a proposition for you."

"Whatever you want or need, I'll do what I can."

"I appreciate that, but this is…ah…above and beyond, so I think it best if you give it some thought before you decide one way or another."

"All right." Jesse held his breath, waiting.

"I've been speaking to first-offender groups," Hank explained. "You know. People who've gotten their first DWIs or DUIs and as a part of their sentence they're required to sit and listen through an impact seminar. Speeches and such, given by people affected by the accidents caused by DUIs."

Jesse swallowed. He'd been to a few himself as a part of his sentence.

"I think they make a difference," Hank continued. "Sometimes, anyway. When I heard you'd gotten out of prison, this idea started niggling at me for how to make a bigger impact on people."

Sarah shifted uncomfortably and Jesse glanced at her. She was upset. For him. He reached out to squeeze her arm and he was surprised to find tears pooling in her eyes. So much emotion in her face, he could hardly stand it.

Hank ran a calloused hand through his hair. "I was wondering—hoping, actually—if you'd consider doing these impact seminars with me."

"*With* you?" Jesse asked, dumbfounded.

"Yeah." Hank nodded. "I think…ah…I think the two of us together would make quite a statement. A much more powerful statement than me being up there all alone."

Jesse tried to imagine standing up in front of a crowd next to Hank in his wheelchair. He couldn't. "Why would you want to do this? Why would you ever want to stand next to me in front of a group like that? Hell, for that matter, Hank, how can you be in the same room with me now? How can you not hate me? You must hate me."

"No, I don't hate you," Hank said. "At least not now. Don't get me wrong. In the beginning I spent a lot of months despising you. There were times when I laid in that hospital bed or was going through painful physical therapy when I wished you…quite literally…dead." He paused. "Most of the time, though, I just wanted to get my hands on your back, snap your spine, so you could experience what I've gone through."

"There would have been some justice in that," Jesse muttered.

"No. There's no justice in revenge," Hank said. "And a man can only stomach so much hate before it turns on him. Starts to eat him up inside. One day in physical therapy it dawned on me that the only way I was ever going to be able to move on from that accident, the only way I was ever going to stop letting that accident define me and my life, was by…forgiving you."

How could Hank forgive Jesse when Jesse couldn't even forgive himself?

"You made a mistake, Jesse. A bad one. We've both paid a high price for it. Life is never fair, but it can be just, and justice was served when you went to prison."

Jesse hopped up and paced.

"I think—I hope—you're a better man today than you were four years ago. That's what matters—"

"What about you? Your life will never be the same."

"You're right." He nodded. "Everything changed for me that night. I'm not trying to suggest that I wouldn't go back in time in a heartbeat if I could and keep this from happening to me. To us. But I can't. I don't want to keep living in the past. I want to move beyond the accident and the only way I can do that completely is if you move beyond it with me."

Jesse turned away and ran his hands over his face.

"I'm not talking about forgetting it ever happened," Hank went on. "Neither one of us will ever be able to do that. I'm talking about turning something bad, something horrendous and painful, into something positive. Turning something destructive into something constructive. You and I standing together have the ability to make a difference in this world. If we can connect with those DUI offenders. If we can make even one of them see the danger in their behavior, we just might save a life. 'Course we'll never know in fact what kind of impact we'll have. But we'll know in our hearts we did our best."

Jesse turned back and held Hank's gaze. He wanted Jesse to stand up in front of a crowd, look them in the eye, and admit that he'd driven drunk and it'd caused a man to lose his ability to walk. Could Jesse suck it up and do that?

"The next seminar I'll be speaking at is a couple weeks from now," Hank said, setting his glass back down on the box. "It's at the community center in Ashland. Starts at 7:00 p.m. I'll email you the details. If you don't come…I'll understand. You are not, for one moment, obligated to do this. You've done your time. Justice has been served. But justice, I've discovered, doesn't always heal the wounds."

Jesse looked away.

"My wounds, inside and out, are on the mend," Hank whispered. "What about yours?"

CHAPTER TWENTY

FOR MORE THAN A WEEK, Jesse had refused to talk with Sarah about Hank Bowman's visit, let alone the proposal Hank had laid out and presumably followed up with emails. Sarah was at a loss as to how to reach Jesse. He'd become a friend, and seeing a friend implode right in front of her didn't sit well.

Since Hank's visit, Jesse had immersed himself in finishing Sarah's house. He was several days ahead of schedule, but the bounce had gone out of his step, the smile had been wiped from his face, and that mischievous glint in his eyes had been doused.

The work on the house, on the other hand, had been going well. Jesse had taken advantage of several warm, dry days and had replaced a couple rotting windows and started painting the entire exterior. All that was left to do on the interior was the fireplace and, finally, the installation of new carpeting. The house was ready for Sarah and Brian to start moving in a few of their things.

Rather than move everything in one fell swoop, Sarah planned on taking things over in chunks and leaving all of her and Brian's essentials in the apartment until the end. She wanted everything perfectly arranged by the time they started actually living in the house.

Driving a golf cart, she moved the first of the many boxes ready to go into storage in the basement—these were holiday decorations—from the apartment to the house. She was so excited she could barely catch her breath.

She maneuvered the cart up to the house, carried the boxes down into the basement and came back upstairs. Several bags of cement mix were stacked onto the porch along with trowels and a wheelbarrow. Jesse was getting ready to lay the fireplace stones.

She would've been excited if not for the fact that Jesse, after Hank's visit, had thrown himself into work like a madman. At his current pace, he would've ended up more than two weeks ahead of schedule had he not tackled the fireplace project and helped Garrett build the deck at Duffy's.

In one day, he'd already removed the old brick surround, set the wood mantel aside and prepped the surface around the fireplace with some type of wiring, presumably to hold the cement. He'd also pounded some type of metal support posts into the wall studs. Most likely these would support the heavy rock.

Rather than being pleased at the progress with her house, Sarah was worried about Jesse. She'd been watching him, working by his side, painting and cleaning, with a newfound tenderness for him in her heart and no idea whatsoever as to how to help him.

"Hey, Sarah, how's it going?"

She spun around to find Garrett standing at the open front door. So preoccupied with thoughts of Jesse, she hadn't heard him come across the porch. "Hi, Garrett. What's up?"

"Just wanted to check on Jesse. Used the excuse of bringing over a few more trowels." He held up a handful of tools. "He's been...kind of withdrawn since Hank came by."

"Tell me about it," she said. "Do you know where he is?"

"If he's not here, then most likely Full Moon Bay."

Located on the secluded northeast shore and accessible only by either kayak or foot, it was one of the best-kept secrets on the island. Rocks piled high near the woods provided a natural retaining wall for the sandiest beach on the island. It wasn't a big bay, but it was as picturesque as it got on Lake Superior.

"I gave him the keys for the maintenance truck this morning. He might be out collecting rock for your fireplace."

"I told him I'd help him."

"Me, too. So much for that."

It was clear both she and Garrett were worried, and neither knew what to do about it.

"I'm going to find him." She started toward the front door.

"Sarah?"

She turned.

"For what it's worth, thank you."

"For what?"

"For giving Jesse a chance, for being his friend. But be careful. I'm not entirely sure he's not going to cut and run before your house is finished."

"He wouldn't do that to me, Garrett. Or to Brian." Holding back a sudden rush of tears, she ran out the door and took the golf cart down the northeast loop of Island Drive.

She found Mirabelle's maintenance vehicle parked beside the overgrown path to Full Moon Bay. A pile of rocks were already stacked in the trailer hitched to the back of the truck. Jesse was down at the shoreline, picking through rock and occasionally tossing one into a wheelbarrow by his side.

His head down, his brow furrowed in concentration, his expression was nothing like the Jesse she'd come to know and...she had to be honest with herself...the Jesse she'd come to love.

And there it was. Against her better judgment, ignoring all the warning bells going off inside her head, her feelings had developed and grown into something so strong there was no fighting it. She'd fallen in love with him.

Dammit. Now what? Now she had no choice but to jump in with both feet.

He glanced up, caught sight of her, but said nothing.

"I thought I was going to help you with this."

"You were busy."

"I'm always busy, but I've still helped with the house when needed."

"Guess I didn't need you after all."

"No," she whispered. "You don't need anyone."

He glanced at her, his gaze wary.

"But that's just what you want everyone to believe, isn't it?"

At that he went back to picking through the rocks and tossing ones that for whatever reason worked into the wheelbarrow.

Well, Sarah had had enough. "You come here with this outwardly happy-go-lucky exterior. Pretending that every bad thing rolls off you like water on a duck's back. Nothing fazes Jesse. No, sirree.

"People won't associate with you because of what you did? So what? They leave restaurants and bars when you appear? Won't sit next to you at a damned funeral? Who cares? Not you. You don't want anybody. You don't need anybody. And you don't want anyone to want or need you.

"Well, guess what? People on this island do care about you. I care about you. But do you let us in? Do you let me in? Do you let any of us give back just a little of what you give to us?

"No! Because Jesse Taylor is a rock." She picked up a stone and threw it in the wheelbarrow. "You think you don't deserve anyone's friendship. Let alone anyone's love. So you're just damned well not going to accept it."

He clenched his jaw and narrowed his eyes at her.

"Well, I got news for you. It's not going to work. You running away, either by burying yourself in a construction job or by literally leaving Mirabelle and moving from town to town isn't going to solve anything."

"Stay out of my life, Sarah," he said through gritted teeth. "I don't want you inside. I got nothing to give. Nothing."

"You're wrong. About everything. So Hank shows up in his wheelchair. Reminding you of what happened. So what? You can work your fingers to the bone. You can run and hide and hide some more and run some more. At the end of the day, Hank will *still* be in a wheelchair. And you will *still* have put him there."

Jesse glared at her, his chest heaving as if it was all he could do to breathe.

"Instead of wallowing around in it—"

"Wallowing?" He shook his head. "I sure as hell am not just feeling sorry for myself!"

"Then what would you call it? Because it's not coping. It's not healing. It's not moving on." She took a deep breath and whispered, "Stop going around in circles, Jesse. Stand still, and make a difference."

Without another word, he turned his back on her, grabbed the handlebars of the wheelbarrow and marched away through the woods. By the time she made it back to her golf cart, Jesse, his truck and all his damned rocks were gone. She may have pushed him too far.

JESSE SPENT THE ENTIRE next week *wallowing*, as Sarah would've called it. Or working, to his way of thinking. Avoiding everyone, particularly Sarah, Brian and Zach. Everyone else, including Garrett, he could manage to hold at arm's length, but not those three.

Sarah was right about everything she'd said out at Full Moon Bay, but for the life of him he couldn't see his way clear of this. All he could think about was the MADD presentation and the overwhelming urge thrumming through him to leave Mirabelle. He'd been so preoccupied it took him twice the time it should have to complete the simplest tasks and half of what he'd finished he'd had to immediately do over as a result of crappy workmanship.

It was close to dinnertime when he heard footsteps on Sarah's porch. The front door opened without a knock. Had to be Sarah. He wasn't holding out any hope that she'd brought him something to eat. After their argument at Full Moon Bay, she'd stopped bringing him meals.

She breezed into the living room. "Hi."

"Hi."

"I thought you were planning on finishing the fireplace today." She studied the stones. "Not a good day, huh?"

"No." He still had a good three feet of rock left to lay down.

"What's going on?"

"It happens. Everyone has bad days every once in a while."

"Not you. On bad days you tend to get even more accomplished."

"Yeah, well, there's a first time for everything."

"Jesse—"

"Sarah, leave it, okay? You said your piece the other day. I don't want to talk about it anymore. You can't fix this."

She didn't say anything.

The moment he glanced back, he regretted raising his voice. "I'm sorry. I just need to be alone."

"No, you don't. You've been alone enough."

Now it was his turn to keep silent.

"You need to go tonight."

There was no need to say where. They both knew.

"It might bring some closure for you. It might—"

"You don't know what the hell you're talking about!" He turned on her. "You don't know what I went through. There hasn't been a single day that I haven't thought of the accident first thing when I wake up in the morning and the last thing before I fall asleep. There is no such thing as closure for me on this."

"How do you know unless you try?"

"I know."

"Jesse, Hank came for a reason. I think he might have hit on something that might help both of you. What have you got to lose?"

What very, very little remained of his self-respect, that's what. Hank's wife and family would be there. It was hard enough having looked into Hank's eyes.

God knows why, but the man had forgiven him. Hank's family hadn't. How could Jesse face them?

"I don't completely understand what you went through," she said, more gently. "Honestly, I can't even imagine it. I can't help but feel like this is the right thing for you. If you don't do it, you just might regret it for the rest of your life. But if you do…"

"Stop, okay! Stop, Sarah."

"If it makes a difference," she whispered, "I'll go with you."

He looked into her eyes, held her gaze. The compassion and friendship Sarah offered was almost too much for him. With her by his side, for a moment, he imagined he could do about anything.

Do something. Anything but nothing.

"Okay," he said. "Let's go."

USING THE CAR that she stored in Bayfield for mainland trips, Sarah drove into the Ashland community-center parking lot and turned off the engine. Jesse had barely said a word since they'd gotten on the ferry and left Mirabelle, and she was afraid to say anything that might make a mess of this already frightening night.

She turned toward him, studied his solemn profile, and suddenly what Hank had asked Jesse to do sunk in for her. "Maybe I was wrong," she said, worried for him. "Maybe you shouldn't do this."

"No, Sarah. You were right. More right than you've ever been about me. So was Hank. I have to go in there."

"Jesse—"

"I *have* to do this. I have to face them. I have to face what I did, but I understand if you don't want to go." He glanced at her. "You don't need to come inside."

"I know."

Abruptly, he climbed out of the car and started toward the main entrance, his head down, his feet moving as if on automatic pilot. Slowly, she followed him, at a loss for what to say, what to do. Her emotions were so conflicted, she wasn't sure she could speak. No matter what, though, she wasn't letting him face this alone. Hurrying now, she finally caught up with him at the door.

"Sure you want to come in?" he asked.

"I'm sure."

He held the door open and then led the way through the building. They found the designated room and stood in the hall for a moment, listening to the presentation. The room was full, holding at least fifty people, and a MADD volunteer was speaking. She introduced a man whose entire family was killed by a drunk driver. The audience was silent as the man relayed the story of his devastating loss.

Jesse bent his head and ran his hands through his hair. When he looked up again, he seemed to spot Hank in the back row of the room at the same moment Hank spotted him.

Hank smiled as he rolled his wheelchair toward them. He was a handsome man, the wheelchair and his thin, almost spindly legs a complete contradiction to the athletic look of his upper body. "I'm glad you both came," he whispered.

Silently, Jesse nodded.

"I'll go up before you. In about five minutes. I'll talk about the impact the accident had on my family, my life. Then it'll be your turn."

"What do you want me to say?"

"That's entirely up to you, Jesse. I'd suggest you

simply tell your story. In your own words. As honestly as you possibly can. Take as much time as you need. Or use as little as you want. Afterward, we'll answer questions."

Jesse took a big breath and stuffed his hands in his pocket.

Sarah lamely placed her hand on his upper back and held it there, not knowing what else to do.

"This is gonna be hard, I know," Hank said. "And I should warn you again. My wife is here. My parents. A couple brothers and sisters."

Jesse had explained earlier that having pled guilty to the charges all those years ago, he'd never been forced to confront Hank's family in court, other than at sentencing. Now there was no way around it.

At that moment, an attractive woman, a brunette with piercing brown eyes, came slowly out into the hall, her eyes boring into Jesse. Sarah reached for Jesse's hand.

Jesse clenched Sarah's hand, but held the woman's gaze. "Mrs. Bowman," he whispered, his eyes misting. "I know this doesn't mean much, but I'm so sorry for all the pain I've caused you and your husband."

She rolled her eyes. "Your apology means nothing to me. You ruined my husband's life—you ruined my life." Resolutely, she shook her head. "I don't know how Hank has been able to forgive you, but I guarantee you that won't be happening with me." Then she walked down the hall, clearly not willing to listen to the program.

Hank sighed. "Sorry about that."

"Are you kidding? She's right."

"Actually, what she is, is bitter. Angry. And damned hard to live with."

"So I can add ruining a marriage to my list of offenses," he said. "I'm sorry."

"No, Jesse. *That* is definitely not your fault. This kind of stress has a way of either cementing together all the fissures in a relationship or…deepening them. I think you can guess which way we went." Hank tipped his head toward the rear of the room. "My parents and siblings are there in the back row. They don't want to meet you, just yet. But I think that'll come. In time."

"I don't blame them. I still haven't forgiven myself. Why should they?"

"Because it's better that way." Hank glanced back at Jesse. "Well, I'm up next. You ready for this?"

"Not even close, but I'll do my best."

Hank rolled back into the room. A moment later, the same MADD volunteer who'd introduced the last speaker, announced Hank's name. He went to the front and introduced himself.

Sarah felt Jesse's hand trembling in hers. She tightened her grip around his fingers. "You can do this." Lame again, but it was all she had.

As if looking at her might be too much for him, he kept his gaze on Hank and said, "Thank you for being here, Sarah." Then he let go of her hand and went to the front of the room.

Sarah slid into an empty seat in the back row, clasped her hands tightly in her lap and prayed that her urging him to come here hadn't been one hell of a big mistake.

"My name is Jesse Taylor," he said, glancing out over the audience. For a second, he caught her gaze. Then he took a deep breath and began. "On a Saturday night in October…about four years ago, I drove…drunk…for the first time. I almost killed a man that night. That

man was Hank Bowman. I hit him with my truck." He
paused to gather himself. "I hit a human being with the
front of my truck. Slammed his body right into a brick
building."

Tears gathered in Sarah's eyes as she tried to imagine the courage it took for Jesse to humbly pour out
his heart and soul to this group. To stand up and face
Hank's family.

"You can all sit there and say to yourselves…well,
that wasn't me," Jesse went on. "But the truth is that it
could've been. I'm here to tell you that once—*once*—
is all it takes to forever change not only the course of
your life, but ruin someone else's…"

CHAPTER TWENTY-ONE

A THUNDERSTORM WAS HEADING their way. As they approached Mirabelle's shores in the water taxi, the wind gusted, and the surface of the water turned choppier by the second. Jesse glanced behind him. Nothing short of a fantastic light display, courtesy of Mother Nature, thunder rumbled miles away, and lightning crackled down from the dark purplish-black night sky.

"Sorry, man," he said to the taxi driver as the man docked his boat in the marina. "Looks like you might get wet."

The man chuckled. "You folks, too, if you don't hurry home."

Jesse hopped onto the dock, took Sarah's hand and helped her up beside him and then paid the driver his fare along with a healthy tip. "Stay safe, and thanks."

"You betcha."

In silence, Jesse walked beside Sarah away from the marina. He felt exhausted and drained, as if adrenaline had been pumping through his veins and his emotions had been on overdrive for hours. Most of him felt just plain heavy with the weight of all that had been said and shared and exposed tonight, but there was a part of him that felt damned close to free. It was a tentative feeling, kind of like stepping through that prison gate and out into the real world all those months ago. It was a feeling he didn't want to put too much hope in, but it was there all the same.

He wasn't fool enough to believe that tonight's admissions in front of that crowd and his commitment to continue to speak about once a month with Hank had taken away his guilt. There were still tough moments awaiting him in his future, moments where he knew he'd hate himself as much as he did that first morning after discovering Hank's spine had been severed. But this was a start, a few steps down a path that with any luck would lead to him being able to look at himself in the mirror again without entirely hating his reflection.

He and Sarah reached Main Street, and he hesitated. "I'll walk you to your apartment."

Nervously, she crossed her arms in front of her as if she were cold and glanced into the sky. A gust of wind whipped her hair into her face. "You don't have—"

"I know." He didn't want her to be alone. He didn't want to be alone. He wanted to tell her how much it meant to him that she came tonight. In no time, they reached the stairs leading to the second floor of her building and they both stopped.

Sarah should've started up the steps, or he should've turned. Instead, neither of them moved. He took a deep breath of cool, sweet spring air, and whispered, "Thank you for urging me to go tonight. For driving. For sticking around. For holding my hand."

"I'm glad I went."

"Good night, Sarah."

She reached up, gently ran her hand down the side of his cheek and then turned and went up the steps.

He wished he could explain to her how much she'd

come to mean to him. He wished… "Sarah, I couldn't have done that tonight without you."

"You'd have managed," she said, looking down at him from the landing above.

Before he realized what he was doing, he was walking up the steps, following her. She'd put the key in the lock and had opened the door. He went to her, not really understanding, but feeling drawn to her all the same. "I wouldn't have managed. Not without you…tonight… having you there…"

"Shh." She touched her fingertips to his lips.

As if God had turned on a faucet in the sky, rain suddenly poured straight down outside in sheets. If they hadn't been under the roofed walkway outside her apartment, they would've been soaked in seconds.

"Do you think He's trying to tell us something?" Jesse grinned as he glanced at Sarah. The moment the worried expression on her face registered, he sobered. "You okay?"

"Sure." She rubbed her arms up and down. "I'm fine."

"No, you're not."

"Honestly? I hate thunderstorms."

She didn't just hate them, she was downright scared.

Lightning flashed over the water, not far off shore, and Sarah started shaking. "I'm sorry," she said.

"No need to be," he whispered. He could think of only one thing that would take both their minds completely off the storm, but that would spell disaster. Instead, he reached for her hand. "It's all right."

"Will you stay with me?"

"Sarah, I don't think—"

"Please?"

"All right, but just until the storm clears." *And keep your hands to yourself.*

They went into her apartment. She closed the door and locked it. "I feel so silly."

"Everyone's afraid of something," he said, trying to make light of the situation.

"Yeah?" She turned. "What are you afraid of?"

You. How I feel when I'm around you. More than anything else, leaving Mirabelle. But he couldn't say any of those things. "June bugs," he said with a smile. "Give me the creeps." He pretended to shiver. "Those big, brown bodies. Those spiny, jagged legs."

She swatted his arm. "That's not the same."

"Like hell. You want to see a grown man scream like a little girl just throw one of those buggers at me sometime."

She chuckled. "I can see you." Then she was laughing and tears started streaming from the corners of her eyes, but within seconds, her tears of laughter clearly turned to tears of sadness.

"Hey," he whispered. "What's wrong?"

"One fall, right at the end of the harvest, my dad and I were in an orchard picking apples." She wrapped her arms around herself. "I was about Brian's age. Without warning, a bad thunderstorm came on us. We were drenched in no time. I've never been as cold as I was that day."

She paused, as if remembering. "We ran to the nearest woods for shelter, and my dad pulled me under a tree," she went on. "Lightning seemed to be hitting all around us. He took the brunt of the weather by snuggling me in front of him and hunching over me." She took a deep breath and a new round of tears fell. "About a week later, he died from pneumonia."

"Oh, Sarah." Without thought to the consequences, he pulled her into his arms. "I'm sorry."

"I know it wasn't the storm that killed him, but I've always felt as if it was my fault that he died." Full of emotions that ran the gamut, she looked into his eyes. "I'd like a reason to no longer hate thunderstorms."

He kissed her palm. As he took her face in his hands, she pulled him toward her. Their lips met in the softest kiss he'd ever known. Their tongues touched and gently explored. Their breath sweetly mingled. For a moment, they clung together as if time had been suspended.

Then, like a wave rolling, cresting to completion, everything changed. Soft turned to hard, sweet to urgent, and gentle to frantic as they tripped sideways down the hallway. She pushed him back against the wall. He ran his hands under her shirt, cupped her breasts over her bra.

He knew it was wrong. He knew it was about as unfair to Sarah as unfair got, but, God help him, he wanted her—needed her—so badly that his insides ached.

When she pulled back for a moment and looked up at him, her eyes so clearly saying she felt the same as him, he simply couldn't find the strength to leave. She needed him tonight as much as he needed her.

"Brian?" he whispered, the air puffing from his chest. "Where's Brian?"

"He's staying at Zach's."

The last barrier fell away.

For her sake he had to try to put a stop to this. Didn't he? "Sarah, this—"

"Oh, no, you don't. You started this. We're finishing it." She tugged his shirt over his head and kissed him, first on his mouth, then on his neck, then down his chest, all the while working on the button and fly on his shorts. She licked the edges of his tattoo, twirled her tongue along the swirling lines and then finally nipped at his nipple.

He sucked in a breath, trying to hold on to his sanity. Then she pushed his shorts over his hips, dipped her hands beneath his boxers and that was all she wrote.

He groaned as her fingers moved over him, pleasure and pain all rolled into one sweet caress. "Sarah, careful." Quickly, he gripped her wrists and drew her hands away. "Condoms?" He sure as hell didn't have any. "Please say you've got protection."

"In my bedroom."

Her room was a surprise, the decor as soft and feminine as the rest of her apartment was bold and brazen. At the moment, though, he didn't care that muted greens and blues mixed with soft whites and pale yellows to create a haven of relaxation. There was only one thing he wanted.

She went to her bedside table, pulled out an unopened box and chuckled. "Wishful thinking."

"About who?"

"You." Her eyes darkened. "I haven't...since Bobby."

Damn. He'd forgotten. "Sarah, are you sure..."

"As sure as I've ever been about anything."

As she walked toward him, she drew her shirt over her head, unzipped her jeans and shrugged out of them. Her bra was a wild pattern of purples, hot pink and black. Her thong, what little there was of the scrap of fabric, was solid black. Like her hair. A bad girl masquerading as a good girl. Every man's dream.

Jesse turned as hard as a rock. When she reached behind her back to unsnap her bra, he reached out.

"No. Let me." He ran his hand along her arm, intent on making the last nine years of her waiting worth every second.

Then he touched her, everywhere, ran his fingers lightly over her cheeks, down her neck, her chest, her belly, wanting to know every inch of her. Her skin was soft and her smell, that ever-present scent of flowers, filled his senses.

He pushed down one bra strap, then the other and freed two dusky pink-tipped breasts. For a moment, he simply gazed at her. Her mouth slightly parted, her eyes heavy-lidded. "You are the most beautiful thing I've ever seen."

"Touch me," she breathed.

"If you say so." Smiling, he cupped her breasts in his hands, bent and took one nipple and then the other into his mouth, laving his tongue back and forth. Then he dipped the fingers of one hand beneath her thong and slid deeply between her thighs. Swollen and wet, she arched to meet him, tilted her head back and groaned.

He wanted nothing more in that moment that to bury himself deeply inside her, but he held back. For her.

She touched him and he jerked back and away. "No, Sarah. I'm already too close. You first."

He kissed her as he laid her back on the bed, un-snapped her bra and dragged off her thong. He spread her thighs with his knee and moved down her body, biting, kissing and licking the whole way.

His heart raced and his hands trembled as he parted her sweet, swollen folds and stroked her tight center with his tongue. She cried out and bucked against him. The instant he slipped two fingers inside her, she came, pulsing violently against him, and he could wait no longer.

He slid back up her body and entered her in time to feel her grip him in the rhythms of her release. "Sarah." He kissed her mouth as he rocked against her. "Sarah!" As he came it was as if his body released in one fell swoop every tense and tight moment of the past four years. He was finally a free man. Free of prison. Free of guilt. If only for a few moments.

THE WEAK RAYS OF SUNRISE filtered through Sarah's bedroom windows as she lay on her side, facing Jesse. His head was on his own pillow, but his arm was wrapped around her side and his legs were entangled in hers. All night, they'd slept in variations of this same pose, always touching, always holding. It'd been the most magical night of her life. Jesse had brought her body to life in a way she'd never dreamed possible. He'd made love to her over and over until they'd both collapsed in sleep, exhausted.

Watching him speak in front of that MADD group had changed everything for her. Everything. The sincerity in Jesse's eyes, the meaning in his voice, the moments his throat had closed with emotion had all worked at softening her heart more than she'd ever expected. Even Hank's parents and siblings had seemed to soften toward Jesse last night. There hadn't been a dry eye in the entire Bowman group.

Jesse had, indeed, paid a price for his mistake. One he'd carry with him for the rest of his life, but he deserved to move on as much as was possible. The Bowman family believed it. Sarah believed it. The only person who didn't was Jesse himself.

This man lying in bed with her was nothing like

Bobby Coleman, nothing like any of the bad boys she'd met in Miami. If any one of them had been in Jesse's shoes that day Hank showed up on Mirabelle, they would've patted Hank on the back and thrown a party in the man's honor. Then they would've turned around and done a line of coke.

Jesse may have thrown himself into work, instead, but at least it was a more productive escape, and he'd come around. He'd faced what he'd needed to do. Jesse was a good man who'd made one terrible mistake, and because he was a good man a piece of him would suffer for that mistake the rest of his life.

There was nothing wrong with her judgment in men. Not anymore. These many years raising Brian on her own had brought reason and clarity. She was attracted to Jesse for damned good reasons. He had all the wonderful bad-boy traits she loved, an easy smile and a zest for life. He knew how to have fun and sought joy—real joy—in life, but Jesse was responsible, dependable and sensitive. He had none of the bad-boy faults, save one. He still believed he was a rolling stone. He still planned on leaving Mirabelle.

She stared at his profile, at his dark lashes fanning out over his cheeks, and sucked in a sharp breath. Good Lord, what had she done? How could she have let this go so far? Now more than ever she knew she would never be happy without Jesse in her life. Well, she wasn't going to let him leave without a fight. If making love with him was playing dirty, then so be it.

In a few hours Megan and Brandon would arrive on Mirabelle, kicking off the first wedding of her busy season, and Sarah wouldn't be coming up for air for several days. But she and Jesse still had this morning, and Sarah planned on making the most of it.

Reaching out, she ran her hand along his muscular chest, down the center of his warm stomach and buried her fingers in the thick curly hair at his groin. His penis, flaccid in deep sleep, didn't stay that way for long.

"Mmm," he murmured, the sound coming from deep in his chest. He opened his eyes and smiled at her. "Sarah," he groaned, his voice raspy with sleep. "What are you doing?"

He loved her. She could see it in his eyes as clear as day breaking outside her window, but even a whisper of her own love, let alone his, would be disaster.

Instead, she grinned. "Making up for lost time."

JESSE CAME AWAKE with a peaceful, lazy smile on his face. Sarah—his sweet, sweet, Sarah—was tucked in front of him. Her smooth back against his chest. Her long black hair splayed out over the pillowcase and under his cheek. Her round bottom pressed against his groin and a nice, stiff morning erection ready and waiting to sink into her tight softness.

He moved against her...and stopped. His Sarah? Who the hell was he kidding? What had he done?

For nine years the woman had sworn off men, and what did he do? He'd slipped right in there and made her forget every promise she'd made to herself. All because he was a selfish son of a bitch. He'd wanted her. He'd needed her. He'd taken her. Hell, he'd even convinced himself that he loved her, but he was merely playing tricks on himself. On her. She deserved so much better than him.

One last time, he buried his face in her hair and breathed her in. Breathed in that fresh breath of life, of love. To which he had no right. Then carefully, quietly, he slid away from her. He sat up and swung his feet down to the floor.

The sheets rustled behind him and he stilled, keeping his fingers crossed that she hadn't woken up, that he didn't need to do this now.

"Don't go," she whispered, her hand resting softly on his waist.

"I gotta get to work."

"No, you don't."

"Yeah, I do." He stood and pulled on his boxers.

"Hey."

He could hear her shifting toward him.

"What's going on?"

"Nothing. I need to get going." He dragged on his jeans.

"Don't, Jesse. Don't do this. Don't make last night— the most perfect night of my life—a mistake."

He turned. She'd pulled the sheet up in front of her. Her face was a mass of emotion, but he made himself face her. Made himself face the beautiful sight of her disheveled hair, her kiss-swollen lips. The whisker burns—from him—on the tender skin on the upper swell of her breasts.

"But that's what it was, Sarah. A mistake. A lapse in judgment. You may not be ready to accept that now, but in a couple days. In a week. It'll hit you between the eyes like a hammer on a nail head. We don't belong together. You deserve—and you know you want— something better than me."

"No. I lov—"

"Don't!" He spun away from the painful sight of her. "Don't say it."

"I love you," she whispered. "I love you. I love you. I love—"

"Well…I don't love you."

"You're lying."

"No, Sarah. It's the truth. Last night was fun. Great, even. But I…don't…love you."

"Then go! Leave!" she threw at him. "It changes nothing."

"Damn right it doesn't," he bit out. The hardest thing he'd ever done was look at the tears in her eyes, tears he'd caused, and hold himself back. He ached to pull her into his arms, to comfort her, to tell her he was sorry. He couldn't. "I'm still leaving as soon as your house is finished."

Then he made himself turn on her and walk out of her bedroom.

CHAPTER TWENTY-TWO

"SARAH!" Megan rushed off the pier. "I can't believe it's finally here."

"It's here all right." Sarah put on the best and brightest smile she could muster, hugged Megan and then shook Brandon's hand. After Jesse had left her that morning, she had no choice but to get up and face the day.

"So what do we do?" Megan asked, her eyes bright with expectation.

"You simply enjoy the experience," Sarah said, motioning behind her toward the horse-drawn carriage. "Hop on board. The driver will take you to the Mirabelle Island Inn. I'll take care of the rest."

The next several days were going to pass in a blur, and for once Sarah found herself extremely thankful for Megan. She'd be too busy to think about Jesse and his insistence about leaving. But when this wedding was over, he was going to find out that she wasn't giving him up without one hell of a fight.

"WHAT ARE YOU DOING?"

At the sound of his brother's voice, Jesse turned off the jigsaw in Garrett's workshop, flipped up his safety glasses and glanced behind him. Jesse had been so intent on following the pattern lines with the saw blade that he hadn't heard Garrett come into the woodworking shop. "Making replacement gingerbread trim for Sarah's front porch," he said. He'd just finished the last of the four arches.

Garrett picked up one of the other arches that had already been sanded and painted, and carefully examined the detail. "Good work, bro. Maybe you *could* make furniture."

Jesse laughed. "Before you get all excited, you should know I didn't design that. Copied the pattern off the old, broken-up chunk still left on her porch."

He set down the arch piece and picked up the triangular gable decoration.

"Now, *that,* I did design, but it's based on the porch arches, so I can't take all the credit."

"No wonder you've been pretty scarce lately. These were a lot of work."

"No kidding. Now I know why custom orders for this kind of trim cost so much. Sarah couldn't afford to pay for premade pieces, so…"

"You made them for her." Garrett glanced at him. "That was nice."

"It's the least I could do. That's pretty cool, too." He pointed to a rectangular piece. "An embellishment for her storm door."

"Good detail. Bot she's excited to see these."

"She doesn't know I made them, so don't say anything."

"You went to a lot of trouble."

"Not a big deal." Jesse brushed away some sawdust from the piece he was working on. "Kind of like a housewarming gift."

Garrett shook his head and laughed softly. "If I didn't know better, I'd say you were one whupped puppy."

Jesse glanced away.

"Is her house finished yet?"

"Yeah. This is the last thing I need to do. I'll be getting this trim up in the next couple of days. While she's busy with that wedding."

"And then what?"

"Then I'm done on Mirabelle. Completely. There's nothing left for me to do here."

"You're sure about that?"

"Positive."

"You could stay, you know. With the way Mirabelle's business is booming, I've had to turn away at least a dozen jobs, both big and small, since I took on this furniture order. One look at what you've done at Sarah's and people will be asking you left and right to man their projects. And…well, hell…Garrett Taylor Furniture Company sounds a little lonely. I'm thinking I like the sounds of Taylor Brothers' Furniture a lot better."

"Garrett—"

"Think about it."

"There's nothing to think about. I'm not right for Mirabelle."

"The old Jesse wasn't right for Mirabelle. This new one? I think he's right where he belongs."

MEGAN AND BRANDON'S groom's dinner went off without a hitch. Sarah had even managed to get home early enough to spend time with Brian. After he fell asleep on the couch while they were watching a movie, Sarah snuck down to her shop to finish assembling the flowers for the wedding. It was well past one by the time she wrapped up and she was likely asleep before her head even hit her pillow.

She woke up Saturday morning, later than she'd hoped, to a sky filled with hazy cloud cover and the kind of cold and heavy drizzle that tended to make a person want to climb back into bed and stay there all day. Not that Sarah ever got to experience that luxury. She slid out of bed, glanced out the window and braced herself for the upcoming day. If the weather was any indication, this wedding was going to be a disaster.

She walked down the hall and found Brian in the kitchen putting away the clean dishes from the dishwasher. "Good morning."

"Morning, Mom."

"What's this all about?"

"You said I should take more responsibility, right? Help out more."

"I appreciate that." She cocked her head at him.

"Jesse's right. You need help. The more I help you, the less work you have to do."

"You really like him, don't you?"

"So do you." He grinned.

"Yeah, I do." She gave him a hug, but stopped short of ruffling his hair.

"You know, it'd be okay with me if you dated him."

"Oh, it would, huh?" She glanced at her son, wishing like hell he was another ten years older and she could spill her guts to him. Someday. "Want some scrambled eggs?"

"I already mixed them up. They're in the fridge."

"You better be careful, mister. I could get used to this."

They made the rest of breakfast, ate and cleaned up together. Then Sarah helped Brian with some homework and they both did a few chores. By the time they were finished boxing up a few more things to move up to the house, the rain had stopped.

They piled the boxes by the door and Sarah glanced into Brian's things. "We won't be staying at the house until later this week. You sure you won't need any of that stuff for a few days?"

"I'm sure," Brian said. "It's just some old video games and books and stuff."

"Did you want to come to the house with me and help unload things?"

"Alex Andersen's birthday party is starting in a few minutes. Remember? We're supposed to meet at Romeo's for pizza for lunch and then we're all going to Alex's house afterward."

To continue the party and a sleepover. No, she hadn't remembered. The change in this wedding date had thrown her schedule out of whack. At least she'd thought to get Alex a present. "Let's wrap his gift and then I'll walk with you to Romeo's."

A few minutes later, they were out the door. She quickly took him to Alex's pizza party, made sure the Andersens had her cell-phone number and that Brian would be with them until morning, and then hustled back to her shop. She grabbed the wedding flowers and a few last-minute things and headed down Island Drive to the Mirabelle Island Inn.

Brittany Rousseau was waiting for her at the front desk. "Hey, there," she said. "You all set?"

"I still have to decorate the chapel and finish in the banquet room, but the wedding isn't until four. I'll be ready by then."

Several hours later, she'd finished decorating both the chapel and banquet hall, had checked in with Megan and Brandon, separately, at least twice. The only snag—so far—had been the color of napkins on the dinner tables. Megan had wanted white, and it was a simple fix. Sarah was going through her checklist one last time before going to collect Megan to get this party started when someone frantically called her name.

"Sarah!" Megan's mother came rushing into the cavernous reception hall. "Sarah!"

She turned. "What? What is it?"

"It's Megan." The woman's face was a mass of worry wrinkles. "She won't come out of the bride's room."

Sarah glanced at her watch. It was only three-fifteen. "Did she say what's wrong?"

"No. She won't talk to anyone. Not even—especially not—Brandon."

Great. Just what Sarah needed. A chilly-footed bride.

"She might talk to you," Megan's mother said. "Through all of this, you've been the only person who's been able to calm her down."

"I'll see what I can do." She took off for Megan's room and found the four bridesmaids hovering at the door, the father pacing in the hall. The mother-in-law, staring with barely disguised disgust at the group, was standing next to her very worried-looking son. Sarah tapped on the door. "Megan, it's Sarah. Can I please come in?"

The door lock clicked, but didn't open.

Sarah turned the knob, snuck inside and quickly set the lock again. She found Megan standing at the window looking out over Lake Superior, the sky blustery and overcast.

Slowly, Megan turned. The very picture of a wedding day gone awry, she was holding her gold calla-lily bouquet as if she was all set to walk down the aisle, but her eyes were swollen and bloodshot from crying, her face blotchy and streaked. She plopped into a chair, her full skirt billowing around her.

"Megan, what is it?" Sarah knelt in front of the young woman.

"Did you know I met Brandon when I was thirteen?" she whispered.

Sarah shook her head.

"He's the only boy I've ever dated. The only boy I've ever wanted to date. We've been talking about this wedding for years."

"If you're worried about the napkins, don't sweat it. They've already been changed out." Sarah smiled. "If there's one guarantee in life, it's that something will go wrong at every wedding. It doesn't mean the wedding's not supposed to happen."

Tears pooled anew in Megan's eyes.

"You know," Sarah said gently. It was time to remind this young woman what weddings were supposed to be all about. "The flowers, guest favors, tuxes, table decorations. None of that is all that important, Megan, when it comes right down to it. Today is about you and Brandon."

"I know that," Megan said. Then she chuckled. "Oh, Sarah. You probably think I'm the most selfish, materialistic, perfectionistic bride ever born."

"Maybe not the most, but darned close."

That brought a small smile and more sniffles. "I'm not, though. Not really. The truth is that I don't give a hoot about any of this." She waved a hand over her dress and then tossed the bouquet onto the table. "It's all for Brandon's mom. And my parents. I'm their only daughter. Brandon's their baby. Everyone's been so excited about today."

Surprised, Sarah took her hand. "Then what is it, Megan?"

"All these months, I've buried myself in our wedding plans, obsessed over every little detail, because…because that way…I didn't have any time to think about… Brandon leaving." Megan took a deep, shuddering breath. "But now it's here and there's no getting away from it," she whispered through her tears. "Three days. And he'll be gone."

Sarah felt her eyes mist up.

"I'd give up this entire day—" Megan glanced into Sarah's eyes "—for one more day with Brandon."

All of Megan's fuss over every tiny detail had been a smoke screen, disguising one very worried bride. For the first time since she'd met Megan, Sarah realized the depth of this woman's feeling for her fiancé.

"What if he never comes back?" she sobbed.

What could Sarah possibly say? Should she lie? Blow it off? But how could she? This was real. This wasn't silly cold feet. Her standard, "You've been planning for this day since you were a little girl, and it's going to be perfect" wasn't going to cut it this time.

"I'm not going to lie to you. You know the risks much better than me. I won't pretend that I know how you feel, either." Sarah paused, grasping for the right words. "But it is what it is, Megan. Brandon's out in the hall right now worried sick about you. He's worried you're having second thoughts about him, and he's wondering whether or not you really love him. This isn't how you want to start off your marriage. I know it isn't."

Megan sniffed, rubbed the back of her hand across her tear-streaked cheek.

"He loves you. You love him. Is there a better way to

send him off than with the memory of you two saying your vows? Than spending his last days—and nights—before his deployment in wedded bliss?"

Megan's smile was so soft and so sad that it nearly broke Sarah's heart.

"If there's anything that will spur Brandon on to do his best to come home safe and sound, it's you, Megan. You're a strong woman. You will find a way to be strong for Brandon and to make it through this until he's home. I know you will."

A soft knock sounded on the door.

"Megan?" It was Brandon. "You all right, honey?"

"Just a minute," Sarah called, and then quieter she said, "Have him come in here alone and share with him what you're feeling."

Megan's eyes went wide. "But he's not supposed to see my dress until I walk down the aisle."

"Is that for you or them?" Sarah cocked her head toward the hall.

"Them."

"Then help him understand this wasn't cold feet. For you. For him. Then pat your eyes dry, touch up your makeup and enjoy this day. Deal with tomorrow when tomorrow comes."

Megan squeezed Sarah's hand. "Thank you, Sarah." Then she took a deep breath, went to the door and let Brandon in.

Sarah slipped out, but not before she heard Brandon softly ask, "Baby, do you not want this?"

And Megan's answer, "I don't care about all *this*. I just want you more than anything in the world..."

Instantly, Sarah's thoughts flew to Jesse. Maybe this last day and a half had done him some good. Maybe by the time this wedding was over, he'd have calmed down, realized how wrong he'd been the other morning in her bedroom. Maybe he wouldn't leave. And maybe she was in denial. Unlike Megan, Sarah couldn't wait until tomorrow to deal with her issues with Jesse.

This wedding couldn't get over fast enough.

CHAPTER TWENTY-THREE

THERE. FINISHED.

Jesse stepped back from Sarah's front door and off the porch to examine the end result. With a critical eye, he looked over every individual angle and line of the exterior of Sarah's house. Then he took a deep breath and took in the whole of it.

"Looks damned good, if I do say so myself," he muttered.

Then he glanced at his watch. It was almost seven o'clock and the sun was dipping low on the horizon. He was cutting it close. The water taxi was scheduled to pick him up at eight. He knew he should get back to Garrett's and pack, but he couldn't resist going through the house one last time.

Despite the wedding happening this weekend, Sarah had somehow managed to move in a fair amount of her and Brian's things. Movers were scheduled to bring up all of their furniture and the rest of their boxes on Monday. If all went according to plan, she and Brian would be sleeping in their new house by midweek. He could easily visualize how Sarah's furniture would look, Brian's collection of baseball caps hanging on his bedroom wall, family pictures, towels, knickknacks. She'd turn this house into a home in no time.

Walking from one room to the next, he relived every moment, both good and bad that had taken place here over the past several months. Sarah…painting here… cleaning there, smiling, laughing and talking with him. Zach and Brian, hanging around and helping.

Finally, back at the front door, he turned and studied the fireplace. He'd done okay. In fact, he was proud of all he'd accomplished here, but as he was imagining Sarah and Brian living here, going about their daily routines without him, emotion clogged his throat. This house felt like home.

But it wasn't his home. It couldn't be.

He tossed the keys Sarah had given him onto the kitchen counter and went outside. After crossing the yard, he looked back at the house one last time. There it was. Sarah's dream come true. Mission accomplished. Time to move on. He took the walk from Sarah's house to Garrett's one last time. Garrett came out of his work-shop just as Jesse hit the steps to the front porch. "Hey." He nodded at his brother.

"Hey, yourself." Garrett caught up with him.

They walked inside, and Jesse immediately noticed the quieter-than-normal house. "Where is everyone?"

"Erica's at Duffy's and the boys are at a birthday-party sleepover at Alex's house. Alex's sister Nikki is babysitting David up at the Andersens'."

He'd hoped he'd have a chance to see Brian, Zach and David one last time, but maybe not saying goodbye was for the best.

"I went by Sarah's today," Garrett said. "The house looks beautiful. That gingerbread…nice touch."

"Thanks." Jesse hung up his jacket.

"You know you can stay with us as long as you want—"

"No, Garrett, I can't." Jesse went into the kitchen and glanced around. He was going to miss this place, too. "Don't get me wrong. I appreciate you and Erica helping me get back on my feet, but it's time for me to stand on those feet alone."

"So rent an apartment or house here on the island," Garrett said. "There's enough work to keep you busy for at least a year. Some woman just bought the old Draeger mansion and is looking for a contractor to turn it into a bed-and-breakfast inn. Hell, I could even use some help with the orders that seem to be coming left and right."

"I've already overstayed my welcome. Hell, I haven't stayed this long in one place since...Chicago."

"You're not that rolling stone anymore, Jesse."

"I'm different in some ways. The same in others." Jesse held his brother's gaze. "If it makes you feel better, I'll wait until tomorrow."

"Promise?"

"Sure." *Why not?*

"All right, then," he said, seemingly satisfied. "I told Erica I'd keep her company at Duffy's. Want to join us?"

Hell, no. The last thing he wanted was to see people. "I'm kind of shot, bro." He glanced down at his dirty construction clothes. "Need to take a shower. Would like a good night's sleep."

"Okay." For an awkward moment, Garrett stood there, and then he suddenly reached out and gave Jesse a hug, almost as if he knew this might be his last opportunity. "See you in the morning."

The front door closed and silence settled over the house. It should've been peaceful. It wasn't. Jesse had grown so accustomed to the sound of children's voices, to the family banter, to the noise of life in this home, that the quiet seemed all wrong. But he refused to go to

Duffy's. He refused to go to Sarah's apartment or her house. God only knew what would happen if he saw her tonight of all nights.

Maybe he should stay until morning to say goodbye to everyone. Maybe that was the right thing. He was so much closer to his brother than he'd ever been. Didn't Garrett deserve as much? What about all the others who had come to mean so much to him? Erica. Brian and Zach. Little Davie.

Sarah.

The memories of her face-to-face. Her scent. The feel of her skin nearly overwhelmed him. Suddenly, he knew he'd never be able to say goodbye to her face-to-face. Never. He didn't have it in him.

Stick to the plan. Leave tonight. Quietly. Even Garrett would have to agree that the word *sure* didn't qualify as a promise. *Make it easy on the boys. Make it easy on Sarah.*

THE WEDDING AND RECEPTION had gone off without a hitch, that is, once Megan had recovered from her near breakdown. The cake had been cut. The bouquet and garter belt thrown. The photographer had called it a night. The wedding guests were busy ripping up the dance floor. And the Mirabelle Island Inn staff would take care of the cleanup. Sarah's job here tonight was finished.

She caught Megan's eye as the bride was walking onto the dance floor and waved goodbye. They'd tie together any loose ends tomorrow.

Megan hiked up her skirts and came rushing toward her. "Are you leaving?"

"Yep. Everything's under control. All you have to do is have fun the rest of the night."

Megan grabbed Sarah's hands. "Thank you, Sarah. This wouldn't have happened without you."

It was her job, but she'd never forget this wedding. She gave Megan a quick hug.

Brandon came to Megan's side. "Thanks, Sarah. For everything."

"You come back safe and sound, okay, Brandon?"

"I'll do my best."

They went into each other's arms and floated onto the dance floor to a soft, slow song, and Sarah made a wish that they'd be happy together. Then she glanced at her watch. It was later than she'd hoped and Brian's party at Alex Andersen's was already in full swing.

Time to find Jesse.

Chances were he'd still be at the house. He'd been working such long hours this last week, trying to get done before the movers came on Monday. Sarah ran to her apartment, changed into jeans and a T-shirt, piled a few more boxes on the back of her golf cart and drove up the hill.

She'd been so busy with the final preparations for Megan and Brandon's wedding and then the actual groom's dinner and wedding that she hadn't been to her house for several days. She couldn't wait to find out how close Jesse was to being finished.

By the time she came to her block, it was almost dark. As her house came into view, her foot slipped off the accelerator and the cart rolled to a stop. "Oh, my God," she breathed. "I can't believe it."

The house and yard looked as idyllic as a picture from a magazine. With the lilacs in full bloom, the spirea bush gushing with little white flowers and the irises popping up in purple glory, the house and yard looked better than when the old couple who'd built the home had lived here.

Jesse had not only finished painting the exterior, he'd also bought pots of marigolds and geraniums for her front steps and hung Boston ferns from her porch. But it was the sight of the white gingerbread trim that caused her to suck in her breath. He'd surprised her completely by creating arches between her porch posts, inserting a triangular section for her gable and custom fitting embellishments on her front storm door.

Jesse had made her dream come true.

Pushing down the accelerator again, she drove the golf cart up the sidewalk to the house and stopped in front of the steps. Glancing up, she got a close look at the trim he'd not only painstakingly tooled, but primed and painted. She went up to the front door and ran her hands along the intricately carved storm-door trim. Smooth as silk.

"Unbelievable."

It would've taken her years to save up enough to buy the premade trim. She couldn't imagine the time this had taken him. How many hours he'd spent all along with the intention of surprising her. When she turned and spotted the swing he'd hung from the porch ceiling, tears pooled in her eyes.

He'd said he didn't belong here. He'd said he didn't belong in her life. Well, if nothing else proved beyond a shadow of a doubt that he did belong with her, this was it.

The pitching machine he'd fixed up for the boys was one thing. All this was nothing short of a true labor of love. Had he been in front of her in that moment, she wasn't sure if she'd hit him or kiss him senseless. Probably one right after the other.

"Jesse?" she called, running into the house. "Jesse, are you here?"

Not a sound. He was gone for the day. Then she noticed the spare key she'd given him lying on the kitchen counter. "He just finished with the house," she whispered to herself. "He has to still be on Mirabelle. He has to be."

Quickly, Sarah carried the boxes into her house and then marched right back to the golf cart. She had a few things to say to Jesse, and if she had her way, he would not only be helping her move in, he'd be moving in with her.

IMPATIENTLY, SARAH KNOCKED on Garrett's door. When no one answered, she rang the doorbell. Still, no one came. There were no lights on in the house and the exterior floodlights were lit. That meant Garrett and Erica were at Duffy's, but where was Jesse?

She raced back down the hill and dropped in at the Nail. No Jesse. Panicking now, she ran down the street, pushed open the door to Duffy's and stalked to where Garrett was sitting at his usual place at the bar. "He's not at my house or yours. He's not at the Nail. Where's Jesse?"

Garrett studied her. "You sure he's not at our house?"

"No one came to the door."

"Dammit! He promised."

"What? You think he might've left. Tonight."

"It's possible."

"No," she whispered. "Give me your keys, Garrett. He's here. He's got to be here."

He pulled his keys out of his front jeans pocket and hesitated. "Maybe you shouldn't go back up there. If he's there, I'm not so sure tonight's a good night to talk to him. And if he's gone…"

"I have to know, one way or another."

"Sarah, wait until tomorrow."

Erica came toward them and stood with her hands on her hips on the other side of the bar. "Don't listen to him, Sarah."

"Erica—"

"Don't." She yanked the keys from Garrett's hand. "If you'd listened to the advice you're giving Sarah, I'd have left for Chicago and might never have looked back."

Garrett sighed, but he kept his mouth shut.

"Go," Erica said, tossing Sarah the keys to their home. "Say what you have to, do what you have to. You may not get another chance."

JESSE STEPPED OUT of the shower, ran a towel over his hair and down his body and then wrapped it around his waist. He brushed his teeth and then gathered a few of his toiletries and threw them in the small leather travel bag.

He looked around the room, making sure he'd left it at least as clean, if not cleaner, as when he'd first arrived on Mirabelle. This was it. Throw on some clean clothes and he was ready to go. He hesitated as a deep, pervasive sadness swept through him. He was going to miss Zach and little David, Garrett and Erica. Sarah and Brian? He couldn't even think about them.

Dammit. Don't do this to yourself. You know this is the only way. Angry now, he grabbed his small bag, opened the bathroom door and stopped dead in his tracks. She was there, standing in his doorway. "Sarah, what the— You shouldn't have come." He threw the rest of his toiletries into the fully packed duffel bag on the floor. "You need to leave."

"I'm not going anywhere. Neither are you."

"Last I checked this was a free country. I'll go wherever the hell I want."

"You mean run away?"

He glared at her, hoping to push her away.

"'Cause that's what you'd be doing if you leave Mirabelle." Undaunted, she stepped toward him.

"I'm not running away," he said. "I'm just doing what's best for everyone. Leaving without a fuss."

"Best for everyone else? Or best for you? I want you to stay. I don't want you to go."

"Sarah…" Wanting her so badly, he closed his eyes. He couldn't look at her. Not if he had any hope of walking away from this without hurting her.

"One kiss," she whispered. "One last kiss."

Her lips pressed against his and he knew it would never be enough. One kiss, hell, one entire night, would never be enough. "Don't," he groaned. "Don't make this more difficult than it already is for either of us."

"Oh, that's exactly what I'm going to do, Jesse. Make this as hard as I possibly can for you."

He could feel her there in front of him. Her heat. Smell her. Flowers and fresh spring air. "Sarah—"

She touched him. Her hands on his arms. His chest. Up his neck and on his cheek. He turned his face and ran his mouth along her palm, but he wouldn't kiss her. No matter what, he would not kiss her.

Then her mouth was on his cheek and he pulled his face away, keeping his eyes firmly closed. Sweetly and slowly, as if they had all the time in the world, she kissed his neck. Then she moved lower, over his collarbone and down to his chest. Her tongue laved his nipple, her fingers dug into his side.

"You're killing me."

"Good," she breathed against him. "It's nothing less than you deserve. If you leave Mirabelle you'll be killing me."

He heard the sound of a match and he could no longer stand it. He opened his eyes and beheld the most beautiful vision he'd ever seen. Sarah was standing in front of him naked, her clothes pooled at her feet. Candlelight flickered in her eyes, on her pale breasts, her belly, the dark shadow at the apex of her thighs. It was all he could do to breathe. "There's a water taxi waiting. I need to—"

"You might as well accept it. You won't be on that boat."

"Sarah—"

"I love you, Jesse." As soon as Sarah said the words, she knew she had never spoken a more important truth in her life. "Stay on Mirabelle. Stay with me and Brian. Build a life here with us."

But there was doubt in his eyes. He didn't doubt her, she knew. He doubted himself.

"You're not perfect," she whispered. "God knows, neither am I, but no one is. You and I have both made mistakes, but we're better people because of those very same mistakes."

He wasn't convinced.

"The least you can do is give me tonight. Give me this night." She kissed his mouth, gave him everything she had to give.

He groaned.

The moment his arms wrapped around her, Sarah knew she'd won. She had him. He was hers, for how long, she didn't know, but at least for the night. To-morrow she'd worry about keeping him for one more night.

You can't do this alone. She warred with herself. *What if he doesn't want to stay? No. He'll stay.* Even if she had to convince him every day for the rest of her life, he would stay.

His hands were on her back, pulling her toward him. His mouth on her lips, her neck, her breast.

She undid the towel from his waist, letting it fall to the ground, letting his erection spring free. Then she wrapped a hand around his velvety softness and he shuddered. He was hers, and she was going to prove it. She kissed his chest, trailed her tongue along his stomach.

"Sarah, don't."

Ignoring his protests, she knelt before him and took him into her mouth, loved him, caressed him until he could barely stand. He moaned and stepped back. None too gently, he gripped her shoulders and pulled her to her feet. "Take no prisoners? Is that it, Sarah?" he growled. "Well, two can play that game."

He crossed the room in two big strides, locked the door and turned toward her. "I hope you're satisfied because you're not leaving this room until the sun comes up."

"Oh, I'm going to be satisfied all right." Her body already trembled with anticipation.

Then he came to her and backed her up to his bed. Kissing her roughly, he laid her back onto the bed, sliding his body against hers from her legs up to her chest. He took her hands and swung them up over her head and kissed her.

Spreading her legs, she bent her knees, bringing

them together, intimately. She shifted her hips, wanting him inside so badly, she was about to cry. Then he pressed her leg up toward her shoulder and entered her quickly, angrily. As if she were the reason for all his pain.

"Don't," she whispered, taking his face in her hands. "Don't be mad at me."

Slowly, as if her words had taken time to register, he stopped thrusting into her and closed his eyes. His chest moved in and out, in great puffs of breath. "I'm sorry," he said against her lips. "So, so sorry, Sarah."

"Don't be sorry, either." She pushed him over, straddled him and made love to him. Softly. Deliberately.

He cupped her breasts as she leaned over him. "Oh, God, Sarah." He thrust more quickly but gently into her, over and over, and suddenly came as she met him one last time. As the breath shuddered out of him, Jesse looked into her eyes. There was so much love in his gaze, she could barely stand it.

Tremors ran through her body as if the earth were quaking beneath them. Then she collapsed on him. He wrapped his arms around her, kissed her neck, and all she could feel was his heartbeat thudding against her chest. His soft breath sounded in her ears. His calloused fingertips lightly caressed her back and Sarah realized she had never felt quite so content.

Finally, she sat up and glanced into his eyes. His tortured gaze told it all. She hadn't changed his mind. In the morning, he still planned on leaving her.

CHAPTER TWENTY-FOUR

JESSE WOKE LATE. From the position of the sun, it looked to be midmorning. Lying on his back, he held Sarah tucked in the crook of his arm, her hand flat on his chest, her face pressed against his side. His body was more relaxed than it'd been in years, but his mind was a jumble of disconnected thoughts.

What the hell are you doing? To Sarah? To yourself? Marry her. Stay. You'll disappoint her. Go. She deserves better. This is home. They believe in you. You have no home. Believe in yourself.

Every time he tried to imagine living here, his heart raced, his hands shook. He wasn't sure he knew how to stop running—he had to be honest—from himself. He had to leave Mirabelle right now. This morning. He had to go. Maybe off the island his thoughts would clear. Yes. Then he could think.

Slipping out of bed, he grabbed his clothes off the floor and quietly dressed. Within minutes, he was out the door and heading toward the marina, everything he owned in his bag. He'd already reached Sarah's street when he heard footsteps running behind him.

"Jesse!"

Sarah. He stopped, closed his eyes for a moment and turned.

Without a word, she came to him, slid her arms

around his waist and moved in close, resting her cheek against his chest.

"Sarah—"

"Don't. Don't say anything. If you have to leave, so be it. Last night, I thought I could convince you to stay, but I was wrong. You have to want to stay." Her body shook. "So go. Do whatever it is you have to do. But come back to me."

He dropped his bag on the sidewalk and wrapped his arms around her. He was resting his chin on the top of her head when a strange smell overwhelmed the floral essence from her hair. The scent got stronger and stronger. "Do you smell that?" he said.

"What?"

He took a deep breath and glanced into the air. "Smoke. There's too much of it to be a fire in someone's fireplace." It was coming from behind them. Down Sarah's street. He spun around. *Son of a bitch.* "Sarah, it's your house!" He took off running. "Get Garrett! Tell him to get the fire truck up here!"

SARAH RACED to the nearest home, Charlotte Day's little Cape Cod, and rang the doorbell over and over.

The Mirabelle librarian yanked open her front door. "Sarah! What—"

"I need to use your phone! Quick!"

Charlotte ran into her kitchen, came back and tossed her the cordless receiver.

Sarah punched in the number to the police station, a number she knew by heart.

Garrett answered on the first ring. "Mirabelle Island Pol—"

"Garrett, my house is on fire!" Sarah cried into the phone.

"Sarah?"

"Get the fire truck up here. Fast."

Her heart already thudding double-time, she tossed the phone back to Charlotte and ran full-out down the street. By the time she got to her yard, Jesse had already pulled out a garden hose and was doing the best he could to spray down the roof. But his efforts were having little to no impact. Unabated, flames poured out of a kitchen window and smoke billowed out the other windows.

"Sarah!" he called. "Stay back."

"Oh, my God. My house." She couldn't move. Her feet felt sunk in cement.

On some level of consciousness, she was aware of Charlotte Day coming to stand behind her. Other neighbors, apparently hearing the commotion, had come out of their houses.

Missy came running down the street. "Sarah!" she called. "What happened?"

"I don't know." Sarah felt herself sway as Missy stopped beside her.

Missy put an arm around her shoulders, steadying her. "Jesse!" Missy called out. "Get back! That wall looks like it's going to cave."

Jesse ignored Missy and kept spraying the house.

"Sarah!" someone yelled.

Sarah glanced down the block to find Erica racing toward them.

"Brian!" Erica shouted. "Brian's in your house!"

"What?" Sarah's stomach pitched. "That can't be. He's with Zach at the Andersens'. They said they'd—"

"They came home! Then he went to get an old video

game he said was at your house!" Erica yelled, terror filling her eyes. "Half an hour ago—"

Sarah ran toward the house.

"Sarah!" Jesse dropped the hose and raced toward her. "You can't go in there."

"Brian's in the house!" she screamed.

"Stay back!" Jesse yelled. "I'll get him!" He bolted up the steps and crashed through the front door.

Sirens sounded around her as Missy and Erica drew Sarah back from the hot flames. The island's only fire truck and ambulance both screeched to a stop on the street in front of her house. By now, a crowd had gathered, but they hung back, letting the island volunteer firefighters make their way with hoses across the yard.

Garrett ran toward them.

"Brian's in the house," Erica cried.

"And Jesse went after him," Sarah sobbed.

"Oh, my God." Garrett hesitated a moment, as if he couldn't think, and then got on his radio.

As several firefighters raced toward the house, the roof caved in over the kitchen in a loud and angry crash.

"Brian!" Sarah screamed. "Jesse!"

Someone grabbed her around the waist, holding her back. She struggled to break free, but couldn't. The flames devoured the kitchen corner of the house and quickly moved to the other side.

"Send the chopper." That was Garrett's voice. "We're gonna have injuries."

"No, no, no!" This couldn't be happening. "Brian! Jesse!" She struggled again.

"Sarah, don't." It was Garrett who had her. "You can't go in there."

"Let me go!" she screamed, and then her legs fell out from under her. As Garrett held her, the world started spinning, and she buried her head in his shoulder. Her beautiful son. The man she'd come to love with a vengeance. *It couldn't be. It couldn't be.*

"There he is!" someone yelled.

She jerked her head up to see Jesse staggering around the far corner of the house. "Jesse," she whispered.

"He's got Brian!" Garrett called. "Sean! They need you!"

He must've broken out a back window and was carrying Brian's limp form in his arms. As Sean shot across the yard, Sarah yanked away from Garrett and bolted toward Jesse and Brian. Suddenly, Jesse, his face and clothes covered in soot, began coughing violently. He dropped to his knees in the grass, but he held on to Brian.

"Jesse!"

Garrett grabbed her arm. "Hold on, Sarah," he whispered in her ear. "Let Sean do his job."

Sean had no sooner lifted Brian from Jesse's arms than Jesse collapsed back onto the ground. "Brian's not breathing!" Sean called as he began performing CPR on her little boy. "We need an airlift to the hospital!"

"Chopper's already on its way!" Garrett called. "It's on its way, Sarah."

JESSE CAME TO in the midst of a coughing fit. Bright overhead lights coupled with the sterile smell and the sight of a privacy sheet hanging from the ceiling told him he was lying in a hospital bed. He reached to rip the oxygen mask off his face, but it wasn't easy. His hands were bandaged. So was part of his face for that matter. Pushing up on his elbows, he struggled to sit.

"Okay, okay," a nurse said, holding Jesse by the shoulders. "Settle down."

"Brian?" The word came out as a hoarse croak and another wave of uncontrollable coughing swept through him. "Where's Brian?"

"The little boy who came in with you is in one of the other emergency rooms."

"Is he all right?"

"I'm sure he's fine."

"No, you're not." Jesse's hands throbbed, his eyes felt swollen, his head ached and he couldn't seem to clear his throat. Still, he had to find Sarah. He had to see for himself that Brian was all right. He swung his feet off the mattress. "I need to find him."

"You're not going anywhere." She tried to hold him back.

"Like hell." He pushed her away and stood, felt the floor shift beneath him and quickly sat back down.

The nurse put the oxygen mask back up to his face. "You have a mild case of smoke inhalation that could turn serious if it's not treated properly."

"Where's Sarah?" he mumbled through the mask. "Brian's mom."

Ignoring him, the nurse poked her head outside the privacy sheet and whispered, "You can come in. He's awake."

A moment later, Garrett and Erica appeared. "How you feeling?" Garrett asked.

"I'm fine. How's Brian?" He couldn't seem to catch his breath.

"We don't know yet," Erica said.

"Sean resuscitated him before you guys were airlifted here," Garrett added. "But we don't know how long he was out."

Sarah had to be going crazy. "Where is he now?"

"Down the way," Erica said. "In a hyperbaric oxygen chamber."

"He's been sedated," Garrett explained. "They think the damage to his airways is minor, but they're worried about carbon-monoxide poisoning."

None of that sounded good. "Sarah." He needed to find her, but another series of coughs wracked his body. He tried to grab the cup of water on the nearby table, but he couldn't get his bandaged hands around the cup.

Erica quickly grabbed the water and put the straw under the oxygen mask and into his mouth. He sucked up some fluids. The moment Erica pulled the cup away, Sarah appeared through the opening in the privacy screen. Her skin was pale and worry creased her brow.

"Sarah," he croaked, flipping up the mask with his bandaged palms. Before he could stand, she came to his side and Garrett and Erica quietly slipped away, closing the privacy sheets behind them.

"Don't get up." She put her hands flat against his chest.

He glanced into her puffy eyes and whispered, "I'm sorry."

"You have nothing to be sorry for."

"Brian. I should've—"

"Jesse, you saved his life." Tears fell unchecked down her cheeks as she looked at his bandaged hands. She caressed the only unbandaged skin on his face. "And now you have serious second-degree burns on your hands and parts of your arms and face."

"Don't worry about me. I'm fine." He wiped her

tears away with the gauze on the front of his fingers. "I want to see him."

"Can you stand?"

"With your help." He put his arm around her shoulder and tentatively stood. "I'm good. Let's go."

Slowly, they moved through the emergency area and into an adjoining ICU unit. The moment the cylindrical, clear-acrylic chamber became visible, Jesse felt his chest constrict. Unconscious and hooked up to various monitors, little Brian lay completely still on his back.

It had to be killing Sarah that she couldn't hold her son's hand. Hell, it was killing Jesse and he wasn't even his father.

"I don't want him regaining consciousness just yet." A man's voice came from behind.

Jesse turned to find Sean coming toward them.

"So I have him pretty heavily sedated," he explained. Then he picked up Brian's chart, flipped through the paperwork and glanced at the readouts on all the equipment.

"Is he going to be all right?" Jesse asked.

"I think so," Sean said, putting the chart away. "A few more minutes in that house, though, and he wouldn't have had much of a chance." He squeezed Jesse's shoulder. "Brian's alive because of you, Jesse."

"I only did what anyone would've done."

"Yeah, sure. A lot of people would've done what you did." Sean smiled. "But then most of them would've been trained firefighters and all of them would've been in full turnout gear." He turned then and walked away, leaving him and Sarah alone with Brian.

Sarah's hand tightened around Jesse's waist, and now he was supporting her. "He's right, you know," she whispered, a new round of tears streaming down her cheeks. She looked into his eyes. "You're a good man, Jesse Taylor."

CHAPTER TWENTY-FIVE

SARAH STOOD in the soft green grass staring at the wet, charred remains of her house. It was all gone. Everything. The only things left standing were the Lake Superior stones Jesse had painstakingly laid one at a time to form her new fireplace. The once subtly colored collection of gray, pink and beige rocks were now black with soot.

She took a few steps into the ash and stopped at the feeling of something solid beneath her foot. An unblemished section of the gingerbread trim Jesse had made for her house stuck through the debris. It was part of the gable decoration he'd designed himself. She ran her fingers along what was left of the intricately carved wood. How many hours had he spent making all that trim? What had he been thinking during that time?

She felt Jesse's presence even before she heard his shoes shuffling against the sidewalk behind her.

He came to stand beside her. "The fire marshall told Garrett the fire started in the basement," he said, his voice still harsh from smoke inhalation. "The wiring in the electrical switch at the base of the stairs."

"I know." She brushed some ash off the dingy white wood. "It wasn't the rewiring you did."

"I'm so, so sorry I didn't fire that son of a bitch of an electrician as soon as he showed up."

"It's not your fault, Jesse." She turned toward him. "Please don't blame yourself."

He wouldn't look at her.

"Your hands," she whispered. The burns on his face and forearms weren't as severe. They'd eventually heal completely, but his hands might be scarred for life. "The doctor said you may need skin grafts."

"Maybe. Just on the back side." He grinned. "I should be able to hold a hammer in a couple weeks."

"Jesse—"

"It's all right, Sarah." He put his hand around her shoulder. "Everybody's okay."

"You worked so hard for nothing."

"We both did."

"There's nothing left to salvage," she said. "Everything's gone."

"Your insurance covers everything. They'll bulldoze over this mess and before you know it, you'll have a brand-new house. You can lay it out exactly the way you want. It'll all be brand-new."

His body heat was the most comforting thing she'd felt all morning and all she wanted to do was curl into him. But not yet. First, they had a few things to settle. "You know what's strange, though? I don't care. About any of it. That house was just wood and paint and glass."

"Sarah—"

"There is no wave without wind. Remember?" She turned toward him, laid her hands on his chest. "No life without love. No me without you. You're alive. Brian's alive." He'd be coming home from the hospital that afternoon. "You two are all that matters to me. I can deal with my house burning down. I can't deal with you leaving Mirabelle. I can't help it. I want those waves, Jesse. I want you."

It was killing him, but he held her gaze.

"I love you, Jesse. Stay. I want to share the rest of my life with you. In that apartment over my shop. In another house. Hell, I'd live in a tent in the woods if it meant you'd be by my side."

"I don't know that I belong here."

"I do. I know. You belong on Mirabelle as much as I do. You deserve to be happy. You deserve to find joy. You deserve a good life."

He wanted to believe that. He wanted to believe he'd done his time, that he'd paid the price for his mistake.

"I'm not perfect either, you know." She gave him a slight smile. "Far from it. So the way I see it is that I have another imperfect person, who happens to be perfect for me."

He wanted to believe it was that simple, but it wasn't.

"Do you love me?"

He looked away, clenching his jaw tight.

"Jesse. Do you love me?"

He closed his eyes. "You know I do."

"Then stay." Sarah cupped his cheeks in her hands and tilted his face back to hers. "Stay on Mirabelle and...build a new house, Jesse."

Build a new house. His heart raced at the possibility. Start from scratch and build an entire house. He could do it. He knew he could do it.

"But don't build *me* a house. Build *us* a house. For *our family*. You, me and Brian. Stay on Mirabelle, and build us a house."

A family. A life.

"I need you, Jesse. Brian needs you. Now more than ever."

Emotion clogged his throat, making words impossible. A part of him still felt as though he didn't deserve Sarah. Very likely that feeling would never entirely go away. No matter what he did or didn't do, he would never completely exonerate himself for taking away Hank's legs.

Still, he was going to spend the rest of his life trying to find the best in himself. If that was good enough for Sarah, it was good enough for Jesse. He gazed down into her eyes and knew that simply staying would never be enough.

"I'll stay," he whispered. "On one condition." If he was going to do this, he was going to do it right.

A tear slipped from her lash. "What's that?"

He brushed it from her cheek and grinned. "You want me to build you a house, boss lady, you gotta offer something in exchange. Cash isn't going to cut it this time."

"Oh, yeah?" She smiled back at him. "What did you have in mind?"

"How does the rest of your life sound?"

"With you?" She swallowed. "Like a dream come true."

EPILOGUE

THERE IS NO WAVE WITHOUT WIND.

His heart calm, his hands steady, his breathing as even as it had ever been, Jesse stared up at Mirabelle's little white church that gloriously sunny and mild weekday evening at the end of May and debated what he was about to do.

Well, hell. Screw the calm-pool, smooth-as-glass theory. Tonight and for the rest of his life he was going to ride the sweetest crest of the biggest wave he'd ever known. Resolved, and about as at peace with his decision as he could get right now, he walked into the church and found Mirabelle Island's retired pastor, John Andersen, waiting for him at the door.

Jesse had the opportunity to get to know John a little bit while he and Sarah had discussed their wedding plans with him, and it had been apparent his wife's death was still at the forefront of his thoughts. "How are you doing, John?"

"As good as can be expected. Thanks for asking, Jesse," the pastor said, his thin lips curving into a slight smile.

"Thanks for doing this," Jesse said. "It means a lot to Sarah."

"She's a wonderful young lady."

"And I'm a lucky man."

"Oh, I have a feeling there's a bit more than luck

involved here." John glanced at Jesse's hands, still bandaged from the fire. "A good woman picked a good man and eventually the rest of Mirabelle will see what Sarah knows in her heart." He smiled. "Now. You ready?"

"Oh, yeah," Jesse said, glancing around. "Is she here?"

"I'm sure she'll be here any minute."

For an instant, Jesse's mind played tricks on him. What if she didn't show? What if she'd changed her mind? What if—

No. Not possible. She would be here. She loved him. Of that, he was absolutely sure. She wouldn't miss today for anything in the world.

From the moment he had asked her to spend the rest of her life with him, she'd told him she knew what her wedding day would be like. Simple. The simpler, the better. She wanted no flowers. No bridesmaids or groomsmen. No sit-down dinner or party favors for guests. No invitations. No champagne flutes. No garter belts or tuxes. No high heels. She didn't even want a wedding dress. The only finery, if you could even call it that, was two plain wedding rings stuffed into the front pocket of his khaki shorts.

Shoes scraped on the concrete steps behind him and Jesse turned to find Missy and Jonas, Erica and Garrett, Zach and David coming toward him. Since Jesse's hands were still bandaged, Erica and Missy kissed his cheek. Garrett smiled and hugged him tightly. "This is it, bro. Your new life starts now."

"You can say that again."

Jonas hung back, waiting for everyone to step away. Then he came to Jesse and patted his shoulder. "I owe you an apology."

"No, you don't."

The man had never once been overtly hostile, only cautious. Who could blame him for that?

"Okay, maybe not." He shoved his hands into his pockets. "In any case, I want you to know that you're welcome in my home anytime. This island is lucky to have not one, but two Taylor brothers call it home. You're as good a man as your brother."

"Well, I wouldn't go that far."

"I would."

As Jonas stepped away, Jesse saw Sarah walking toward the church, holding Brian's hand. She wore a simple shirt and a flowing skirt, both in white. Her hair was down and straight, and all he wanted to do was run his hands, bandaged or not, through the long black strands.

Grinning at Jesse, Brian went to stand by Zach, and the group behind Jesse filed into the church. He and Sarah were alone in front of Mirabelle's little white church.

Slowly, her eyes never leaving his face, Sarah climbed the steps and stood before him.

"You look...so beautiful," he whispered.

"So do you." She smiled, a little bit shy, but a lot happy.

"I know you wanted today simple, but every bride should have flowers." Jesse drew from behind him the bouquet of island wildflowers he'd collected. "Picked them myself."

"With your hands still bandaged?"

"Well, cut them is more like it." Took him longer than he'd expected, but he'd managed. "I have no idea what they are." All he knew was their colors—blue, white, yellow and red—looked pretty and seemed to suit Sarah and the kind of wedding she wanted.

"Perfect, is what they are." Her eyes misted with tears. "Thank you."

"Well," he said, grinning. "You ready for this?"

"Never been more ready for anything."

He placed her hand on his arm and walked to the front of the little chapel with her. The service from start to finish took all of ten minutes, with the very thorough kiss taking up most of the time. When it was over, they turned around to clapping and laughter.

"I made dinner," Erica said, "at Missy and Jonas's house."

"You weren't supposed to do that," Sarah protested.

"She knows," Missy said. "But *we* all wanted to celebrate."

They walked as a group the few blocks to Missy and Jonas's house, and as they approached, it was clear the backyard was full of people.

"You didn't have to plan it," Missy said. "So it's okay if we invited a few people, right?"

Sarah laughed. "It's more than okay. It's wonderful."

The crowd hooted and clapped when they appeared, and there were more introductions for Jesse. He could see in Sarah's smile that the best surprise of all was that Ron and Jan Setterberg and Arlo and Lynn Duffy had returned to Mirabelle a week early for this special occasion. Even Natalie and Jamis Quinn and their brood of kids had made a special trip to celebrate with Sarah and Jesse.

These people, some of whom he'd never met before, hugged and congratulated him as if they'd known him their entire lives. All of Sarah's people. People Jesse had no doubt would soon be his, as well. Even Jan

Setterberg pulled him aside for a moment. "I apologize for being rude to you at the funeral. I was wrong." She glanced at Brian and her eyes filled with tears. "I just can't imagine… I'm glad you're here on Mirabelle."

"Thank you, Jan. That means a lot to me."

Ron patted him on the back. For several long moments Jesse was more than a little overwhelmed.

"So what do you think?" Sarah whispered in his ear.

"I think you're the best thing that's ever happened to me." He kissed her.

Then Hank spun out from where he'd been unintentionally hiding behind a group of people and rolled toward them through the grass. "Congratulations," he said, smiling.

"Hank." Jesse shook his hand. "Thanks for coming."

"Thanks for inviting me," he said to Sarah.

"You are more than welcome," Sarah said. "Anytime, anywhere on Mirabelle."

"I'm sorry about the fire." Hank glanced from Sarah to Jesse, taking in Jesse's bandaged hands. "I'm glad you're okay."

"Brian's okay," Jesse said. "That's what counts."

"I have a toast!" Jamis called out, holding a bottle of beer in the air. Everyone grew quiet as they glanced at him. "And just like that," he said, shaking his head, "another one bites the dust."

Natalie laughed and raised her own glass of wine in the air. "Congratulations, Sarah and Jesse!"

"Hear! Hear!" Hank said, wheeling out of the way.

"Way to go, little bro!" Garrett called out. "And Sarah!"

"Ayep," Arlo agreed, holding baby David in his arms.

"Cheers!" Ron and Jan said in unison, each holding one of Missy and Jonas's baby boys.

Missy handed Sarah and Jesse glasses of sparkling water. "Your auras today are as beautiful as I've seen them," she said, tears in her eyes.

"Thank you, Missy," Sarah said, "for doing all of this."

"Me?" Missy laughed. "I made a few calls. Erica did all the work."

Erica had, indeed, prepared a feast. Two big pans of lasagna, salad and bread, an antipasto tray, flatbread pizzas and a triple-layer cake.

"You outdid yourself, sis." Jesse gave Erica a hug after he and Sarah had finished eating.

"You know how much I love cooking for anyone who shows up at the table."

He laughed. "Thanks for putting up with me in your house all those months."

"You and Sarah going to stay in her old apartment?"

"For a while yet," Sarah said.

"I've got a whole summer's worth of construction projects scheduled, so the house is going to have to wait. The plan is to get the shell of a new house done before the snow flies."

"We'll work on the interior over the winter," Sarah added.

"And it'll be better than ever," Hannah said as she came toward Sarah and Jesse, her arms outstretched. "Congratulations. I'm so happy for both of you."

"Thanks, Han," Sarah said.

"This is as good a time as any to tell you some news of my own."

"Yeah?"

"I'm moving to Madison."

"What?"

"We had such a great time over Valentine's Day and in Florida over spring break. He asked me to move in with him."

"That seems fast."

Hannah chuckled. "I've known him longer than you've known Jesse."

Sarah laughed. "You got me there."

"But I decided to get my own place. Subleasing an apartment for six months to see how it goes. So...as soon as school's out, I'll be moving."

"I'm going to miss you, but I get it."

"I'll only be a few hours away, and you know I'll be back to visit. Who knows? Maybe someday soon you'll be planning *my* wedding." Hannah grinned as she walked away.

As the food slowly disappeared and the sun started to set, someone lit a bonfire and brought out a radio. Jesse found himself blissfully alone with Sarah in the dark. "Well," he murmured in her ear, "the day didn't turn out exactly as you planned. But did it work?"

"It's been nothing short of magical."

Brian ran up to them. "This is awesome," he said, grinning as he glanced up at Jesse. It was amazing, but the boy hadn't gotten a single burn from the fire. "Now can I call you Dad?"

Dad? Whoa. Jesse swallowed down a sudden lump in his throat. "You serious?"

"Dude. I've always wanted a dad." Brian glanced at Jesse's bandaged hands. "And you're gonna be the best ever."

Jesse looked at Sarah. The love he saw in her eyes

filled him with joy. Real joy. The kind of joy that life was supposed to be all about. "Yeah, Bri. I'd be honored to have you call me dad."

"Sweet. *Dad.*" Brian laughed and ran off with Zach toward the fire.

Jesse reached for Sarah and pulled her close. "That sounded so weird."

"How does husband sound?" she whispered against his lips.

He closed his eyes, buried his face in her hair and breathed in the scent of flowers, something he was going to enjoy doing for the rest of his life. "Like the most right thing in the world. Wife."

* * * * *

*Grace Andersen comes home to
Mirabelle Island for good.
Be sure to look for
Helen Brenna's next book,
HER SURE THING,
and find out who tries to claim Grace's heart!*

Harlequin
Super Romance

COMING NEXT MONTH

Available August 9, 2011

#1722 STAND-IN WIFE
Twins
Karina Bliss

#1723 THE TEXAN'S SECRET
The Hardin Boys
Linda Warren

#1724 ONE GOOD REASON
Going Back
Sarah Mayberry

#1725 HER SURE THING
An Island to Remember
Helen Brenna

#1726 FULL CONTACT
Shelter Valley Stories
Tara Taylor Quinn

#1727 FEELS LIKE HOME
Together Again
Beth Andrews

HSRCNM0711

REQUEST YOUR FREE BOOKS!
2 FREE NOVELS PLUS 2 FREE GIFTS!

Harlequin

Super Romance

Exciting, emotional, unexpected!

YES! Please send me 2 FREE Harlequin® Superromance® novels and my 2 FREE gifts (gifts are worth about $10). After receiving them, if I don't wish to receive any more books, I can return the shipping statement marked "cancel." If I don't cancel, I will receive 6 brand-new novels every month and be billed just $4.69 per book in the U.S. or $5.24 per book in Canada. That's a saving of at least 15% off the cover price! It's quite a bargain! Shipping and handling is just 50¢ per book in the U.S. and 75¢ per book in Canada.* I understand that accepting the 2 free books and gifts places me under no obligation to buy anything. I can always return a shipment and cancel at any time. Even if I never buy another book, the two free books and gifts are mine to keep forever.

135/336 HDN FC6T

Name _____ (PLEASE PRINT)

Address _____ Apt. #

City _____ State/Prov. _____ Zip/Postal Code

Signature (if under 18, a parent or guardian must sign)

Mail to the **Reader Service:**
IN U.S.A.: P.O. Box 1867, Buffalo, NY 14240-1867
IN CANADA: P.O. Box 609, Fort Erie, Ontario L2A 5X3

Not valid for current subscribers to Harlequin Superromance books.

**Are you a current subscriber to Harlequin Superromance books
and want to receive the larger-print edition?
Call 1-800-873-8635 or visit www.ReaderService.com.**

* Terms and prices subject to change without notice. Prices do not include applicable taxes. Sales tax applicable in N.Y. Canadian residents will be charged applicable taxes. Offer not valid in Quebec. This offer is limited to one order per household. All orders subject to credit approval. Credit or debit balances in a customer's account(s) may be offset by any other outstanding balance owed by or to the customer. Please allow 4 to 6 weeks for delivery. Offer available while quantities last.

Your Privacy—The Reader Service is committed to protecting your privacy. Our Privacy Policy is available online at www.ReaderService.com or upon request from the Reader Service.

We make a portion of our mailing list available to reputable third parties that offer products we believe may interest you. If you prefer that we not exchange your name with third parties, or if you wish to clarify or modify your communication preferences, please visit us at www.ReaderService.com/consumerschoice or write to us at Reader Service Preference Service, P.O. Box 9062, Buffalo, NY 14269. Include your complete name and address.

HSR11

*Once bitten, twice shy. That's Gabby Wade's motto—
especially when it comes to Adamson men.
And the moment she meets Jon Adamson her theory
is confirmed. But with each encounter a little something
sparks between them, making her wonder if she's been
too hasty to dismiss this one!*

*Enjoy this sneak peek from ONE GOOD REASON
by Sarah Mayberry, available August 2011
from Harlequin® Superromance®.*

Gabby Wade's heartbeat thumped in her ears as she marched to her office. She wanted to pretend it was because of her brisk pace returning from the file room, but she wasn't that good a liar.

Her heart was beating like a tom-tom because Jon Adamson had touched her. In a very male, very possessive way. She could still feel the heat of his big hand burning through the seat of her khakis as he'd steadied her on the ladder.

It had taken every ounce of self-control to tell him to unhand her. What she'd really wanted was to grab him by his shirt and, well, explore all those urges his touch had instantly brought to life.

While she might not like him, she was wise enough to understand that it wasn't always about liking the other person. Sometimes it was about pure animal attraction.

Refusing to think about it, she turned to work. When she'd typed in the wrong figures three times, Gabby admitted she was too tired and too distracted. Time to call it a day.

As she was leaving, she spied Jon at his workbench in the shop. His head was propped on his hand as he studied blueprints. It wasn't until she got closer that she saw his eyes were shut.

He looked oddly boyish. There was something innocent and unguarded in his expression. She felt a weakening in her resistance to him.

"Jon." She put her hand on his shoulder, intending to shake him awake. Instead, it rested there like a caress.

His eyes snapped open.

"You were asleep."

"No, I was, uh, visualizing something on this design." He gestured to the blueprint in front of him then rubbed his eyes.

That gesture dealt a bigger blow to her resistance. She realized it wasn't only animal attraction pulling them together. She took a step backward as if to get away from the knowledge.

She cleared her throat. "I'm heading off now."

He gave her a smile, and she could see his exhaustion.

"Yeah, I should, too." He stood and stretched. The hem of his T-shirt rose as he arched his back and she caught a flash of hard male belly. She looked away, but it was too late. Her mind had committed the image to permanent memory.

And suddenly she knew, for good or bad, she'd never look at Jon the same way again.

Find out what happens next in ONE GOOD REASON, available August 2011 from Harlequin® Superromance®!

Celebrating

Blaze™ **10** years of

red-hot reads

Featuring a special August author lineup of
six fan-favorite authors who have written
for Blaze™ from the beginning!

The Original Sexy Six:

Vicki Lewis Thompson
Tori Carrington
Kimberly Raye
Debbi Rawlins
Julie Leto
Jo Leigh

Pick up all six Blaze™
Special Collectors' Edition titles!

August 2011

Plus visit
HarlequinInsideRomance.com
and click on the Series Excitement Tab
for exclusive Blaze™ 10th Anniversary content!

---

www.Harlequin.com

Harlequin®

SPECIAL EDITION

Life, Love, Family and Top Authors!

IN AUGUST, HARLEQUIN SPECIAL EDITION FEATURES
USA TODAY BESTSELLING AUTHORS
MARIE FERRARELLA AND *ALLISON LEIGH*.

THE BABY WORE A BADGE
BY *MARIE FERRARELLA*

The second title in the **Montana Mavericks:
The Texans Are Coming!** miniseries....

Suddenly single father Jake Castro has his hands full with
the baby he never expected—and with a beautiful young
woman too wise for her years.

COURTNEY'S BABY PLAN
BY *ALLISON LEIGH*

The third title in the **Return to the Double C** miniseries....

Tired of waiting for Mr. Right, nurse Courtney Clay takes
matters into her own hands to create the family she's
always wanted— but her surly patient may just be
the Mr. Right she's been searching for all along.

**Look for these titles and others in August 2011
from Harlequin Special Edition wherever books are sold.**

BIG SKY BRIDE, BE MINE! *(Northridge Nuptials)* by *VICTORIA PADE*
THE MOMMY MIRACLE by *LILIAN DARCY*
THE MOGUL'S MAYBE MARRIAGE by *MINDY KLASKY*
LIAM'S PERFECT WOMAN by *BETH KERY*

---

www.Harlequin.com

SEUSA0811